The Rancher and the Girl Next Door

JEANNIE WATT

KU-319-308

First published in Great Britain 2009
by Harlequin Mills & Boon Limited,
Eton House, 18-24 Paradise Road, Richmond, Surrey TW9 1SR

MILLS & BOON®
Pure reading pleasure™

© Jeannie Steinman 2008
(Originally titled *The Brother Returns*)

ISBN: 978 0 263 87378 8

38-0709

Harlequin Mills & Boon policy is to use papers that are
natural, renewable and recyclable products and made from
wood grown in sustainable forests. The logging and
manufacturing processes conform to the legal environmental
regulations of the country of origin.

Printed and bound in Spain
by Litografía Rosés S.A., Barcelona

ABOUT THE AUTHOR

Jeannie Watt lives with her husband in an isolated area of northern Nevada, and teaches science in a town forty miles away from her home. She lives off the grid in the heart of ranch country, and considers the battery-operated laptop to be one of the greatest inventions ever. When she is not writing, Jeannie likes to paint, sew and feed her menagerie of horses, ponies, dogs and cats. She has degrees in geology and education.

To Gary, with love.

CHAPTER ONE

NO ONE EXPECTED Claire Flynn to last long in Barlow Ridge. Even Claire had her doubts about making the transition to life in the tiny Nevada community, but she had sworn to herself that no matter how great the emergency or how dire the circumstances, she would not ask for help. It was a matter of pride.

And now here she was, going in search of help.

Drat.

She trudged up the rickety wooden steps leading to Brett Bishop's front door. Technically he was her landlord and therefore the logical person to help her with domestic emergencies. But he was also her sister's new brother-in-law, and a bit of an enigma. *An interesting combination,* Claire mused as she raised her hand to knock on his weathered kitchen door. It opened before her knuckles touched wood.

Brett did not look pleased to see her, but then he never looked too pleased about anything. That enigma thing. Claire enjoyed enigmas.

"There's a snake in my house."

His brown eyes became even more guarded than usual. "What kind of snake?"

"Grayish, no markings, maybe twelve to eighteen inches long. Very fast and uncooperative."

It had scared the daylights out of her when she'd moved a box and found it curled up in a corner. The feeling had apparently been mutual, since the creature had shot off toward the washing machine before Claire's feet were back on the ground. It was then that she'd decided to go for reinforcements. If her computer had been connected to the Internet, she might have done some quick research on snake removal, but it wasn't, so she took the coward's way out. When she'd made her vow of independence, she hadn't factored in reptiles.

Brett regarded her for a moment, his mouth flattening exactly the way it had when she'd made the mistake of flirting with him during their wedding-duty dance just over a year ago. And then he gave his dark head a fatalistic shake.

"Let's go see what you've got," he said.

WHEN CLAIRE FLYNN SMILED, she looked like she knew a secret, and if you treated her right she might just tell you what it was. Brett did not want to know Claire's secrets. He'd had enough secrets for one lifetime.

He stepped out onto the porch, preparing himself for the inevitable. His brother, Will, had asked him to give Claire a hand when necessary, and Brett had agreed, but he hadn't anticipated snake removal as one of the services required.

"I appreciate this," Claire said as he pulled the door shut behind him.

"No problem." But he did wonder how much more help she was going to need before her year of teaching was over. And he also wondered just how well she was going to fit into this small community, with her choppy blond hair and trendy clothing. Not many women in Barlow Ridge wore skirts that clung and swirled, strappy tops or flimsy sandals. In fact, none of them did. He imagined the locals were going to have a fine old time discussing her.

Claire walked briskly beside Brett as they left the homestead house and headed across the field toward the single-wide trailer she was now calling home. The field had just been mowed and baled with third-cutting alfalfa, so although the walking was easy, he expected the hay stubble was probably scratching up Claire's bare ankles pretty good. She didn't say a word, though, which kind of surprised him.

And she hadn't whined about the condition of the trailer—the only place to rent in Barlow Ridge—which happened to sit on the edge of his hay field. Another surprise. The previous teacher to rent it, a guy named Nelson, had registered at least a complaint a day.

"Where'd you last see the snake?" Brett asked when they were a few yards from the house. Dark clouds were moving in from the south. The evening thunderstorm was brewing early today and Brett hoped he'd be able to get rid of the snake and return home before lightning began to strike.

"It went behind the washer."

Brett grimaced. Nothing like moving a heavy major appliance with his worst nightmare lurking behind it.

Claire opened the trailer door and stood back. The interior smelled of industrial-strength cleanser. Brett wheezed as the stringent odor hit his nostrils.

"You know," he said, "if you just close the

door and give the snake a little time, it'll probably pass out from the fumes."

"Very funny."

He sucked in a breath of fresh air, then stepped inside and headed down the hall to a narrow alcove where the washer was installed. Claire was close behind him. He grabbed a broom propped against the wall and handed it to her before taking hold of the washer, keeping his feet as far away as possible.

"What am I supposed to do with this?" she asked, lifting the broom, a clunky wooden bracelet sliding down her arm in the process. Who cleaned house wearing a bracelet?

"Defend us."

Brett took a firm hold and started rocking the appliance toward him, fully expecting the snake to shoot straight up his pant leg at any moment. Damn, he hated snakes.

He finally got the heavy machine pulled out far enough so that he could see the snake coiled in the corner, looking as threatened as Brett felt. A blue racer. Fast but not dangerous. Unless it went up your pant leg.

He reached his hand out for the broom. "Better stand back."

Brett gently nudged the snake into the hall, trying not to dance too much as he blocked the reptile's repeated escape attempts with the broom, before finally managing to send it sailing through the front door. For several seconds it remained motionless, but then it came back to life and slithered off into the grass.

From behind him, Brett heard Claire sigh with relief. He turned to give her an incredulous look.

"Just because I don't want it living with me doesn't mean I want it to get hurt."

Brett closed the door. Sweat beaded his forehead, and it wasn't entirely due to the hellishly hot interior of the trailer. He set the broom back against the wall, noticing that it was damp. He touched the surface again, experimentally, with the palm of his hand. She'd washed the walls.

"Are you some kind of germophobe?" he asked as he pushed the door wide to let out both the heat and the cleaning fumes. She had the windows open, but the air was still in the heavy pre-thunderstorm atmosphere.

"I prefer it to ophidiophobia."

"Ophidio…"

"Fear of—"

"I know what it is," he snapped. Or at least he could make a good guess. He hadn't realized it was that obvious. "I'm not afraid of snakes. I'm just cautious." Like all sensible Nevadans. He wiped his sleeve over his damp forehead. "Why don't you turn the cooler on?"

"It made a funny noise, like it was losing a bearing." Her green eyes were steady on his. "I didn't want to bother you. I thought I'd find out who the local handyman was."

Brett walked over to the cooler panel and flipped the pump switch, followed by the blower switch. A low screech became progressively louder as the blower wheel began to turn. He quickly snapped both switches off. Yes, it did sound like a bearing was going, and for some reason he hated the fact she had figured that out.

"I'll have a look at it." He could not leave her in a hotbox until Manny Fernandez had time to come round and fix the cooler. She'd likely be using the furnace by that time—which was also probably in need of repair.

"I don't suppose you have any tools?"

She walked into the kitchen and returned a few seconds later with a zebra-striped tool kit.

"It was a gift," she said before he had time to comment. "From the class I student—taught last year."

Brett felt an unexpected desire to smile at the

defensiveness in her voice. So Claire's fashion sense had its limits. "They must have liked you."

"We...developed a rapport," she said cryptically, as she followed him outside.

There was an old wooden ladder lying beside the trailer, and Brett propped it up against the siding. A sudden gust of wind almost knocked it over again. He waited a moment until the wind settled down, making the air seem heavier than before, and then he began to climb.

Swamp coolers were not complex machines, and it wasn't too difficult to tell that this one was on its last legs. Claire was in for a warmish time in her trailer. He'd have to see about ordering parts, if they still made them for this dinosaur.

The ladder shifted, and a moment later Claire climbed up onto the roof herself. Somehow he wasn't surprised.

"Another snake?" he asked wryly.

"Just curious. Someday I may have to fix this thing myself."

"You going to be here that long?"

"Ten months, and then back to grad school. What's the prognosis?" she asked.

"Terminal." The wind gusted again and the first faint rumblings of thunder sounded in the distance. The storm was moving in fast. "We'd better get down to the ground." He closed the cooler's heavy hinged cover.

Once they were back on solid earth, Brett put the ladder beside the trailer and handed Claire her tools. "I'm going to Wesley tomorrow. I'll see about getting some parts, if they still make them. If not, I'll see about a new cooler." He felt bad leaving her in an oven. "It's going to be kind of hot without it."

"That's the beauty of being a Vegas native. I'm used to it." She pushed her choppy bangs away from her forehead. They stuck up, giving her a punk rock look. She smiled. "So… You want to go down to the bar and grab a bite or have a drink? As a thank-you?"

He hesitated just a little too long.

"I take it that's a no."

He wasn't sure how to say what he needed to without being insulting and possibly pissing off his brother for not being nice to Claire. "Look," Brett said in what he hoped was a reasonable tone, "I'll help you out whenever you need it, but I'm not much of a socializer."

"What does that mean?"

That I'm not going to risk screwing up again with someone so closely tied to my brother?

"It just means I'm not much on socializing,"

he said with a touch of impatience. "It's nothing personal." Not the total truth, but close enough.

"All right." She didn't look particularly offended, but the smile was gone from her eyes. "I guess I'll get back to work. Thanks for the help. I'll call you if I need anything." She started for the trailer door.

"There's something you should know, Claire."

She looked back. "What's that?"

"I don't think it was an accident that there was a snake in your house. There was a bunch of kids hanging around, just before you got here. I went to see what they were doing, and they took off running."

"You think they were my students?"

"I'd say it's a real possibility."

Claire considered his words for a moment. "Should make for an interesting year, don't you think?"

"Uh, yeah." That was one way of putting it.

"I think I can probably handle anything they might dish out." She sounded confident.

Brett nodded, wondering if she knew what she was up against. Apparently not. There was a flash of lightning, followed by thunder. "I think I'll head back before it rains."

So HER STUDENTS HAD PUT a snake in her house and Brett didn't want to socialize with her. Claire shook her head as she went through the door. Not exactly a welcoming beginning to her new life in Barlow Ridge. She was surprised about her students, and not so surprised about Brett. She'd only met him three times before deciding to take the teaching job here, but every time they'd been together she'd been struck by his standoffish attitude. With her and with his family.

Well, Claire didn't do standoffish. With the exception of her mother, Arlene, who could still make her quake in her boots, she'd never met anyone who intimidated her. Maybe she should thank her mother for that.

The trailer was starting to cool off as the wind grew stronger, blowing in through the open windows. Another flash of lightning lit the sky, and Claire wondered how safe it was being in a metal can during a thunderstorm. It had to be safe, though. There were lots of trailers in the world and she'd never heard of one being struck by lightning. But leave it to her to be the first.

She sank down in the reclining chair, pulling her knees up to her chest as the sky flashed and a blast of thunder shook the trailer almost simultaneously. This was not only her first night alone in her new home, it was one of her first nights really alone anywhere. As in, no family down the hall, no neighbor on the other side of the wall. No neighbors within a quarter of a mile, for that matter.

It felt…strange.

But she could handle it.

In fact, she had a feeling that she might even grow to like it. If not, she only had ten months to get through before she moved back to Vegas.

Her cell phone buzzed. Claire glanced at the number, debated, and then gave in to the inevitable.

"Hi, Mom." She forced a note of cheerful optimism into her voice. Nothing set her mother off like Claire doing what she pleased and enjoying it. Arlene had wanted her to be an engineer. Claire was talented in math, but hated the cut-and-dried engineering way of thinking. She was more free-form—*way* more free-form—and didn't understand why Arlene couldn't see that a free-form engineer who hated to double-check her equations was probably going to be a dangerous engineer. Arlene resented the fact that neither of her daughters had gone into the high-profile, high-paying professions she had chosen for them before they'd entered preschool. And she still hadn't given up on turning their lives around.

"I called to see how you're settling in."

"Just fine," Claire said breezily, deciding not to share her snake adventure just yet. "I'll be going to school tomorrow to see my new room and do some decorating."

"Any regrets?" her mother asked hopefully.

"Not yet, but there's still time." Claire knew that Arlene wanted her to at least entertain the possibility that she'd be sorry for putting off grad school for a year.

"Well, there's a reason they can't keep a teacher at that school."

"Any idea what it is?" Claire asked innocently.

Arlene did not deign to answer, and Claire decided to change the subject while they were still on polite terms. She sifted through several topics and dismissed them all. Her stepfather, Stephen, was off-limits, since he had moved out of the house, informing Arlene that he would not come back unless she decided being a companion was as important as running her business. Claire wasn't all that sure that Stephen would ever be coming back.

She couldn't ask her for career advice—or decorating advice, since she was living in a run-down rented trailer on the edge of a hay field. But she could try cooking, their only common ground.

"Hey, Mom…" A boom of thunder nearly drowned out her words.

"What on earth?"

"Thunderstorm."

"You shouldn't be on the phone."

"It's a cell phone." Claire decided not to argue. "You're right." She smiled slightly. "Thanks for calling, Mom. I was lonely."

"Goodbye, Claire. It was good talking to you."

Claire pushed the end button. It really hadn't been too bad a conversation. They'd both behaved fairly well. She held the phone in her hand for a moment, then punched in her sister's number. Regan answered on the first ring.

"I've been waiting," she said.

"Why?" Claire knew why. For about nine-tenths of her life, she'd run every decision past Regan, even if she rarely followed her sister's advice. It was a habit that had started when they were young, and continued well into college. It wasn't until Regan had moved away from Las Vegas that Claire realized maybe life wasn't always a joint venture.

"Because you've never lived alone before."

"Well, I've *been* alone," Claire said, "and this isn't all that different."

"So how are you settling in?"

"Fine, now that Brett got the snake out of the house…"

"The snake?"

"My students hid a snake in my house before I got here. It scared the daylights out of me when I found it, and since I don't know anything about snakes, I had Brett come and remove it. Then I asked him out for a beer as a thank-you and he told me he doesn't socialize."

There was silence on the other end of the line, and then Regan murmured, "Don't take it personally."

"That's what he said," Claire replied, swinging her legs over the one arm of the chair and leaning back against the other. "And I'm not. I just thought it was odd, which makes me wonder, why are the gorgeous ones always tweaked in some weird way?"

Regan laughed.

"What?"

"Oh, I was just thinking that you could take a long look in the mirror and ask yourself that same question."

"Ha, ha, ha." They talked for a few more

minutes, making plans to meet when Claire made her next trip to Wesley for supplies.

"Speaking of shopping," Regan said, "Kylie is planning an Elko trip and she wants to know when you can come. She says your taste is better than mine, which, I have to tell you, worries her father a bit."

"Tell her to name the day," Claire said with a laugh. Elko shopping was nothing like Vegas shopping, but it was a heck of a lot better than Barlow Ridge shopping or Wesley shopping. And Kylie, Regan's stepdaughter, was a girl after Claire's own heart. A true renegade.

Claire finally hung up and set the phone back on the side table. The thunderstorm had passed without dropping any rain, but the air in the trailer felt fresher, cooler. She got to her feet and headed down the narrow hallway to her bedroom, walking a little faster as she passed the washing machine. Logic told her there were no more snakes lying in wait for her, but her instincts told her to take no chances. She'd yet to have much experience with animals, but when she did, she wanted them to be furry and friendly.

"YOU THE NEW TEACHER?"

Claire smiled at the grouchy-looking woman behind the mercantile counter. "Yes, I am."

"Gonna stay?"

"One year." Claire spoke easily, truthfully.

The woman snorted. "That's the reason the kids are running wild, you know."

"What is?"

"The fact that none of you will stay."

"Yes, well, there's not a lot to do here, is there?"

The woman gave her another sour look, but didn't argue. It would have been hard to. The community had one store, a bar that served food and a community center that looked as if it was well over a hundred years old. Actually, everything in the town looked a hundred years old. Including the proprietress of the store, who was still glaring at Claire as if it were her fault teachers didn't want to settle permanently in a community a zillion miles from civilization.

"I'm Claire Flynn," she said with her best smile.

"Anne McKirk," the woman grudgingly replied.

"You have a nice store." It was definitely an everything-under-the-sun store. Food, hardware, crafts, clothing. One of the soda coolers held veterinary medications. It wasn't a large space, but it was packed to the rafters.

"I try."

Claire unloaded her basket on the counter. She would have liked some fresh fruit, but considering the circumstances, she'd take what she could get.

"Your sister taught here."

"Yes. Three years ago."

"She was good, but she didn't last long."

"She would have had a bit of a commute if she'd stayed," Claire pointed out. Will Bishop, the man Regan had married, lived seventy miles away in Wesley, Nevada, where she now taught.

"Well, it would have been nice if Will had taken over the old homestead, instead of his brother. Then she would have stayed."

"Yes, she would have," Claire agreed. But it hadn't worked out that way, so now the town was stuck with the wrong brother and the wrong sister.

"You interested in joining the quilting club?"

"I, uh, don't know," Claire hedged. She had never done anything more complicated with a needle than sew on the occasional button. She did it well, but she had a feeling that quilting was more difficult than button attachment.

"I'll have Trini give you a call. Everybody joins quilting club."

"Then I'll join."

Claire said goodbye, then strolled down the five-block-long street to Barlow Ridge Elementary, which was situated at the edge of town. Her trailer was only a half mile away, so she could walk to work on the nice days.

The school, constructed in the 1930s, had a certain vintage charm, but Claire knew from her initial visit that it would have been a lot more charming had it benefited from regular upkeep. It consisted of three classrooms—one used as a lunchroom—a gymnasium with a velvet-curtained stage at one end, two restrooms and a tiny office barely big enough to hold a desk and a copy machine.

Claire unlocked the stubborn front door and went into her room, setting her lunch on the shelving unit just inside. The space was of adequate size, but the equipment it contained was old, tired and makeshift. With the exception of a new computer on the teacher's desk, everything dated from the previous century. There was no tech cart for projecting computer images, only an old overhead projector. No whiteboards or dry-erase markers, but instead a grungy-looking blackboard and a few small pieces of chalk.

She went to run her hand over the board, and found the surface grooved and wavy. Picking up a piece of chalk, she experimentally wrote her name. The chalk made thin, waxy lines, barely legible. Something needed to be done about this.

The desks came in a hodgepodge of sizes and shapes, all of them old-fashioned, with lift-up lids. She'd been thinking about how she would arrange them. Rows…a horseshoe…in groups. The students should probably have a say.

Behind her desk was a door in the wall that opened into a long, narrow closet jammed to the ceiling with junk. Probably seventy years' worth of junk, from the look of things. She'd be doing something about this. Claire hated disorganization and wasted space.

She left her classroom and walked through the silent school. There was another mystery door, at the opposite end of the hall from the restrooms. She pulled the handle, and though the door proved to be a challenge, it eventually screeched open. A set of stone steps led downward.

A school with a dungeon. How nice.

There was no light switch, but a solitary bulb hung from a cord at the bottom of the steps, adding to the torture-chamber ambience.

Claire started down the steps. The smell of

dampness and mildew grew stronger as she descended. She pulled the string attached to the light, illuminating most of the basement and casting the rest into spooky shadows. The floor was damp and there were dark patches on the walls that looked like moss. A frog croaked from somewhere in the darkness.

Stacks of rubber storage bins lined the walls, labeled Christmas, Halloween, Thanksgiving, Easter. Others were marked History, English and Extra. Probably some great stuff in that last one, Claire thought as she went to lift the corner of a lid. The bin was filled with old blue-ink ditto papers. There were also several tables, a plastic swimming pool and a net bag of playground balls hanging from an antique metal hook on the wall.

The frog croaked again and Claire decided she'd seen just about all there was to see. She went back upstairs, the air growing warmer and dryer with each step. Once she reached the top she wrestled the door closed and pushed the latch back into place.

"Is that you, Claire?"

The unexpected voice nearly made her jump out of her skin. She pressed her hand to her heart as she turned so see Bertie Gunderson, a small yet sturdy-looking woman with short gray hair, peeking out of the office doorway. Claire had met her the first time two days earlier at the district staff development meeting.

"Darn it, Bertie, you scared me."

The other teacher smiled. "It's refreshing to hear that I'm more frightening than the basement."

Claire followed her back into the office, where she was copying papers on the antique copy machine—a hand-me-down from another school, no doubt. Regan had told her that Barlow Ridge Elementary got all the district's reject equipment. "I was wondering about the blackboards."

"What about them?"

"They're unusable. Is there any chance of talking the district into putting up white-boards?"

Bertie cackled. "Yeah. Sure."

Claire felt slightly deflated, which, for her, was always the first step toward utter determination.

"You can try," the veteran teacher said.

"I'll do that."

Bertie was still in her classroom working when Claire finally left three hours later. She'd started sorting through her storage closet but gave up after a half hour, concentrating instead on making her first week's lesson plans. She would be teaching five different subjects—some of them at four different grade levels. Regan had already explained that she could combine science and social studies into single units of study for all her grades, but English and math had to be by grade level. The challenge was scheduling—keeping one grade busy while another was being taught.

But Claire loved a challenge, and this would be just that. Plus, she'd have an excellent background for her planned master's thesis on combined classroom education. Old equipment and a wavy blackboard were not going to slow her down.

BRETT'S CELL PHONE RANG at seven-thirty, while he was driving the washboard county road that led to Wesley.

Phil Ryker. His boss.

"Hey, pard," Phil drawled, setting Brett's teeth on edge. He had to remind himself to practice tolerance. Phil was an urban boy who wanted to be a cowboy, and being heir to the man who owned most of the land in the Barlow Ridge area, including Brett's family homestead, he was wealthy enough to indulge his dreams. Brett considered himself fortunate to be leasing his homestead with an option to buy, which he was close to exercising, and also to be working for Phil, managing the man's hobby ranch during the three hundred days a year he was not in residence. Those two circumstances were enough to help Brett overlook a fake drawl and words such as *pard*.

"Hi, Phil."

"I won't be able to get to the ranch next week like I planned, but I did buy a couple of horses and a mule, and I'm having them shipped out."

"All right." What now? Brett knew from past experience that the horses could be anything from fully trained Lipizzans to ratty little mustangs.

"One of them is a bit rough. I thought maybe you could tune him up for me."

"Define '*a bit rough.*'" Brett's and Phil's idea of rough were usually quite different.

"Seven years old and green broke, but he's beautiful," Phil said importantly. "You'll see what I mean when he arrives."

"He isn't…"

"He's a stud. I'd like to show him, so I need him fit for polite society." Phil laughed. "I'll get a hold of you closer to the delivery date. Hey, did you figure out that problem with the north well?"

"Yeah. Yesterday. The water level is fine, but the pump needs to be replaced. I sent you an estimate."

"Just take care of it. We can't have that pivot go down."

"Sure can't." Because that would mean that he wouldn't be able to grow hay at a loss. Brett figured Phil knew what he was doing. A hobby ranch that was slowly losing money was a tax write-off and apparently Phil needed write-offs. Brett had tried to interest him in a number of ideas that would make the ranch more economical, perhaps even profitable, but he had his own ideas. Brett gave up after the third set of suggestions was rejected, finally understanding that Phil wasn't particularly concerned about losing money. Must feel good, he mused as he hung up the phone.

Amazingly, Brett found the parts he needed for the swamp cooler at the hardware store in Wesley. Now all he needed to do was go home and get them installed—with luck, while Claire was still at school mucking out her classroom.

He didn't want to spend a lot of time around her. It wouldn't be prudent, since he found her ridiculously attractive, and he was really trying to mind his p's and q's where the family was concerned. He'd spent more than a decade being the missing brother, and before that, he'd been the rebellious brother.

Now he owed it to his family to be the *good* brother. And this was one time he was not going to fail.

CHAPTER TWO

CLAIRE SMILED AT HER NEW class—all ten of them—and wondered who'd masterminded the snake incident. They all looked more than capable of it, but at least the younger students, the fifth and sixth graders, were smiling back at her with varying degrees of curiosity and friendliness. By contrast, the five older students, the seventh and eighth graders, stared at her with impassive, just-try-to-engage-us-and-see-how-far-you-get expressions.

"I'm Miss Flynn," Claire said, as she wrote her name on the overhead projector.

"We know who you are," one of the kids muttered snidely. Claire glanced up, startled by the blatant rudeness, but she couldn't tell who'd spoken. "I'm looking forward to a pro-ductive year, and I thought that in order to—"

One of the eighth-grade boys raised his hand.

"Yes?"

"Do you think you'll be here for the whole year?"

"It's one of my goals," Claire said dryly. She knew that her class had had three teachers in two years, each less effective than the previous one. "As I was saying, in order to get to know each other better, I thought we could all introduce ourselves and tell one thing we did this summer. How about starting on this side of the room?" She nodded at the boy in eighth grade, Dylan, who sat farthest to her right.

"I think everyone knows who I am. This summer I slept." He fixed her with a steely look.

Claire quelled an instant urge to jump into battle, as her instincts were telling her to do, deciding it would be wiser to bide her time and get a read on her opponent.

"How nice," she said. She nodded at the girl sitting next to him.

"I'm Toni."

"Did you accomplish anything this summer?"

"No." But then Toni suddenly made an O with her mouth. "Yes," she amended, with a satisfied expression. "I *almost* talked my mom into getting rid of her bum of a boyfriend."

Claire gave the girl a tight smile and moved on.

"My name is Ashley," the redheaded girl sitting next to Toni chirped. "This summer I totally revamped my wardrobe." She jangled the bracelets on her wrist as if to prove the point.

Claire was saved from the remaining introductions by the sudden appearance of a first grader.

"Mrs. Gunderson said to tell you we have sheep!" he squeaked, his eyes wide with excitement.

"Sheep?"

"On the play field."

"And…?" Claire asked with a frown, but her students were already out of their seats and heading for the door. She followed them, wondering if this was an elaborate ruse and if she should order them back into the classroom, but then Bertie emerged from the office.

"Sorry about this. The older kids herd sheep better than the younger ones. It should only take a few minutes. I've just called Echetto and told him to get his buns over here and take care of his flock. The man really should leave his dog when he goes somewhere. The dog works a lot faster than the kids."

A thundering herd of woolly bodies circled past the front of the school and disappeared around the side. Bertie's class was crowded onto the steps. Trini, the school aid, had the four kindergarten kids perched on the window-sills in Bertie's room, where they laughed and giggled as the sheep ran by again, the older students in hot pursuit.

"They like to watch," Bertie explained, before cupping her hand to her mouth and yelling at Claire's students, "Just get them into Echetto's front yard. He can put them away when he gets back."

Claire was impressed by the way the kids worked in unison to gather the sheep and herd them off the play field, onto the road and then halfway down the block to the house that apparently belonged to Echetto, whoever he was. Ashley and Toni hung toward the rear, but when a couple of ewes made a break for it, they expertly chased them back into the flock. A few minutes later all the kids returned, filed past Claire into the school and took their seats. They'd been smiling while they were outside, but the older ones were once again stony faced—except when they looked at each other.

"Well, this is a first," Claire said. "We don't have many sheep emergencies in Las Vegas."

No one smiled back. In fact, they were making a real effort to make her feel stupid for trying to talk to them like people. "Are you always this rude?" she asked softly.

The younger kids glanced down. The older ones continued to stare at her.

"We can work on manners," she added.

No response, although she noticed the younger kids were now watching the older students, looking for cues.

"This morning I'm going to have you take placement tests, so I can plan the English and math curriculums. Then, after break, we'll do a writing activity. I need you to clear your desks and we'll get going on the tests right now, while you're fresh."

The older kids grudgingly shoved notebooks into their desks, a couple of them muttering under their breath.

The rest of the day passed so slowly and dismally that Claire was beginning to wish the sheep would escape again. She knew the younger ones were not on board with the older ones—yet. But they were watching and learning.

She had to do something. Fast. The headache that had begun shortly after the sheep roundup was approaching migraine status by now.

"I have a list of supplies I'd like you to have within the next week," she announced just before afternoon recess.

Ashley raised her hand and Claire nodded at her. "What about the kids who can't afford supplies?"

A reasonable question, and one that might have denoted concern for those with financial limitations—if it hadn't been for the girl's condescending tone. Ashley, with her salon-streaked hair, Abercrombie T-shirt and Guess jeans, was obviously not going to have difficulty buying five dollars' worth of supplies. And then, as if to make it perfectly clear that she was establishing her own status, she glanced pointedly over at one of the fifth graders, a rather shabbily dressed boy named Jesse.

Claire looked Ashley straight in the eye. "If you have trouble affording supplies, please see me in private."

The girl flushed. "I wasn't talking about myself," she snapped.

"Well, it is kind of you to be concerned about others," Claire interjected, before the girl could name names. "If any of you do not have the opportunity to buy supplies, we'll work something out. Please see me." She smiled at Ashley. "Does that answer your question?"

The girl did not bother to reply. Claire decided to fight the politeness battle later. She noticed a couple of the younger kids trying not to smile. Apparently they appreciated Ashley getting hers, and Claire made a mental note to find out more about the girl and her family.

The last two hours of the day passed without incident, although it became apparent by then that Ashley held a grudge and owned a cell phone. Ashley's mother arrived just before school ended. She waited in the hall outside the classroom, marching up to Claire as soon as the room had emptied of students.

"Miss Flynn. I'm Ashley's mother. Deirdre Landau."

Claire could see the resemblance in both features and clothes. In fact, the mother was dressed almost exactly like the daughter, in pricey jeans and T-shirt, with expensive hair in a make-believe color. Claire was in no position to comment on make-believe hair colors, since she was a little blonder than nature had ever intended, so she overlooked that detail.

"You embarrassed Ashley today."

"I apologize for that," Claire said honestly. And she was sorry. She wished the incident had never happened, but she wasn't going to let Ashley humiliate a defenseless fifth grader, either.

There was a silence.

"That's it?" Deirdre finally asked.

"What more would you like?" Claire asked reasonably.

The woman's mouth worked as she fought for words. She'd received an apology. Readily and sincerely. And that was the problem. She'd wanted Claire to grovel. Or protest. Or, at the very least, put up a struggle. She tried again.

"A promise not to do it again."

"Fine. As long as Ashley understands that I will not tolerate an intentional attempt to hurt another student's feelings."

Deirdre looked shocked. "Ashley would do no such thing."

"Then perhaps I misread the situation," Claire said in an agreeable tone. "So the next time it happens, I'll just give you a call and you can come to the school and we'll discuss it while it's fresh in everyone's mind."

"I would welcome that."

"Great, because I believe that communication among parents, students and teachers is imperative in an educational situation."

Deirdre blinked. "And I want you to apologize to Ashley in front of the class. After all, she was embarrassed in front of the class."

"Sure." Again, Claire did not hesitate in her

response, and it seemed to confuse Deirdre. She frowned suspiciously.

"Tomorrow."

"First thing."

"All right." It was obvious the woman didn't trust Claire's easy acquiescence. "Ashley's waiting. I need to be going."

Claire refrained from saying "See you soon," even though she had a feeling it wouldn't be long before she and Ashley's mom were face-to-face again.

Claire called Regan that night. "What do you do when you're teaching the undead?" she asked as soon as her sister answered the phone.

"Excuse me?"

"Zombies. My older kids behave like zombies, except for when they're herding sheep or sniping at me."

"Echetto's sheep got out again?"

"This is common?"

"Couple times a year."

"Sheep I can live with, but these older kids are mean, Reg. I thought I'd have a group of sweet rural kids who'd been left to their own devices for too long. And instead I have three snotty ringleaders trying to get the best of me, and a bunch of younger kids learning to follow their lead. Can you tell me anything about Toni

Green, Ashley Landau and Dylan Masterson that might help me?"

"Not a lot," Regan confessed. "The only one I know is Dylan, and he wasn't bad as a fourth grader. He just needed a strong hand."

"Well, he didn't get it."

"As to the zombie issue, you're going to have to live with it."

"Meaning?"

"It's a control thing, and you can't force them to be enthusiastic learners. But you can do what Will does when he trains a horse. If they show an appropriate response, reward them. If they act like zombies, ignore it and do your job."

"Kind of like the extinction theory?"

"Pretty much." Regan's voice softened. "You do know you may have a power struggle for a while?"

"I'm getting that idea."

"Stay consistent. Stay strong."

"I'll be Hercules."

"You may have to be," Regan said with a laugh. "Call any time you need moral support, all right?"

"Are you sure you mean that?" Claire asked ironically. There was a time when she'd automatically called Regan before even thinking about a problem.

"I mean it. Anytime." A muffled voice sounded in the background. Regan laughed, then said, "Kylie wants you to promise to come watch her ride at the regional horse show and to wear something to impress her friends."

"Tell her I'll get right on it."

Claire felt better for having called. She had no intention of crying on Regan's shoulder every time something went wrong, but it was good to know she had backup if she needed it.

"BEFORE WE START CLASS, there's something I need to attend to," Claire said as soon as the students were seated following the Pledge of Allegiance. Ashley was already smirking.

"Yesterday I embarrassed Ashley, and I want to apologize for that."

The girl nodded, like a queen granting pardon to an offending subject.

Claire hitched a hip onto the edge of her desk and swung her foot. "In order to avoid this happening in the future, I think I should explain some things to you as a class. I don't want *anyone* to be embarrassed, but if I see you trying to hurt someone else, I will call you on it. It may embarrass you. It's called a consequence. I don't know how many of you have been following the latest developments in self-esteem studies…" The class stared at her blankly. "But the pendulum is swinging from the stroking of egos back to consequences for actions."

Rudy tentatively raised his hand.

"Yes?"

"Would you please translate that?"

"If you do the crime, you'll do the time."

A look of dawning awareness crossed ten faces. Ashley's mouth flattened so much that Claire wondered if it would stay that way forever.

"I'm not exactly stupid," Claire continued. "I can tell when someone is trying to hurt someone else, and I will not put up with it. Any questions?" Several kids shook their heads. "Great. Please get out your math homework."

The fifth and sixth graders had their homework ready. One of the seventh graders had half of the assignment done. The remaining four older students had nothing.

"Where's your homework?" Claire asked.

"I didn't do it," Dylan answered nonchalantly.

"Any particular reason?"

He shrugged. "Mr. Nelson never made us. Homework was just practice. It was the tests that counted."

"If we could pass the tests, he said we really didn't have to do the homework," Lexi chimed in.

"And did you pass the tests?"

"Yes," the older kids said in unison.

Which made Claire wonder if Mr. Nelson had even bothered to grade the tests. Because after looking at the math placement results from the day before, she was thinking these kids had either gotten a case of collective amnesia over the summer or they hadn't learned the concepts in the first place.

"Well, things have changed," Claire said. "Homework is no longer optional. It is very much required. If you don't do your homework and show me your work, you will not pass math."

The kids looked as if she'd just told them that lunch was canceled for the year.

"But if we can pass the tests…"

"I'm sorry," Claire said pleasantly, "but this is not a negotiable issue."

"That's not fair."

She simply smiled. "In order to be fair, I'll let you do last night's homework tonight. We'll review today. Then, starting tomorrow, homework counts. Now, let's see what you remember from yesterday."

It was another long day. With each lesson she taught, it became more and more apparent that these kids had some serious holes in their education.

After school, Claire was sitting with her elbows planted on her desk, her forehead resting on her fingertips, pondering the situation, when she heard the door open. She shifted her hands to see Elena standing there, biting her lower lip.

"Hi, Elena. What can I do for you?"

"I forgot my math book." The girl went to her desk and took out the book. She hesitated, then asked, "Are you feeling all right?"

Claire smiled. "I'm fine. Just a little tired." *And discouraged.*

"We've never had a teacher that looked like you before," the girl said shyly. "I like your shoes."

Claire smiled again. She liked her shoes, too. It had taken her most of the summer to find the shade of green that perfectly matched her skirt. "Thanks. Hey, can I ask you a question?"

Elena nodded.

"Do you understand the math?"

"I do now."

"Did you yesterday?"

She shook her head, her dark braids moving

on her shoulders. "Today you went slower, and I think I got it."

"Thanks, Elena. I'll see you tomorrow."

"See you, Miss Flynn."

So she needed to slow down. All right. She could do that. But it killed her to be reviewing multiplication facts and long division, when she was supposed to be moving on into other aspects of math.

And as far as English went… She glanced down at the stack of poorly punctuated drills in front of her. *Yowza*. She hadn't created this monster, but she was supposed to tame it.

Welcome to the real world of education.

BRETT SAT DOWN at his computer and took a deep breath. The chores were done, and there was nothing pressing at the Ryker place. It was time. In fact, it was well past time.

Brett was going to college. Online. He just hoped no one found out—in case he failed.

During junior and senior high he'd been a poor student—not because he couldn't do the work, but because he wouldn't. His dad had made a career of comparing Brett's achievements to Will's, and Brett had invariably failed to measure up. Finally, he'd accepted the fact that in his dad's eyes he was never going to be as good at anything as Will was, so he quit trying, telling himself he wasn't really a loser, since he wasn't playing the game.

But still, he had silently resented Will for being so damn good at everything, and resented their dad for constantly reminding him of it.

Brett had eventually gotten his petty revenge, though, and had done a pretty fair job of messing up a number of lives in the process. Not bad for an underachiever.

Okay. First lesson. Concentrate.

Brett started by reading the introduction. Then he reread the introduction, and wondered if maybe he should start with his humanities class instead of algebra.

There was a knock on the door and he literally jumped at the chance to put his education on hold again.

And then he looked out and saw who it was. Claire. With a bottle of wine, no less.

This could not be good.

He opened the door, but only because he had no other option.

"Yes, I know," she said, as she walked in without waiting for an invitation. "We're holding on to our personal space, but I need some help, and damn it, Bishop, you're the only one who can give it to me." She handed him the bottle and walked to the cupboards. "Where do you keep your glasses?"

"Has anyone ever told you that you're pushy?"

Claire smiled at him over her shoulder as she opened a cupboard. "All the time."

"And it doesn't slow you down?"

"Not in the least."

Brett gave up. "Next to the fridge."

Claire opened the cupboard he indicated, then frowned as she pulled out a smallish glass. "What's this?"

"It's a wineglass."

"No. This is an overgrown shot glass. And where's the stem?"

"It's a poor man's wineglass. I can't afford stems. You're lucky it's not a jelly glass."

She smiled again as she took out a second one. "All right. But it's small, so we'll have to fill them more often."

"How long do you plan on staying?"

"Has anyone ever told you you're tactless?" she asked.

He smiled instead of answering.

"And *that* doesn't slow you down?"

"Not in the least."

Brett pulled a corkscrew out of the utensil drawer before Claire had a chance to tear the kitchen apart looking for it. He plunged it into the cork with a little more force than necessary.

"White wine?" he asked.

"Is that a problem?"

"I prefer red wine when I solve problems."

"I'll make a note of that."

"Actually, I can't see us doing a lot of joint problem solving," he said pointedly.

Claire settled herself on one of the mismatched kitchen chairs. "I know that Will asked you to help me when you could. And I may need a lot of help before this year is over."

She accepted the glass he offered, took a bracing drink, then reached up with her free hand to ruffle the top of her hair in a gesture that clearly suggested exhaustion, or possibly frustration. "Are you renovating?" She looked down the hall to the living room, where he was in the process of tearing up the old floor so he could lay a new one.

"The place needs work, so I try to do a little every month. Now, what can I do for you?"

"I'd like some information."

"On…?"

"My kids. My students. I've survived day two, and I'm not ashamed to admit that these kids are close to getting the best of me. That means I have to plan a strategy."

Brett was impressed, in spite of himself. He'd always admired proactive people, as long as they weren't running roughshod over him—or trying to.

"I'll tell you what I know, but you gotta realize I haven't lived here that long."

"But you're a native of the area."

"My grandfather and great-grandfather were natives. Granddad sold."

"Well, you've got to know more than I do." Claire reached down for her purse and pulled out a small spiral notebook. "I'm thinking that if I can just understand the lay of the land, who's related to whom and who does what, maybe I can connect better with the kids. I don't want any dirt or gossip. Just information that's in the public domain."

Brett lifted the wine to his lips, sipped. It really wasn't that bad for white wine. "Don't you have school records with that kind of information?"

"Allegedly, but they're in pretty bad shape. The district is sending me copies of missing documents, but I want to know about families. Where they live. What they do."

Brett shrugged. "I'll tell you what I can."

"Okay, first off, tell me about the Landaus."

"They're rich." Claire waited, and he expanded. "They're one of the few families here that are not land rich and cash poor. Landau's a nice guy. Ashley is his stepdaughter. Only child. He married the mother about three years ago, I think."

"How about Jesse Lane?"

Brett shook his head. "Don't know any Lanes. They aren't locals. It might be that new guy who has the trailer north of town."

"Elena and Lexi Moreno."

"They're related to the Hernandezes."

"Ramon and Lily?"

"Hardworking families. The Hernandezes work for the Landaus. The Morenos have their own place."

"So I have cousins in the classroom, as well as brothers and sisters," Claire said musingly. "Okay. Rudy Liscano."

Brett smiled slightly. Everyone knew Rudy. Everybody liked Rudy. "Rudy's another cousin to the Hernandezes and the Morenos. His dad works for the county-road department. He's the one you yell at when you blow a tire."

"I see. How about Rachel Tyler?"

"Her family has the oldest ranch in the area. They raise nice horses."

"Dylan Masterson?"

"I'm not certain. The Mastersons aren't local. I think they own some businesses somewhere and are out here escaping. I know they built a hell of a place on the other side of town."

"You mean, that A-frame?"

"That's it." Brett drained his glass. "I think she's an artist or something."

"And Toni Green."

"Her mom works at the bar. They live in the rooms over the bar." Brett had been invited to see those rooms before the latest boyfriend had taken up residence, but he'd declined the invitation. "I think she's escaping, too, but for a different reason."

Claire flipped her notebook shut. "Thanks."

"I didn't give you all that much information."

"I just want enough to understand where my kids are coming from, and I didn't want to ask Bertie. I think the ones who are ranch kids for real probably have different references and values than the imports." She refilled their glasses without asking. "In one of my college classes, the prof said that home visits were a must in order to understand your students, but… I think in a community like this, visits might be seen as nosiness unless the families invited me."

"You're right," Brett agreed.

"So, I decided to rely on hearsay."

"Then you should hit the post office and the mercantile."

"You gave me what I need." She leaned back in her chair, studying him in that steady way of hers. Her lips curved slightly. She had a really nice mouth. "So, tell me again, Brett. Why is it that we can't socialize?"

Brett felt his own mouth tighten.

Claire shrugged. "Hey. You're the one who laid down the rules. I was just wondering why."

And then he saw that he'd probably made a major tactical error. He'd already figured out from their first few encounters—and from the fact that she'd taken a teaching assignment in Barlow Ridge—that Claire was a woman who loved a challenge. And that was exactly what he'd given her. Stupid move.

"I didn't say we couldn't socialize. I said I wasn't *much* on socializing."

"You seemed to do okay at the wedding, except with me."

"Claire."

She raised her eyebrows, making her green eyes even wider beneath her pearly lavender eye shadow. He frowned, annoyed at the way she shook his concentration.

"We can socialize, but it has to be on a certain…level." She tilted her head inquiringly, but Brett had a suspicion that she knew exactly what he was referring to. "You were coming on to me at the wedding."

"A little," she agreed, totally missing his point.

"We can't... I mean, we're practically related, and I don't want to create a situation."

"Wow." Claire took a careful sip of wine, her expression maddeningly calm. "You certainly extrapolate things out, don't you? That's almost like jumping from a simple hello into marriage."

"No. It's not." He didn't like the way she made him feel foolish for a perfectly logical statement of fact.

"Well, I think you're dodging stones that haven't even been thrown."

"I like to err on the side of caution."

"That's not what I hear," she said softly. "Rumor has it you were a wild guy back in the day."

"Where'd you hear that?" he asked in an equally quiet tone.

"Around."

"Regan?" Damn, he hoped not. He didn't want Claire to know his story. But she and Regan were sisters.

"No. Actually, a couple of women were discussing you in the bar when I went in for a sandwich yesterday. You were a rodeo star, according to them."

"Yeah. I was."

Too close for comfort. Those rodeo days had ended up being the dark point of his life, and he wasn't going to discuss them. Period.

Brett slid the cork back into the bottle. Rudeness and tactlessness seemed to be his best strategies. He pushed the bottle across the table toward her. "I was kind of in the middle of something when you came."

She nudged it back toward him before she stood. "You keep it."

"You'll probably need it more than me." He picked up the wine and pressed it into her hands.

"Thanks for the help, Brett. See you around." A few seconds later, the screen door banged shut behind her. Brett watched her walk down the path for a moment, admiring the subtle swing of her hips beneath the swirly skirt in spite of himself.

Claire Flynn was not going to be good for his peace of mind.

CHAPTER THREE

CLAIRE GAVE HERSELF a good talking to as she walked home across the bristly hay field. Once upon a time she'd berated Regan for dating the wrong kind of man—which was truly a case of the pot calling the kettle black, since Claire also tended to pursue guys for the wrong reasons.

She liked to attain the unattainable.

It was a bad habit, and one she was trying to break herself of. Being attracted to Brett Bishop was not a step in the right direction, since she suspected her interest in him was sparked solely by his corresponding lack of interest in her.

But she couldn't get around the fact that there was something about him that made her want to know more. Like, why the barriers? With her, with his brother, and with his niece, Kylie.

There was probably a simple explanation.

Claire wondered how long it was going to take her to figure it out.

ON MONDAY MORNING Claire started her school day by handing out progress reports listing the students' grades in each subject.

"What are these?" Dylan asked with a sneer. Claire was going to start working on his attitude just as soon as she'd made some headway with Ashley.

"Those are your grades for your first week of school. I'd like you to show them to your parents, have them sign the bottom and then bring them back by Wednesday at the latest." The grades were, for the most part, dismal in math and English. Primarily because few of the students were doing their homework.

Dylan frowned. Elena Moreno's mouth was actually hanging open. Only Rudy and Jesse seemed satisfied with what was on the paper. Rudy had all A's. Jesse had straight C's, and apparently that was good enough for him. He was an earnest kid who tried hard, but it was especially obvious he had some holes in his education. His records had yet to arrive from his previous school, and Claire had no idea what his background was.

"Are you going to do this every week?" Ashley asked with disbelief.

"Every Monday. This way there will be no nasty surprises at the end of the quarter.

Everyone will know their grades, and your parents will be aware of your progress."

"But making us bring them back signed shows you don't trust us."

"You do know that trust is earned, don't you? I doubt we'll do the parent signatures all year, but I want to start out that way, until everyone is aware of what to expect."

"What're you going to do if we don't bring them back by Wednesday?" Dylan asked in his most obnoxious tone.

"I'll phone or e-mail your parents. Now, please get out your math homework."

Dylan blew out a disgusted breath and made a show of shoving the grade paper into his pocket in a big wad. The other kids tucked their slips away less dramatically, some in notebooks, some in pockets, and started digging for their math books.

"My mom is going to kill me," Toni murmured to Ashley later, as the class left for morning break.

"Mine won't," Ashley responded with a smug lift of her chin. She spoke loudly enough to make certain Claire heard her. Claire smiled, but it was an effort. She didn't even have the pleasure of knowing that real life would teach Ashley a lesson or two. Ashley's family probably had enough money to cushion her from reality.

Pity.

Ashley didn't have to grow up to be a shallow, arrogant person, but there didn't appear to be much to keep it from happening. And then, as if to solidify Claire's opinion, she heard Ashley through her open window after school, making fun of Jesse.

"Do you live here or something?" Ashley asked in a snooty voice.

"No. My dad works late." The poor kid was often sitting on the swings, waiting for his father to come pick him up, when Claire went home, and she left late most nights.

"Well, I hope he works overtime, so he can buy you some decent clothes."

Claire barely stayed in her seat. But she knew Jesse wouldn't appreciate his teacher coming to the rescue. He probably wouldn't appreciate knowing that she'd overheard the conversation, either.

"Hey, at least people like me," Jesse said.

"That's what you think," Ashley retorted smugly. "Come on, Toni. Let's go."

Claire drew in a breath, let it out slowly, and after a quick look out the window, forced herself to continue her grading. Jesse was still sitting on a swing, and he seemed to be okay. And Claire was going to see to it that he remained okay, at least while he was at school.

THE FIRST MEETING of the school parent-teacher organization was called to order that evening by Ashley's mother, who'd once again raided her daughter's wardrobe. There were at least twenty parents in attendance, in addition to Trini and Bertie. Claire was impressed. The parent-teacher organization of her old school had been comprised of approximately twenty percent of the parents. The Barlow Ridge PTO attendance seemed to be hovering around the one hundred percent mark. Claire was even more impressed with the treasurer's report. These people were either prolific savers, or they were talented at fund-raising. It turned out to be a combination of the two.

They discussed the year's fund-raisers—a Christmas craft show, a chili feed and a quilt auction. Claire knew of the quilt auction via Regan, who now owned two heirloom-quality hand-pieced quilts.

Almost twenty minutes were spent debating whether the PTO's Santa suit would last another season, or if they'd need to buy another before the Christmas pageant. And then they went on to folding chairs. Were there enough? Should the broken ones be fixed or replaced? And when had the piano last been tuned?

The meeting was almost over when Deirdre focused on Bertie and Claire, who were seated at the back of the room. "Have we covered everything?"

"I, um, have a request," Claire said.

Everyone half turned in their chairs to look at her. Claire decided it was a good thing that she enjoyed public speaking, because all eyes—some of them not that friendly—were on her.

"First of all, I'm enjoying working with your kids. We have some ground to make up because of teacher turnover during the past few years, and I was wondering if the PTO would purchase math manipulatives and four novel sets, one for each quarter."

Claire could tell by the way expressions shifted and glances were exchanged that she'd accidentally hit on a sore spot. She wondered what it could be. It certainly wasn't finances, from the sound of the treasurer's report. She tried again.

"The novels in the storeroom are not only old and not entirely grade appropriate, they're in really bad shape," she explained. "I don't know if they'll survive another reading. And as far as math manipulatives go, there aren't any."

"There's a reason for that," one of the parents said. "We've bought several programs in the past that other teachers packed up and took with them when they left."

"You're kidding!"

"Not at all. And I think our new novel sets and some reference books ended up in Wesley at the elementary school when a teacher transferred there. We also bought a pricey math program that left with another teacher, and she didn't even stay with our district. She moved out of state."

Another parent smiled condescendingly at Claire. "How long are *you* planning on being here?"

"I'm going to graduate school next fall. I made that clear when I interviewed here." *And I was hired because no one else would take the job.* Under normal circumstances Claire wouldn't have held her tongue, but she had enough of a fight on her hands bringing her students under control. She needed parental support, or her battle was going to be twice as hard.

"Couldn't you borrow what you need from one of the schools in Wesley?"

"I'll ask."

"It's nothing personal, Miss Flynn." Claire was getting very tired of hearing how nothing was personal in Barlow Ridge. "It's just that we've been burned in the past."

"And I don't think our kids need fancy programs and gimmicks." An older woman near the front spoke up. "They need a good teacher."

Claire was beginning to see that isolation might not be the only problem with teaching in Barlow Ridge. She composed herself before going on the offensive.

"Your children also need discipline and development of a work ethic, if they are going to achieve grade level."

Her statement caused a ripple. "What do you mean by '*achieve* grade level'?" Deirdre demanded in a shocked tone.

Claire frowned. "I mean, that many of my seventh and eighth grade students are behind in at least one subject area—primarily math. They need to catch up. Didn't you get standardized test scores last year?"

There was another ripple as the parents exchanged puzzled looks.

"No."

"None of you received scores?" Bertie asked. The group shook their heads in unison.

"I gave them to Mr. Nelson. He was supposed to staple them to the year-end report cards."

"And when did Mr. Nelson do anything he was supposed to do?" Trini muttered.

"Didn't you wonder why the younger kids had scores and the older ones didn't?" Bertie asked the group.

"I just assumed that the upper grades weren't tested. You know how they've messed with the tests lately, changing dates and grade levels…" Deirdre said.

"We have copies in your children's files," Bertie said, with a frustrated sigh. "We'll need some time to locate and duplicate them, but you'll get the scores before Friday."

The meeting was adjourned shortly thereafter, and Claire went into her room to collect her jacket and purse. She had no new novel sets, no math manipulatives—just parents who didn't think she was up to the job of teaching their children. Parents who hadn't been aware of how far behind their kids were.

And even though she didn't need the point hammered home that the parents weren't supporting her, it *had* been hammered home.

"What really fries me," one parent said as she passed by Clare's open door on the way to the exit, "is that the school district must know we have low scores, but they send out the most inexperienced teacher they can find."

"Well, she certainly isn't engaging Lexi," her companion responded. "It looks like all she's doing is drawing lines in the sand and daring the kids to step across. That's not teaching."

Claire swallowed hard and turned off the lights. She and Bertie stepped out of their rooms and into the hall at the same moment. Bertie signaled for her to wait a minute as the two parents made their way to the exit.

As soon as the door swung shut, Bertie said, "Try not to—"

"Take it personally?" Claire shook her head. "It's kind of hard not to."

"These kids haven't had a real teacher since Regan left, and the parents are getting frustrated."

"Well, I can't blame them, but I hate being prejudged."

"That's a tendency here," Bertie said. "You're newly graduated, which is a strike against you. And the kids are complaining, which is another strike. Plus…" She hesitated, then said, "You dress kind of…fancy. Which might put some parents off."

"They don't like the way I dress?" Claire

was wearing a knee-length chiffon skirt in a bright floral pattern, a silky peach T-shirt and a chunky necklace. Normal fare for her. But she remembered Elena saying they'd never had a teacher that looked like her.

"Well…" Bertie looked down at her own clothing, which consisted of brown corduroy pants, a white cotton T-shirt and well-worn athletic shoes. "I think it's been awhile since they've seen anyone wear hosiery to school."

"I'm not buying a new wardrobe to fit in," Claire muttered. "I like my clothes." She and Bertie walked down the hall together, exiting the school into the inky darkness of a cloudy night.

"I like your clothes, too. I wish I had the energy to dress better, but I don't." Bertie stuck her key in the lock and abruptly changed the subject as she twisted her hand. "This test thing really annoys me. It's good that Nelson got out of teaching, because I think the parents have cause for legal action."

"Would they do that?"

"Barlow Ridge parents are not passive parents." She smiled grimly before asking Claire, "Where's your car?"

"I walked."

"It's going to storm. Do you want a ride home?"

She shook her head. "Thanks, anyway."

"Coming to quilting club on Wednesday?"

"Will it be friendlier than the PTO?"

Bertie smiled ruefully. "There's some crossover—Deirdre, Willa, Mary Ann. I think they're already betting you won't show."

Claire smiled humorlessly. "In that case, I'll show." She couldn't sew a stitch, but she figured she could either be there, trying to do her part for the quilt auction, or sitting home alone with her ears ringing as the other women discussed her.

PHIL'S HORSES AND MULES arrived while Brett was in the middle of his online class. Horses he understood. Reacquainting himself with math was going to take some time. He was making headway, but he was glad to give himself a break in order to drive over to the ranch, less than a mile away, and take delivery.

He went to meet the shipper, who opened the door of a trailer to reveal a handsome black mule. Beyond that Brett could see two broad chestnut-colored backs, but the dividers kept him from seeing the horses' heads.

"They're tall," he commented to the driver.

"Yeah. And Numb Nuts, up front, doesn't have any manners."

"Good to hear."

Brett stepped in and ran a hand over the mule's neck. The big animal gave him a get-me-out-of-here look. Brett complied, leading the big guy out of the trailer and over to one of the many individual corrals adjacent to the barn. When he released it, the mule circled the pen once and then went to the water trough for a long drink.

"Where're you from?" Brett asked, suddenly realizing that he had no idea where these animals were being shipped from.

"San Diego. I left them in the trailer last night, because I didn't know if I could get the stud back in."

Phil wouldn't like that, Brett thought. Phil couldn't tell a good animal from a bad one without help, but he insisted that all of his animals be treated right. It was the one thing that helped Brett overlook his boss's other foibles, which included a healthy dose of arrogance coupled with ignorance about matters he wanted to look like an expert in. Such as horses.

Brett stepped back into the trailer to unload a very nice quarter horse. The mare followed him placidly to her pen, and then she, too, went straight for the water.

And now for Numb Nuts.

He had a feeling from the way the trailer was rocking, now that the stallion was alone and wondering where his mare had gone, that his nuts were actually not all that numb.

Brett opened the divider and the horse rolled an eye at him, showing white. And then the animal screamed. Brett untied him, taking a firm hold on the rope close to the snap, and started to lead him to his pen. The stud danced and rolled his eyes again, but he respected the lead rope, and Brett got him shifted safely. As soon as the stallion had drank his fill, however, he started pacing the fence, back and forth, back forth, punctuating every turn with a fierce whinny.

The driver smiled and headed for his truck, obviously glad to be on his way.

Brett decided to let the horse settle in for a day or two before he attempted to tune him up. And as soon as he could, he was going to suggest to Phil that unless he wanted to make a complete spectacle of himself, perhaps he might want to find a calmer animal to show.

When Brett pulled into his driveway, he saw Claire walking across the field toward his house. What now? She met him at his truck.

"I need a favor."

"So do I," Brett said wearily, pushing his hat back.

"What do you need?"

"I need someone to tactfully tell my boss that he's in over his head."

Claire frowned. "Who's your boss?"

"See that ranch over there?"

She nodded.

"It's one of many around here owned by the Ryker family. They have a land company and they lease ranches—including the one that I'm living on. Phil Ryker decided to become a cowboy a few years back, and took over that ranch as his personal hobby. I take care of it for him while he's away."

"I see."

"And he likes to buy horses. And cows. And mules. He even bought some llamas, once."

"And he's just bought something you don't think he can handle?"

Brett smiled wryly, wondering why he was unloading on Claire. She didn't seem to mind, though. "He bought something I *know* he can't handle, and now he has to be convinced of it before he hurts himself."

"Good luck," she said with a smile. Damn, but she had a nice smile.

"Yeah," he said, sobering up. "What favor do you need? Snake removal? Cooler renovation?"

"I'm joining the quilting club and Regan has a bag of stuff for me at her place. If you're going to Wesley this week, could you pick it up?"

"Yeah. I can do that."

"Thanks." She smiled again. "Well, I have a ton of planning to do, so I'll see you later." She took a few backward steps before turning around. "Good luck with your boss."

"Thanks," he muttered. He was probably going to need it.

The next morning Brett made his weekly trip to Wesley, picking up groceries, animal feed, hardware, and vaccines for the new horses. He put off stopping at his brother's place until last.

It was close to four when he knocked on the door. It swung open almost immediately, Kylie's wide smile fading when she saw him. She forced the corners of her mouth back up again.

"Hi. I thought you were someone else."

Obviously. Kylie had grown into a beautiful girl—almost a carbon copy of her mother—which added to Brett's awkwardness whenever he had to face her alone. Kylie always picked up on the vibe and reflected it back, making their one-on-ones a tad uncomfortable.

"Regan has a bag of quilt supplies for Claire that I'm supposed to pick up."

"Oh. Right. I was wondering what this was." Kylie stepped back to retrieve a large plastic bag, which she handed to him. For a moment they stared at each other, neither certain of what to say. As usual.

"Are you coming to watch me ride?" There was a regional 4-H horse show in Elko in two weeks, and Kylie had qualified in several events.

"Yes, I am." He made it a point to watch her ride or play basketball whenever he could. It hurt in some ways, but it was a price he was willing to pay.

"Do you know about the barbecue afterward?"

"What barbecue?"

"Regan wanted to have a get-together since Claire is here, so that she can introduce her around."

Brett automatically shook his head. "No. I probably won't be coming."

"All right." Kylie seemed fine with it. Relieved, in fact. Brett felt the usual twinge of regret.

A truck pulled into the drive behind his, and a kid who looked too young to be driving jumped out. Kylie's face lit up and Brett felt a stirring of protectiveness. Surely Will wasn't letting her date already? She was only fifteen.

"Hi, Kylie. Hi…" The boy's face contorted in confusion for a second and then he said, "I thought you were Mr. Bishop."

"He is," Kylie said. "This is my uncle."

"Oh. Hi. I'm Shane." The boy extended his hand, and Brett gave him points for manners.

"Nice to meet you." He glanced over at Kylie, encountering eyes exactly like his own. "I gotta get going. Nice meeting you, Shane. Bye, Kylie."

"See ya."

CLAIRE PERCHED ON the edge of her desk, an expectant look on her face. After a few seconds of staring silently, she asked, "Is there a problem with the topic?"

The students shook their heads, then began writing in their journals.

Claire waited the full fifteen minutes before asking, "Does anyone want to share?"

As usual, the students sat staring straight ahead. Even the young ones. They were learning fast. Claire sighed and told the kids to get out their social-studies texts. When she'd informed Brett that she could take whatever these students could dish out, she'd meant challenges such as snakes—not things like a stupefying lack of response. And she was fairly certain it wasn't too late for the younger kids, that they *would* respond if it weren't for fear of being laughed at by the older students.

What to do?

Claire drummed her fingers on her desk, then stopped when a few kids looked up at her. She opened her grade book and pretended to study the columns of numbers. The obvious answer was to separate the younger students from the older ones, but she couldn't do that in the space she had available.

She thought back to her professors, with all their pie-in-the-sky educational theories. Never once had it been mentioned that she might be faced with kids who simply refused to engage themselves. Kids who did not want to learn.

Regan had advised her to ignore the stony stares and reward the behavior that met her expectations, but hadn't mentioned what to do if the behavior of the older kids was tainting the younger ones.

Claire headed for the office phone. Something had to be done before it was too late.

Back in the classroom, she told the fifth and sixth graders to go outside for recess. When the older kids also rose to their feet, she asked them to remain. She spoke quietly, but there was no doubt that she meant what she said. The seventh and eighth graders sat back down.

"We need to talk. You guys are role models for the younger kids. I want to know if you think you're setting them a good example?"

They did not even have the grace to appear ashamed. If anything, they looked smug, and Claire felt her anger growing.

"You guys are acting like a bunch of jerks, and it has to stop. I will not have you ruining the education of the other students. I've phoned Principal Rupert, and if this behavior continues, he will be driving out to have a talk with each one of you on an individual basis."

Dylan and Ashley both smirked. Toni gave Claire a stony stare.

"He's also calling your parents today."

Ashley looked unconcerned, but Dylan and Toni paled slightly. So there was *some* fear. That was good. Maybe there was hope.

"I don't hold grudges," Claire continued. "I'm willing to let bygones be bygones, if you start acting the way you know you're supposed to act." She drew in a breath, wondering if the kids knew how much she was winging it. "Instead of recess, I would like you to write about how your behavior is affecting the other kids. Ashley, I want to talk to you privately."

"Sure," the girl said with a toss of her head. She followed Claire out into the hallway.

"I know you feel safe, Ashley—like no consequence can touch you."

The girl smiled.

"And I want a straight answer. Are you going to set a better example with your behavior? Or are you going to continue as you've been doing?"

"I don't see anything wrong with my behavior, and neither does my mother."

"You don't see how the younger kids are learning from watching you?"

She shook her head.

"Then my only option is to put you where they can't watch you. Your desk will be in the hall for the remainder of the day and tomorrow, until we talk to the principal. We'll reevaluate then."

"I'm going to sit in the hall?"

"Yes."

"How will I hear what you're saying?"

"What would that matter, Ashley? You seem to think you already know everything. Stay here. I'll go get your desk."

Claire took a few steps toward the room, angry with herself for sniping at the girl. She turned back, wanting to give it one last stab. "This is your choice, Ashley. I don't want you out here. If you'll participate in class in a respectful way, I want you in the room with everyone else. You're a bright girl, and you can help the younger students learn."

She raised her chin and narrowed her eyes. But she did not respond.

A steaming Ashley was sitting at her desk in the hall when the younger kids came traipsing in again. Claire stood next to her door and watched the procession. The kids looked first at Ashley, then at Claire. No one said anything.

There was a definite change in attitude, now that Ashley was no longer in residence. Claire took her the work for the afternoon, then closed the classroom door. There would, no doubt, be a hot phone call from Deirdre Landau later. Maybe even a personal visit. But it was worthwhile, if Claire could save her younger students from going over to the dark side.

Surprisingly, Ashley left school that afternoon without summoning her mother. She walked away, her chin held high and her books pressed close to her chest. Toni walked with her, but their heads were not together as usual.

Claire felt a little bad, but knew she had to draw the line somewhere.

She graded papers until three-thirty and then went into her storage closet, prior to her usual trip to the basement before going home. Every evening she sorted and carted one shelf of stuff off to the nether regions. She almost had space in her closet now to store the textbooks that were shoved into boxes under her counters. And in the process she had uncovered some useful supplies, as well as some hilarious artifacts of days gone by. She figured that with her box-a-day strategy, she'd have decades worth of haphazardly stored items properly sorted and put away by the end of the semester. If nothing else, she would leave the school better organized than she'd found it—and the students better educated. Even if it killed her. And them.

Claire pulled open the stubborn basement door and started down the stairs, descending into the earthy coolness, which felt good after the heat of the classroom. She had just heaved the box up on top of the lowest stack of rubber bins when she heard a heavy scraping noise, followed by a dull thud.

The door. Someone had closed the basement door.

Bertie must have come back, seen it open…

Claire trudged up the stairs and pushed. The door didn't budge. She controlled a twinge of panic, twisted the handle and pushed again. Nothing. Someone had thrown the dead bolt. She began to pound with the heel of her hand.

"Bertie!"

No answer. Claire pounded until her hand was bruised, more in frustration than from any hope of being heard. It was pretty obvious she'd been locked in on purpose. Three guesses as to who had done it.

She sank down onto the top step and stared at the dangling light. About time for the bulb to burn out, the way things were going. She had a flash of inspiration and shot a glance over her shoulder at the door.

But the hinges were on the outer side. Drat.

The frog croaked and Claire's shoulders slumped.

Could it be she was going to spend a night in the basement? Not if she could help it.

She rose to her feet and tromped down the stairs. The ventilation windows were covered with screens, and they were quite small. And high—probably seven feet off the floor. Claire glanced down at her hips, then back up at the window. What would be worse? Spending the night in the basement or spending the night stuck in a window?

It was a no-brainer. She was going for stuck-in-the-window.

Claire searched for some moderately safe way to get herself up there. With all the stored files and equipment, would it have been too much to ask that a ladder be among them? Apparently so. The only bits of furniture were rickety or broken. An old file cabinet wobbled when she tried to move it, so she started stacking rubber bins. The ones that were full enough to support her weight were also quite heavy. She managed to pile them three high and then climbed on top, grimacing as her hands pushed the damp, mossy wall when she steadied herself.

The window was now at shoulder level, and it wouldn't open. It had no latch.

Claire said a word that was normally frowned upon in a school setting, then climbed off the stack of boxes to find something she could use to break the glass.

THE PHONE RANG just as Brett started working on his algebra assignment. He'd already done all the damage he could to his humanities lesson, and it was time to move on.

"Hi, Brett," Regan said. "Have you seen Claire?"

"Uh, no. I left the bag of supplies inside her door. She wasn't home."

"She's not answering her phone, and I'm getting concerned."

"Maybe she's in the shower."

"For two hours?"

Actually, he could imagine that. Brett glanced out the window and saw the lights weren't on in the trailer, shooting that theory to hell. "I'll walk over to her house."

"Thanks, Brett. I appreciate it."

"No problem."

Maybe it was quilting night, Brett reasoned as he headed across the dark field, flashlight in hand. Or maybe she had a date. On a Thursday? Probably not. Maybe she was still working. That seemed the most reasonable answer, even if it was going on seven o'clock.

Claire pulled into her driveway just as Brett rounded the rear of her trailer. He turned off the flashlight and thought about disappearing when she got out of her car, but then noticed that she was looking…rough. Her white blouse and her face were smeared with a dark substance, which he hoped wasn't blood. It was hard to tell in the fluorescent glow of the yard light. And her skirt was ripped up the side.

Alarmed, he stepped out of the darkness, his movement obviously startling her, and then he saw to his relief that the stains were not blood.

"What are you doing here?" she asked with a remarkable amount of dignity, considering the fact that she was green.

"Regan called. She was worried about you."

"Oh, that's right. I was supposed to—" She broke off and frowned at Brett. "Well, thanks for checking on me. I'll give her a call."

"You want to tell me what happened?"

She shook her head. "No. I think I'll employ that we-need-to-keep-our-own-space rule you invented."

"Suit yourself." His mouth tightened as he fought with himself. She was vertical, obviously not hurt—physically, anyway. He'd love to know how she'd gotten smeared with green gunk, but it was none of his business. Still... "Are you sure?"

"Positive," she said. "Now, if you'll excuse me?" She walked past him into her house, the tear in her skirt exposing a lot of leg as she disappeared. The door closed with a thump.

Brett stared at it for a moment, then turned

his flashlight on again and started back across the field.

This was not going to be a restful school year.

CHAPTER FOUR

A GROAN ESCAPED Claire's lips as she saw her reflection in the living-room mirror. She was green.

How had Brett kept from laughing? Or asking more questions?

She blew out a breath that lifted her short bangs, and headed toward the bathroom, where she cranked on the hot water and stripped off her ruined clothing.

Claire had made a career out of trying not to let problems bother her—instead, she let them bother Regan. Regan was a caretaker by nature, and Claire was more than happy to let her sister smooth out the wrinkles in her life. At least until that unhappy day when Regan had moved from Las Vegas to Wesley, and suddenly Claire had found herself dealing with her issues on her own. But to her amazement, after a few false starts and many long phone calls, she had done all right.

She wasn't going to tell Regan about this escapade. Not just yet, anyway. She braced her hands on the sink and let her head droop as she waited for the water to warm up.

Reaction was setting in. Anger. Bewilderment. And a grudging appreciation for Ashley's style of revenge. The kid was good. Now, Claire would have to be even better.

BRETT PACED THROUGH his house. He was supposed to be finishing his math, since it was due the next day, but he also had some work to do in his living room. He'd torn out the existing floor and was down to subfloor. There were bundles of interlocking hardwood flooring sitting there, and they weren't going to lay themselves.

Algebra or flooring? He headed for his computer. When a guy felt like doing flooring, it probably meant he was avoiding something that needed his attention more.

Brett had figured it was going to take some work to bring himself up to speed in his studies, but he hadn't realized just how much he'd forgotten, or at the very least, misplaced in his brain. And it wasn't as if he hadn't used math throughout his adult life, calculating animal dosages, fencing footage, acreage, amounts of feed. But somehow, that came easier than solving for X.

He pulled his yellow legal tablet closer and copied a problem. And then, as he launched into step one, he found himself wondering again just how Claire Flynn had ended up the color of slime.

CLAIRE SPENT MOST of the night staring at her dark bedroom ceiling and debating about how to deal with the situation. Ashley had gotten her revenge, but there was no way for Claire to prove it. So what to do? Confront her and listen to the denial? Contact the principal with nothing but a hypothesis?

Ignore the incident?

Ask Bertie for advice?

She hated to do that, and hated to admit what had happened, but she was going to have to explain the situation to Bertie. The work order to fix the basement window would have to go through her as lead teacher.

Drat.

Claire took extra care with her hair and makeup the next morning. She even wore her favorite dress, hoping she wouldn't be squeezing through any small spaces in it, and she drove, instead of walking, arriving early.

The basement door was still latched from the outside.

Bertie came in just after Claire, and found her standing there.

"Working up courage to go downstairs?" she asked as she went into the office and dumped a cardboard box on the floor.

"No. Surveying the scene of the crime."

Bertie reappeared. "What does that mean?"

Claire shrugged. "Someone locked me in the basement last night."

"No." But even as she spoke, it was obvious from the older woman's expression that she believed her. "Ashley?"

"That's who my money's on. No proving it, though." Claire sighed again. "Any ideas on how to handle this?"

Bertie leaned back against the copy machine and studied the floor tiles for a moment, a deep frown pulling her gray eyebrows together.

"Not an easy one."

"One of the basement windows needs to be repaired." Bertie's eyes snapped up and Claire told her the entire story.

"You know, Wanda would have been here at ten o'clock."

"I hadn't thought of that." Wanda, whom

Claire had yet to meet, was supposed to clean the school between the hours of three and five, but she preferred to work between ten and twelve, after her kids were in bed. The district office was unaware, and Bertie saw no reason to enlighten them.

"I wasn't thinking all that clearly, to tell you the truth. I just knew I didn't want to spend the night in the basement."

"I don't blame you. Not with Jim Shannon down there."

"The frog has a name?"

Bertie slowly shook her head. "No. Jim is a ghost."

Somehow Claire wasn't surprised. "Ghost?"

"Yes. It's a long story that has been embellished for years, but to sum it up, someone called Jim Shannon fell down the stairs about eighty years ago, shortly after the school was built. Apparently, they hadn't installed a hand railing and he slipped."

"And he died?" If so, Claire was glad she'd been happily unaware last night, when it had been just her and Jim and the frog.

"The story gets a little hazy there. The consensus is that he lived another ten years after his tumble, but had a permanent limp and held a grudge because of it." Bertie started pulling reams of colored paper out of the storage cupboard. "He's buried on the other side of the fence, and the kids swear that they can hear him moaning in the basement."

"How can someone be buried on the other side of the fence?"

"Family plot. They don't allow it anymore, but sixty or seventy years ago they weren't so particular."

"Well, I wasn't feeling any vibes from Jim. But I was mad enough that he may have been afraid of me."

Bertie smiled and lifted another stack of paper onto the counter.

"What should I do?"

"We have two choices here. We can call Rupert and see what he wants to do about it, which will be nothing, because he won't want to get off his lazy keister and drive out here unless we have the suspect in custody."

"And choice number two?"

"We report the broken window, have the district repair it, pretend nothing has happened and listen for information." Claire cocked her head and Bertie explained. "My little guys are a fountain of information. They hear things from the older kids and share among themselves. All I have to do is keep very busy at my computer. For some reason they think that if my back is turned, my ears don't work."

Claire laughed. "I like plan number two. And now I guess I'd better go and decide how to wage my counterattack."

"Good luck," Bertie called as Claire left the office.

Claire was afraid she was going to need it.

CLAIRE WAS TALKING TO Mr. Rupert on the phone when the students came in at the morning bell, so she didn't see Ashley's expression as she entered the classroom. Claire ended the call a few seconds later and went over to Ashley's desk.

"Would you like to stay in here today?" she asked.

The girl's eyes narrowed as she considered Claire. Their gazes held for a moment as they sized each other up, each of them a little more impressed with the other's abilities than she'd been the day before. "Yes," Ashley said.

"I've spoken to Mr. Rupert. First sign of rudeness and you're back in the hall and he's on his way out for a meeting."

"I understand," Ashley said.

"Good. Maybe we can start over."

But Ashley wasn't interested in starting over. In spite of her promise to avoid being rude, she shot daggers at Claire when she didn't think she was looking, and Claire noticed the kids forming a tight knot around her during recess, probably being filled in on what had happened to Claire the day before.

And even though she didn't need confirmation that the story had been told, she got it shortly after school, when Elena Moreno came in for the coat she'd left behind.

"Did something happen to you, Miss Flynn?"

Claire managed a perplexed expression. "No, why do you ask?"

"No reason."

Mmm, hmm. Well, at least the girl looked concerned.

"Some of the kids kind of noticed a window got broken," Elena added, as she bunched her coat into a wad and stuffed it into her backpack, apparently hoping to jog Claire's memory.

"Mrs. Gunderson has already phoned it in to the maintenance department. But thanks for reporting it." Claire gave her most serene smile. "I'll see you tomorrow."

Elena smiled back, obviously confused. "Well, see ya."

"See ya."

She headed for the door, glancing at Claire over her shoulder before disappearing from view.

Claire let out a small sigh as she heard the outer door bang shut. She hadn't lied to the girl so much as sidestepped her question. And she was going to keep sidestepping until she had this situation under control.

THE QUILTING CLUB MET on Wednesdays at seven o'clock, and Claire was determined to attend every meeting—at least until she'd made some inroads into the community. She wasn't going to impress anyone with her sewing ability, but she figured the more she was around them, the more the townspeople would get used to her, and the more parent support she'd have.

Claire had spent her time after school that day catching up on her grading rather than organizing the storage closet. No more trips to the basement for her unless Bertie was in the building and aware of where she was going. The basement buddy system. At exactly 5:00 p.m., she gathered up her tote bag of quilting supplies and locked the school.

Jesse was still waiting by the swings. Ramon had been with him up until 4:30 p.m., but now the boy sat alone, making patterns in the dirt with his tennis shoe.

"Waiting for your dad?" Claire asked as she walked by on the way to the gate.

"Yeah." Jesse twisted the swing sideways. "He's usually here by now, but he had a longer trip today."

"Trip?"

"He's a salesman. He has a route and today's his long day."

"I see." Claire smiled, wondering why a salesman was living in such a remote area. Maybe the guy just wanted to get out of the rat race. Claire had yet to meet Jesse's dad, but parent-teacher conferences would be coming up, and she'd meet him then.

"You know, if you ever need a ride home, I can give you one."

Jesse shook his blond head. "No. Dad doesn't want me home when he's not there."

So instead, he wanted the poor kid sitting in a deserted school yard? Alone. That made tons of sense.

"I was wondering…"

"Yes?" Claire asked when the boy's voice trailed off.

"Do you have any chores or anything that need doing around your place?"

"Are you hiring out?" Claire asked.

Jesse glanced down at his pants, which had a hole in the knee, and it wasn't too hard to follow his train of thought. "Yeah," he said matter-of-factly. "I was thinking that I could, you know, buy a few clothes."

"It's always fun to buy clothes." Claire gave no indication that she didn't think a ten-year-old should be buying his own clothing. "Yes, I can come up with one or two things."

"Is Saturday morning all right?"

"Can you come on Sunday, instead?" Kylie had a horse show on Saturday, and Claire wasn't going to miss it.

"I can come Sunday."

"Other people might need work done on Saturday, you know."

"Yeah," he said with a bright smile. "I'll check around."

An older model Ford Explorer pulled up in front of the school then and Jesse jumped to his feet. "That's Dad. See ya." He grabbed his backpack and trotted off. "Thanks," he called as he closed the school-yard gate.

Claire stood near the swing for a few minutes after the boy had climbed in and the vehicle had driven away. She'd lifted a hand in greeting to the driver and had gotten a quick, rather distracted wave in return.

She wasn't quite sure what to make of Mr. Lane.

"IS IT TRUE THE KIDS locked you in the school basement?"

Claire had barely taken her seat at the quilting meeting when Anne McKirk, the mercantile owner, growled her question. Fortunately, she was sitting next to Claire and hadn't growled all that loudly. None of the other women seemed to have heard.

"Where on earth did you hear that?" Claire asked.

"From pretty much everyone."

"Did you hear who did it?" Claire asked, without really expecting an answer.

"That Landau girl," Anne said promptly. She opened the large plastic bag sitting at her feet and pulled out a quilt hoop with a red-and-blue square stretched across it. "What are you going to do about it?"

"Make her learn something, whether she likes it or not."

Anne didn't say anything more, but she was smiling as she placed her hoop on the long table at which they were seated.

Trini pulled out the chair directly across the table from Claire. "So you came," she said with a smile. "Do you have your stuff?"

Claire plopped her own plastic bag on the table. "Yes. I just don't know what to do with it." Regan had bought the things on the list that Trini had supplied, sending them along with Brett, and Claire had examined them. But she was still unclear on how it all became a quilt.

"Great. Come on over to the cutting table and I'll show you how to make the pieces. We're each making a square for this Fourth of July quilt, so you can learn the ropes and contribute."

Ten minutes later, Claire was back at the long table with a stack of precision-cut red and blue triangles, parallelograms and squares.

"Thread your needle," Anne instructed, without looking at her. She said it in a voice that made Claire believe the older woman thought her incapable of the single act. Well, she happened to be a fine needle threader. It was the sewing part she'd have to fake.

Claire quickly got the hang of the running stitch used to sew the pieces together, and she concentrated on the task, while conversation floated around her, providing a pleasant background. She soon abandoned the flat surface of the table and held the fabric pieces on her lap, frowning as she bobbed the needle up and down, attaching bits of fabric. She'd felt awkward at first, but sewing was becoming more natural to her.

She picked up the two pieces she had just joined, pressed the seam to one side with her fingers, as Trini had shown her, and then pinned a long parallelogram to it and put it back on her lap to stitch.

The other women seemed to have forgotten she was there. She didn't really have anything to say, so she remained quiet and sewed, feeling a sense of satisfaction to be doing something so useful. Maybe she could actually make a quilt.

"What do I do once I get the square sewn together?" Claire asked no one in particular.

"Lap quilt," Anne murmured, her glasses slipping down her nose as she concentrated on her hoop. "Each square is individually quilted to a square of batting and backing of the same size. Then we join *those* quilted squares together and—"

"Instant quilt," Trini finished. "We don't have to use big frames this way, and we can quilt anywhere."

"How many quilts do you need for the spring auction?"

"As many as we get done. We try to finish one for each member, so that would be twelve, including you."

"If you stay that long," Anne said.

Claire pursed her lips and focused on her stitches. Just a few more and the square would be done. She ended the longest seam she'd yet attempted, knotted it off the way Trini had shown her and clipped the thread. Done.

She lifted the square off her lap and felt a breeze as her skirt came with it.

She frowned and gave a small tug. Her skirt refused to let go of the square, and vice versa, and then one of the older women across the table started laughing.

"You…" she pressed her lips together, but couldn't contain her mirth "…you sewed it to your skirt."

Claire gave another experimental tug. "Yes, I did," she agreed. She looked up, her expression serious. "Surely this isn't the first time this has happened?"

Lips quivered and then several of the smiles turned into giggles.

"I can see that the club is going to be a more active place with you here," Anne said, passing Claire a small pair of scissors. "Just clip the knot and pull the thread."

"And this was my best seam, too," Claire said as she followed directions. The square lifted free a few seconds later.

"Why don't you sew up on the table?"

Lexi's mom, who had ignored Claire up to this point, suggested.

"Good idea," she agreed. It felt more awkward sewing on the table rather than on her lap, but she could see she'd have fewer mishaps that way.

"Is this the first time you've quilted?" someone asked.

"Is it that obvious?" Claire replied.

The woman shook her head. "Not at all," she said wryly. "By the way, I'm Elena's grand-mother, Gloria."

"Nice to meet you," Claire stated. She re-threaded her needle and started sewing. "Elena's a very nice girl."

"Who wants green shoes just like yours."

"Really? They're quite practical, you know. Green goes with almost everything."

"But do you have any idea how hard they are to find?"

Claire grinned. "As a matter of fact, I do."

The rest of the meeting went better than she had expected. She couldn't say she was a fully accepted member of the group by the time she left, but she had the feeling the others weren't going to mind having her there. Not all of the PTO moms had warmed up to her, but she'd made some headway, and she understood their cautiousness. Even though Claire was by nature an all-or-nothing girl, she'd take what she could get in this case.

BRETT SHOWED UP at the horse show just as it was beginning, and settled in the middle of the stands, using two large family groups as cover. He wanted to watch alone, and if Claire saw him he had a feeling that wouldn't be possible.

The morning air was crisp, but by afternoon he knew he'd be glad to be under the canopy. Even in late September, the midday temperatures could become uncomfortably hot.

Kylie was entered in three events, all of which were scheduled for that day. He'd watch, maybe stop by and give her an "atta girl," then head back to the ranch to put some time in on Phil's killer stud. He knew Regan wanted him to go to the family picnic, play nice and act like he belonged, but the truth was that he *didn't* belong.

The stands were almost full when the show started. He could see all of the fairgrounds from his vantage point—Will's trailer, Kylie cantering her horse in the warm-up arena prior to her first event and Will and Regan sitting side by side on the running boards of the trailer. Claire was standing next to Regan, watching

Kylie. She was wearing jeans, something he'd never seen her in before, with a formfitting shirt and white sunglasses.

Brett pulled his attention back to the arena, where the halter classes were taking place. He was here to watch a horse show, not Will's sister-in-law.

CLAIRE HAD SPENT surprisingly little time at horse shows, considering the fact that Regan had once been a show jumper. This show was her third.

"See? It's not all dust and horse manure," Regan commented as they made their way back to the trailer from the arena where Kylie had just taken the reserve champion ribbon in a class called reining. Claire had no idea how the horse or rider were judged, but she could tell from Will and Regan's reactions that Kylie had done a bang-up job. Even Kylie, who had a tendency to be overly critical of her own performance, was grinning widely.

Claire skirted a pile of the stuff that horse shows weren't made of. "I have to admit, it's nice being out in the sun, watching the kids. What's Kylie's next class?"

"Barrels. It won't be until after lunch."

"Cool. I'm starving."

"We're eating light, because of the barbecue later."

"Fine with me. I just need something to take the edge off."

Kylie and Will were already at the trailer, unsaddling the horse.

"My stop could have been better," Kylie told her father. "He was slow. I think that's why I got second."

"We'll work on it," Will agreed.

Claire wandered to the front of the truck and leaned against the sun-warmed hood, facing the stands. Brett was there, near the top. She'd spent a good deal of time that morning surreptitiously searching the crowd until she'd finally zeroed in on him. Now she found herself checking periodically to see if he was still around.

He was. He hadn't moved, even now when the lunch break had been announced.

Regan came to lean beside her, following her sister's gaze.

"Why is he up there?" Claire asked.

"Better view."

"Will he be coming to the barbecue?"

"I'd be surprised," Regan said softly.

And for reasons she couldn't quite figure out, Claire refrained from asking why.

CLAIRE DIDN'T COME HOME Saturday night. Must have been a helluva picnic, Brett thought as he propped the ladder next to his house. The place needed a new roof, which he'd be paying for now that he'd successfully negotiated the option to buy, but not for a year or two, the way things looked. So in the meantime, he'd have to continue climbing onto the roof after each windstorm to replace missing shingles.

He's just finished hammering the last asphalt beauty into place when he noticed a kid walking down the driveway. Brett descended, hitting the ground about the same time the light-haired boy reached the gate.

"Hi," Brett said, wondering if he was there to sell something. Brett had only lived in Barlow for a year, but he knew the school was hell-bent on fund-raising.

"Hi." The kid shuffled his feet. "I'm kinda looking for a job, and I was wondering if you have any chores that need doing. Miss Flynn said—"

"Miss Flynn sent you over?"

"Yeah."

Brett glanced toward the trailer. No car. Claire wasn't there. Maybe she'd told the boy to hit Brett up while they were at school.

"Well…" He really didn't want a kid hanging around.

The boy's face fell. "Thanks, anyway."

Brett groaned inwardly. "Now that I think about it, I have a few things I could use a hand with. Are you any good with a shovel?"

"I guess."

"You guess?"

"Never did a lot of shoveling." He spoke cautiously, obviously wondering if this admission would be a deal breaker.

"Then it's about time you learned. Are you interested in working hourly or for a flat rate by the job?"

"Flat rate."

Brett almost smiled. The kid spoke authoritatively, but Brett had a strong feeling he had no idea what the difference was between the two.

"Flat rate it is. You got a name?"

"I'm Jesse Lane."

"Nice to meet you, Jesse. I'm Brett."

They were almost to the barn when Claire's car pulled into her driveway. Good. He and Claire would be having a discussion about this matter after Jesse went home. Brett didn't appreciate her sending a kid over without so much as a heads-up. *She* might be out to save the world, but that didn't mean Brett Bishop had to help her.

CHAPTER FIVE

CLAIRE WAS PLANTING BULBS in the long-neglected flower bed that ran the length of her trailer when Brett arrived from across the field, determined to set a few things straight. He almost turned back when he saw what she was doing. He'd never had a tenant who'd tried to improve the place before. Most of them just complained a lot and then moved on.

"We need to talk," he said, in what sounded to him like a reasonable voice.

"About what?" Claire used both hands to pat dirt over the top of a bulb.

"Jesse Lane."

"What about him?" She pushed the hair away from her forehead with her wrist.

"I'd appreciate it if you'd talk to me before sending kids over looking for work."

"I didn't send him."

They regarded each other for a moment, and

Brett knew they were thinking the same thing. Jesse wasn't a liar. The kid was too earnest.

"You didn't tell him I'd hire him to help with chores?"

Claire stuck the trowel into the dirt. "He's doing some chores for me today, but I told him I'd be gone Saturday and he might want to see if anyone else had chores that day."

"Maybe that was what he meant."

Claire cocked her head. "Did you hire him?"

Brett didn't like the way she was looking at him, as if she'd just decided he might actually be redeemable. "Yeah."

"That was nice of you."

"I can be nice."

"If you say so," she said in a skeptical voice, but he knew she was playing with him. Sometimes he wondered if there was ever a time when she wasn't.

Brett debated for a moment, then asked the question that had been driving him crazy. "How did you get to be green the other night?"

Claire stood up and took her time brushing the dirt from her knees. She didn't seem at all surprised by the abrupt change of topic. "From being in close contact with some rather slimy moss."

"And how did you come into contact with moss?" In Nevada.

"I was in the school basement."

Oh, that made perfect sense. What had she done while she was down there? Rub her face on the wall?

"Run into Jim Shannon?" he asked conversationally.

"Fortunately, I didn't even know about Jim Shannon then."

"What happened?"

"Someone shut the door while I was down there and latched it, so I had to break a window and climb out."

"A kid?"

"Probably."

He tried not to look surprised either by the student's actions or her own. But he was. "That's not a good start to the school year."

"No." She reached down for the trowel, idly wiping dirt off the metal with a gloved finger. "These kids play hardball."

"Hey. You gotta be tough to survive in Barlow Ridge."

"I guess."

"What are you going to do about it?"

"Nothing. If I get some solid evidence—which is highly unlikely at this point—I may change my mind, but for now it never happened."

"That's probably better than making a big deal over it."

"I guess we'll see. As I figure it, one of two things can happen. Either they give up, or they try harder. And I've got to tell you, I'm really hoping for the former."

WHEN CLAIRE ARRIVED at school the following morning, Jesse was already sitting in his swing, but this time he was not alone. Cuddled in his lap was a fluffy tabby cat.

Claire got out of her car, slung her tote strap over her shoulder and walked to the playground. When Jesse looked up at her, she could see that his eyes were swollen, red rimmed. He had been crying.

"Hi, Jesse. I see you brought a friend to school."

He nodded.

"I don't know if Mrs. Gunderson is going to like that."

"I know." He bit his lip.

"Is there a reason you brought your cat to school?"

"We have dogs and they attack cats."

"How long have you had the cat?"

"Awhile. But Dad is tired of the litter box and he says I have to get rid of her. I can't let her outside to go to the bathroom, because the dogs'll get her."

The boy's voice started to break. Claire lowered herself into the other swing, ignoring the fact that her skirt was now resting in the dust. "Is there someone…"

The boy raised sad eyes and Claire had her answer.

She reached out to stroke the cat, which huddled closer to Jesse. Then she dug a hand into her bag and pulled out her keys.

"You can take her to my house." There was plenty of time for him to walk over there and back before school began.

"Really?" And then his face fell. "She'll need a litter box."

"She'll be all right until lunch, won't she?" Jesse nodded.

"I'll run to the store during lunch." Surely Anne had kitty litter among her assortment of animal supplies.

"Thanks, Miss Flynn." Jesse stood, hefting the cat up higher on his shoulder. "I'll be back in time for school."

Claire watched him let himself out the gate, and wondered what she'd gotten herself into.

THERE WAS A KID in Claire's trailer. Brett had just finished his morning chores when he glanced across the field and saw a small boy disappear inside.

Brett decided, in spite of his vow to keep his nose out of Claire's business, to investigate. It beat trying to find a snake later on.

It took only a few minutes to cross the field. He was quietly mounting the steps when the door opened and Jesse came backing out. The kid jumped a mile when he saw Brett, and a scarlet flush stained his cheeks.

"Shouldn't you be in school?" Brett asked gruffly.

"I was dropping something off for Miss Flynn."

"Like what?"

"My cat."

"Your cat? Why?"

The boy swallowed and the story poured out. Brett nodded as Jesse talked, thinking that he could see the dad's point of view where the litter box was concerned, but all the same… Making your child get rid of his pet? It seemed a bit harsh. Especially when Jesse was so attached to it.

"And Miss Flynn is going to keep it for you?"

"She just said I could keep it here today. She didn't say anything about how long."

Brett considered the situation, and then he

did another nice thing that Claire would probably find hard to believe.

"Well, you know, I don't have any dogs. And I do have a lot of mice in my barn."

Jesse's eyes widened and he started to smile, but fought it, just in case he'd misunderstood. It gave Brett the feeling that he'd already had too many disappointments in his short life.

"I think if she lived in the house for a few days, she'd probably call my place home."

"And I could visit her?"

"Hell…" He caught himself. "Uh, yes. In fact, let's just say I'm boarding her."

"What's that?"

"That's where someone takes care of your animals for you."

"And I pay you?" Jesse asked cautiously.

"You do chores to *help* pay for cat food."

"*Help* pay for it?"

"She'll probably be eating mice and making my barn a better place to be, so we'll go halves. You'd still make some extra money for yourself."

The kid was grinning widely now, and Brett felt an odd sensation spread through his midsection. "Shouldn't you be getting to school?"

"Oh, yeah. Can you catch Sarina if I unlock the door?"

"I imagine I can."

Jesse fitted the key in the lock and turned until the latch popped open.

"Don't forget to lock it," he admonished as he trotted down the steps. "Oh, and Miss Flynn is buying kitty litter at lunch."

"Tell her I'll take care of it," Brett said. "Don't be late for school."

He watched for a moment as Jesse hurried down the drive, his big feet out of proportion with his skinny body, and wondered if the boy was getting enough to eat.

A few minutes later, as Brett hefted the cat, he wondered again. He was no cat expert, but this one seemed bony despite the massive quantities of fluff that enveloped it.

"Hey, kitty." He rubbed a hand over its ears. "Looks like we're roommates for a while." And what a strange turn of events. This morning he'd woken up cat-free, and now here he was, about to bunk with a feline.

He held the cat against his chest, taking a quick survey of the trailer before he started for the door. It was homier than the last time he'd been here, on snake disposal duty. And it smelled good. A subtle odor of spices and perfume teased his senses and his imagination. A couple of camisoles lay draped over the back of the sofa, spread out on a towel to dry. He remembered the lavender one. She'd been wearing it when she'd come to his place, toting her bottle of wine. And though there were now candles and pillows and bric-a-brac on display, the place was surprisingly neat and organized. Somehow he'd had a feeling that Claire would live in a more cluttered environment. With the exception of the camisoles, it looked like a place where an engineer might live—which was exactly what she'd been training to be before the education bug bit her. He remembered her explaining that to him when they'd danced at the wedding, just before she'd started to nuzzle his neck.

Brett let out a breath and headed outside. His cell phone rang as he exited the trailer, startling the cat.

"Easy, kitty," he muttered, juggling the phone up to his ear.

"Hi, Brett," Phil said. "I thought I'd give you a heads-up. I'll be arriving this Friday. You need to contact Marie and tell her to give the house a once-over."

"Sure." Brett held the cat with one hand and the phone with the other as he walked.

"Have you had time to get the stud tuned up for me?"

"It's going to take more than a tune-up."

Which was something he planned to discuss with his boss once they were face-to-face.

"Really." The word was delivered flatly. Phil was a wannabe cowboy, and he genuinely loved animals—even if he didn't totally understand them. But he hated to hear the word *no* in any context. Brett hadn't had to say it too often, but this was going to be one of those occasions when no other word would do. He'd just try to say it in a way that Phil could accept.

"Really," Brett said firmly. "This boy needs serious work."

"I bought a new saddle for him."

"It'll fit other horses."

"I'll make an evaluation when I get there," Phil said curtly. "I'll see you Friday."

Make an evaluation... Brett shook his head. Funny how the CEO replaced the cowboy whenever Phil encountered a roadblock. Well, Phil could evaluate that stud until the cows came home. It wasn't going to change the fact that the animal was too much horse for him.

JESSE SHOWED UP at Brett's home at 3:05 p.m. in the afternoon. He must have run the half mile from school.

"Is she doing all right?" he asked as soon as Brett opened the door.

"She's doing fine." He had just got back from the Ryker ranch a few minutes before Jesse's arrival, but the cat was still there, sitting on the back of the sofa, right where he'd left her. "I bought some food and litter at the mercantile. She's all set up."

Jesse dug around in his pocket. "Here," he said, pulling out a small greenish wad of paper. "This'll help until my first payday."

Brett solemnly took the dollar. "Thanks."

The kid smiled. "Where's she at?"

"Living room. Come on in."

"I can only stay for a minute. My dad is coming early tonight, so I have to go back to the school." The cat jumped off the sofa and trotted over as soon as the boy entered the room, throwing herself against his skinny legs.

"Hi, Sarina. Are you being good?" he asked as he lifted her, nuzzling his nose in her fur. Brett could hear her purring from across the room. After a few minutes of mutual affection, Jesse put the cat down. She rubbed her head on his leg. "Can I stop by tomorrow and see her?"

"You bet. We can work up an after-school chore schedule—if your dad doesn't mind."

"He won't care," Jesse said solemnly. "He's glad I have something to do."

Probably glad to have a free babysitter. But Brett didn't know the circumstances, so he decided to give the guy the benefit of the doubt. For now.

THERE WAS A quilting session that evening, but thanks to Brett taking custody of Jesse's cat, Claire was able to work late at school without worrying about the animal making confetti out of her laundry or doing whatever bored felines might tend to do.

A smile played on her lips as she stacked her last pile of grading. Brett, who was ticked off because she'd sent Jesse to ask about chores, was now going to board the boy's cat. Brett was obviously more of a softie than he let on, something else for Claire to add to the enigma file.

Most of the quilters were already at the community hall when Claire came in, her tote bag laden with new quilting fabric.

She took a seat across from Deirdre and Trini, then lifted her washed and ironed yardage out of her bag and stacked it on the table in front of her.

"What are you going to do with *that?*" Deirdre asked sharply.

"Make a quilt."

"With those colors?"

Claire was about to explain that she'd matched the colors to the Gauguin print that hung over her bed, but Elena's grandmother, Gloria, interceded before she had a chance.

"I think those are lovely colors," she said, her needle poised in the air. "One of the things I like about quilting is that you can find color combinations to fit any personality." She glanced over her glasses at the beige and white fabric pieces Deirdre was meticulously sewing together. "Everything from exciting brights to ho-hum neutrals." She turned back to Claire just as Deirdre realized she'd been insulted. "So, how are things at school?"

Claire held her breath as Deirdre slowly lowered her eyes to her sewing, her jaw firmly set, then said, "I think things are starting to go more smoothly."

"We're glad you're here," Gloria said, in a tone that dared anyone to disagree with her. "Elena likes your class."

Deirdre looked up, her needle hovering for a second in midair, and even though she didn't say anything, Claire knew what she was thinking.

Not every student liked her class.

BRETT EXPECTED CLAIRE to stop by that night. Jesse had to have explained to her that she was no longer a cat sitter, but to Brett's surprise she didn't show up, and her trailer remained dark. Around nine o'clock, just when he was thinking he should probably check the school basement, he saw headlights pull into her drive. Lights came on in the trailer a few seconds later. No visit tonight. Claire must have faith in his cat-sitting abilities.

The cat had spent most of the evening on the back of the sofa, pretending to be asleep while watching him out of slitted eyes as Brett sat at the computer and tried to beat concepts into his head that he should have understood years ago. He did her a favor and ignored her. She wasn't any trouble, which made Brett wonder again what kind of guy made a kid give away his cat.

Strange situation.

He was going to have to make a point of meeting Jesse's dad. He'd seen him driving through town a few times, but the man never seemed to get out of his vehicle.

The phone rang and Brett answered it, once again expecting Claire. But this time it was Regan.

"Kylie made it!" There was only one "it" his sister-in-law could be referring to, since the horse show season was over and fall rodeo was winding down. Basketball. Kylie's other fixation, which Brett thought might be genetic, since he loved the game and Will hated it.

"Varsity?" He realized he was smiling broadly. Kylie had played junior varsity basketball during her freshman year—much to her disgust. She'd set herself the goal of making the varsity squad the following year, come hell or high water, and now she'd done it.

"I guess that expensive camp paid off," Regan said happily. "The game schedule is on the school Web site. Will isn't home yet, so he doesn't know, and Kylie made me promise to let her tell him, but I *had* to tell someone and I knew you'd want to know."

"Thanks. I appreciate it."

"Hey, have you heard anything about my sister through the grapevine? She's been very uncommunicative lately."

Brett rarely got close enough to a grapevine to hear anything. "I think she's doing fine," he said, telling Regan what she wanted to hear, and hoping she wouldn't ask him to investigate, since he wasn't going to. He wondered if she knew about the school basement, but then decided it wasn't his place to say anything.

"Just checking," Regan said. "Claire has a tendency to do things the hard way."

"No kidding," he said.

Regan laughed. "Getting to know my sister, are you?"

"Only in the landlord sense," Brett said abruptly. "Thanks for calling, Regan. I'll be at that first game."

CLAIRE SLID LOWER in the tub. The water had finally cooled to the point where she could stretch out and enjoy the flicker of the candles and the heavy scent of lavender. For a few seconds, anyway, before the phone rang.

Drat. She'd meant to turn it off. She splashed water as she got out of the tub and wrapped herself in a thick towel, catching the phone on the third ring.

"Hi, Mom." It was a wild guess, since she hadn't bothered to check the number, but Claire knew it made her mom crazy when she answered that way. Some things were too much fun to give up cold turkey.

"Hello, Claire." Arlene's voice was carefully modulated.

"Are you all right?"

"Of course I'm all right. Why would you ask that?"

"You've called twice this week." Claire headed back to the bathroom, eyeing the tub longingly and wondering if she could get back in without dropping the phone in the water and ruining it. Of course she couldn't. "I thought you might be lonely."

"I'm not lonely." Arlene made loneliness sound like a character flaw. "I just want to keep in contact with my daughters. Is that so unusual?"

Yes. Arlene was not a chitchatter.

"No. Not unusual at all," Claire stated, settling on the edge of the tub, her back to the water. "Any word on Stephen?"

"Windsurfing, I believe." There was a pause, and then she said, "I was wondering if you knew when you might be coming down to Las Vegas next?"

"I could come for Thanksgiving."

"I'll be at a conference in San Diego."

"Over Thanksgiving?"

"It butts up against the holiday. Travel is a nightmare, so I thought I'd stay until the following Monday."

And Stephen was windsurfing. Maybe there was a method to Arlene's madness.

"I could pop down some weekend." Four-hundred-mile drive. Slightly more than a pop, but still…

"No. I don't want you to do that."

"What do you want, Mom?"

Arlene let out an audible sigh. "I don't know."

And that was the first time in her life Claire had ever heard a hint of self-doubt from her mother.

"Well, will you let me know when you do know? Or if you want to talk?"

After another heavy silence, Arlene seriously alarmed her daughter by calmly saying, "Yes, Claire. I will."

CLAIRE WAS STILL THINKING about her mother's call the following day at school. Arlene had not said one word about Claire's current situation. She hadn't asked about graduate school or demanded reassurance that Claire was indeed going to continue her education. No. She hadn't really talked about anything. She'd just seemed to want to make contact. Which made Claire wonder if she and Regan should strong-arm their mother into getting a medical checkup.

She called Regan right after school. "I think something's wrong with Mom."

"Why?" Regan asked cautiously.

"She's been calling just to chat."

"Sometimes mothers and daughters do that."

"Not our mother and not this daughter. If she wanted to chat, she'd call you."

"Maybe she's changing."

"I prefer the old Mom. At least I knew how to handle her."

"Change is good," Regan said dryly.

"Not when it took me way more than twenty years to figure out how to handle the original."

THERE WAS A NEW GUY in town. Claire couldn't say she knew everyone in Barlow Ridge, but it was a small place and she figured she'd seen almost everyone who lived there. She'd never seen this guy, though. Tall and well-built, blond hair, blue eyes—an Adonis in cowboy boots. Lizard-skin cowboy boots, to be exact.

He nodded at her as he hefted a twelve-pack of beer from one of the mismatched standing coolers. "Can I get you something?" he asked politely.

"One of those six-packs of grapefruit juice?"

"Sure." He grimaced a little as he handed her the juice.

"Not a fan?" she asked, wondering how many lizards had given their lives for his boots.

"I'm more of an orange-juice man," he said with a crooked smile.

Claire put the grapefruit juice into her

basket, debating whether she should allow herself to be charmed. She was leaning toward yes. "It's actually quite good."

"I'll just have to take your word for it." He paused, his eyes never leaving her face. "I'm Phil Ryker."

"Claire Flynn. I think I'm one of your neighbors."

"In this place everyone is your neighbor."

"True, but I'm closer than most. I live in the trailer at the edge of the field."

His smile widened. "You're the new schoolmarm."

Claire regarded him for a moment. "What exactly is a marm?"

"Damned if I know. Are you going to last longer than the other teachers?"

"I think I already have."

He laughed. "I need to get going, but I'll see you around, Claire." It sounded like a promise.

She continued her shopping, picking up some nails to fix a loose board on her porch, a jar of peanut butter, some fairly fresh bread, a box of cereal. She stopped there, since she was walking and didn't want to be toting more than was comfortable.

"So what do you think?" Anne asked as Claire set her purchases on the counter.

"Of him?" Claire guessed, since Phil Ryker had exited the store a few minutes before and there was no one else there.

"Yeah."

"He seemed all right."

"He owns half this valley, you know."

"How nice. Hey, we missed you at quilting the other night."

Anne gave her a nice-try smirk. "Watch him. He thinks if he snaps his fingers he can get anything he wants."

"Thanks for the warning," Claire said as she took her bag. "I'll keep that in mind."

"So, you're telling me the horse needs more work."

"I'm telling you the horse will kill you." An overstatement, but Brett was trying to make a point.

Phil laughed. Brett bit the edge of his lip as he studied the horse that was standing with his chest pressed against the rails of his pen. His head held high and his body quivering, he sniffed the air for his mares. This was no joke.

"How much more time?" Phil asked patiently.

Brett counted to ten.

"I mean, if I can't make the first show in the spring, I understand."

"If you plan on riding this horse in a show, you'll need to find a different trainer."

That got his attention. Finally.

"Like your brother?" Phil asked pointedly.

"Will wouldn't take on this horse for the purposes you intend." Brett glanced over at his boss. He didn't like what he saw. The man's face was set in stubborn lines. "*I* wouldn't ride this stud in a show, and I used to ride bronc. If you lose control of him, he may hurt someone else in the ring. He's an unpredictable horse. Use him for breeding."

That was all the horse had been used for thus far. Had the animal been of a gentler nature, or if Phil had about a decade more experience, Brett could see trying to show the stud. But the way things stood now, it was a wreck waiting to happen.

"I'll make some calls," Phil said in a clipped voice. The man was not used to being contradicted—even if it was for his own safety, as well as the safety of anyone else in the arena with him.

Brett moistened his lips and tried to come up with a way to make the guy listen to reason. The problem was not only that Phil had rarely heard the word *no,* but that he also had a pretty damn big ego. Not a good combination.

"And I expect you'll find someone who'll take on the job," Brett agreed. "But be careful. There're a lot of guys out there pretending to be trainers who aren't."

"So it seems."

Brett pushed off from the fence. "I've got some work to do." He hoped. He started walking toward the barn. Phil didn't yell after him that he was fired, but he had a feeling it could happen at any time—which meant that his ability to make the payments on the homestead would be jeopardized. But on the other hand, he wouldn't have a dead urban cowboy on his conscience, either.

CHAPTER SIX

"WHAT'S THE PROBLEM, Ashley?"

The girl had been muttering under her breath all afternoon, and when Claire finally called her on it, Ashley had requested an after-school meeting.

"This," she said, showing Claire her social-studies paper. "I answered all the questions right and you gave me a C."

"You were supposed to use the format given in the directions. That was a big part of the grade." And she'd stressed that point when handing out the assignment.

"But a C? That's stupid."

"That's following directions. A life skill."

"My mom says that you don't know what you're doing." Ashley shoved the paper into her notebook.

"Is your mom trained in the field of education?"

"What?"

Claire leaned back against her desk and folded her arms over her chest. "Does she have training that enables her to judge whether or not I know what I'm doing?"

"You don't need special training to see when someone is doing something wrong."

"So what am I doing wrong, Ashley? Maybe you could tell me so I can work on things."

"You want me to make a list?" the girl asked sarcastically.

"Yes. Consider it homework, instead of today's English homework. I want you to go home, sit down with your parents and make a list of what I need to work on. I'll even send a copy to Mr. Rupert."

Ashley laughed. "You don't mean it."

That was when Claire's easygoing expression shifted to no-nonsense. "I mean it. How can I improve, if I don't know what is bothering you? And since Mr. Rupert is evaluating me, he'll need the list."

"Fine. I'll make a list. You want me to use complete sentences?" Ashley added snidely.

"No. Just make a list."

Claire had a major headache by the time she left that day. No matter how many times she told herself it didn't matter, the situation with Ashley and her mother bothered her. She was trying to help these kids, yet Deirdre seemed to think Claire had moved out to the middle of nowhere in order to pick on her little girl.

Maybe it was time to cart another bottle of wine over to Brett's. He was good at giving her something to think about besides school. In fact, he gave her a lot to think about, and she rather enjoyed it.

Ultimately, though, she didn't go to Brett's. She stayed home and tallied grades in preparation for the upcoming report cards, losing herself in numbers and analysis. Ashley was passing all her classes, but with B's and C's instead of the A's she thought she deserved simply for being cute.

And the math scores for all the students were still disturbingly low. Toni had a natural aptitude and she was picking things up quickly, but she was also careful not to look as if she was enjoying her success when Ashley was around.

Claire knew that one of the biggest problems was that the students needed immediate feedback on their work, to prevent them from repeating mistakes over and over again. The blackboards were unusable, bumpy and shiny from years of being painted and repainted with blackboard paint, to the point where chalk would no longer adhere. She needed the whiteboards she'd ordered the first day of school. That way she could watch the kids work, and correct errors as they occurred. She was doing what she could with slates, but they were not good enough.

Claire called the district procurement department as soon as she got to school the next morning. "I really need the whiteboards I ordered," she said pleasantly.

"We're doing what we can, Miss Flynn."

"Can you do it faster?"

"Miss Flynn, we have a procedure we have to follow. Let me familiarize you. Again."

Claire hung up the phone after being informed of procedure—again—and was about to dial her sister when Ashley strode into the room.

"My mom said she didn't want to make a list off the top of her head. She wants time to think."

"And you couldn't come up with anything on your own?"

"I want to wait for Mom, so I did my English instead." She popped the paper into the hand-in basket, then pivoted and departed, her chin high in the air.

As soon as the outer door had swung shut,

Claire went to the office and punched Regan's number into the phone. Her brother-in-law answered.

"Hi, Will. I need a favor."

THREE SHEETS OF WHITE enameled Masonite, purchased from the Wesley lumberyard, came into Barlow Ridge on an empty hay truck late that afternoon. Will had accomplished in half a day what the school district had failed to achieve in two months. Now all Claire had to do was to get the boards mounted without calling on maintenance. The broken basement window had gaped open until one of the PTO dads had finally screwed a piece of plywood over it to keep adventuresome kids from daring each other to spend the night with Jim Shannon. The plywood had yet to be replaced with glass. Barlow Ridge school maintenance was obviously not a district priority, so Claire was going to have to handle the whiteboard installation on her own.

Just a matter of a few screws and something to attach them to. No big deal. Or so she hoped.

AFTER EVALUATING THE situation, Claire came to the sad conclusion that there were some things a zebra-striped tool kit couldn't handle.

Mounting whiteboard was one of them. She needed a drill—preferably cordless—and an extra set of hands.

"Do any of you have a cordless drill?" she facetiously asked her class right after taking attendance. It was the first time she'd ever seen a glimmer of interest on every single face in the room.

"What are you going to do?" Dylan asked.

"We're putting up whiteboard."

"*We're* putting up whiteboard?" Toni asked. "Why are *we* doing it?"

"Because I'd like to *use* the whiteboards before spring break."

"I can bring a drill," Rudy said.

"Great," Claire said.

"Do you know how to use a drill?" Ramon asked curiously.

"How hard can it be?"

"Have you ever used one?"

Claire pretended to give the matter some thought. Then she shook her head and the kids laughed. Even Ashley smiled before she caught herself.

"Are you going to do your drilling in a dress?"

"Is there some kind of law against that?" Claire asked, leaning back against her desk.

"The law of normal behavior," Dylan said, but his sarcasm didn't have its usual bite.

"I might dress for the occasion."

"Wear jeans," Elena said.

"Teachers shouldn't wear jeans to school," Claire said.

"Why not?"

"Because it's important to show respect for your profession."

"You can show respect, no matter what you wear," Elena said.

"Is that a fact? How?"

Elena started to speak, but Claire held up a hand. "Why don't you write your answers in your journals?"

There was a collective groan, but she put up her hand again. "It'll be like a debate. You read your responses and I'll answer them. If you can convince me you're right, I'll…" she glanced at the clock "…give you ten extra minutes during afternoon recess *and* I'll wear jeans to school. But only if you come up with decent arguments."

For the first time since she'd started teaching at Barlow, all her kids started writing at once.

CLAIRE WORE JEANS to school the next day. And boots and a University of Nevada—Las Vegas sweatshirt. Part of the deal. As promised, Rudy showed up with a drill and Dylan had a box of two-inch wood screws. The kids had already toted the sheets of Masonite into the classroom and leaned them against the bookcase.

"Now what?" Elena asked. She, too, was wearing jeans. And green shoes.

"We'll need to find the studs…"

"The *what?*" Ramon demanded. Toni giggled and Claire gave her a sharp look. In Ramon's world, a stud was an animal used for breeding. Claire could understand his confusion.

"A wooden support beam, usually a two-by-four."

"Oh."

"Everybody knows that," Toni muttered.

"Do you know how to find a stud?" Claire asked the girl.

"You use a stud finder."

Ashley smirked, thinking her friend was being sarcastic, but the smirk disappeared when Claire said, "Right." She handed the girl a small plastic box. "Have at it."

Toni went to the wall and started running the box over the surface. "Here's one."

"How do you know this geeky stuff?" Ashley demanded, and Toni looked embarrassed.

"My mom's last jerky boyfriend was a contractor," she said as she handed the stud finder back to Claire.

"Your mom needs to…" The sentence went unfinished as Claire shot a warning look in Ashley's direction. She noticed that Toni, tough as she was, seemed to automatically assume that Ashley's opinion was more important than her own.

"Here, Ashley. Find a stud on the other side of the board."

Ashley drew in a breath and looked as if she wanted to protest, but by some miracle she didn't. She snatched the stud finder and began tracing it over the wall as Toni had done. After a few seconds, she said, "There isn't one over here."

"Give it to me," Dylan said with impatience. He took the device and quickly located another stud.

"How did you…?"

"I have skills," he said. He tossed the little box in the air, then handed it off to Jesse.

"Okay, now, let's measure the distance and calculate where we need to drill holes in the whiteboard. Elena, you and Lexi can do that, and then Jesse and Ramon will measure it out on the board."

"IT WAS SO MUCH FUN. We figured out how to put the whiteboard over the chalkboards, and we measured so that we hit the studs just right with the screws. Miss Flynn let all of us use the drill. Then when we were done, she had Oreos for us and we got to draw on the boards. She has tons of dry-erase markers."

Brett smiled tolerantly as Jesse bounced along next to him on the way to check the electric fence that surrounded his back pasture.

"So nobody gave her trouble today?"

Jesse thought for a moment. "Nope." He watched with interest as Brett disconnected the hot wire from the fence. "What are we doing?"

"Looking for places where dried grass or weeds are touching the wire. It grounds the fence and then it doesn't work."

"Why do you use an electric fence?"

"It keeps the cows where they belong."

"Oh." The kid nodded. "Does it hurt a lot if you touch it?"

"Some."

Brett thought about teaching Jesse how to lay a piece of grass on the wire in order to see if electricity was flowing, but then decided against it. If the weed was wet, the kid would get shocked instead of just feeling a mild vibration. Better that he thought all electric fences were hot.

"If you see these insulators on the fence posts, you need to stay away, okay?"

"Okay."

They continued around the perimeter of the fence. Every now and then Brett stopped to whack some high weeds down or pull a tumbleweed free. When they got back to the gate, he put the hot wire back into place.

"Is it on now?"

"It's on. I can put the cows out here tomorrow." They started for the house. "Where's your dad meeting you tonight?"

"The school."

"He can pick you up here, you know." Brett would really like to have a chat with the guy. He wanted to figure out what Jesse's situation was because, frankly, the kid was kind of growing on him. He wanted to make sure he was being taken care of.

"I'll tell him." Jesse jumped over a big rut, then glanced at Brett. "What were you doing when I came today?"

He'd been sweating over his math lesson. He'd had to redo the previous one because he'd failed the quiz, which made him feel like the king of all losers.

"I have an online class and I wanted to submit the lesson before I forgot."

"What kind of class?"

"Math."

"You're taking math?"

"No big deal."

"Yeah, but you're old."

"So?"

"Well, didn't you learn all this stuff a long time ago?"

"I was supposed to, but…" He hesitated, not wanting to confess to this kid that he'd made some stupid choices for some stupid reasons. "Long story."

"I've got time," Jesse said in a grown-up way.

Brett reached out and ruffled the kid's hair. "No you don't."

"What kind of math are you learning?" Jesse asked as they approached the house.

"Algebra."

"Is it easy?"

"I wish," Brett muttered.

"Not easy?"

"I've done easier stuff."

"You need help?"

Brett shook his head.

"Because Miss Flynn is *really* good in math.

I didn't understand a lot of stuff when school started, and she made it easy to understand. And she says that if we fifth graders work hard, she'll have us ready to take pre-algebra in seventh grade and algebra in eighth grade!"

"That sounds good. You'd better work hard."

"But…"

"I'm doing all right. I only meant I wish it was easier. I didn't mean I couldn't do it." *Yes, you did.*

"Oh." Jesse was quiet for a few minutes, then said, "Miss Flynn said that if we do pre-algebra before we go to high school, then we'll be able to get all the way through calculus before we graduate." He frowned. "What is calculus?"

"It's…" Brett almost said "hard math," but he caught himself. No sense giving the kid ideas. "It's upper-level math. And it's important to take it, if you plan to go to college. You are planning to go to college, aren't you?"

"Yep. Did you go?"

Brett opened his mouth to sidestep yet again, when Jesse said, "No, I guess you didn't, if you're taking algebra now."

"I wanted to go."

"Really? What'd you want to be?"

"I don't know. I just thought it was important to go. To use the brain God gave me."

Which he'd failed to do, time after time. "Since I didn't go right after high school, I decided to go now. Online."

Jesse nodded approvingly.

"What does your dad do, Jesse?"

"Sales. He has a route and he travels."

"What does he sell?"

"Different stuff. It changes."

"Why'd you move here?" Barlow Ridge wasn't exactly a hub of sales activity.

"Dad said it was quiet and he wanted a quiet place. We used to live in Reno. We lived in a trailer park, but Dad couldn't leave me home alone while he did his route, because it wasn't a good part of town."

"So you like it here?"

"I liked living with my grandma in Carson City the best, but this is all right. I like coming here and working for you."

"You used to live with your grandmother?"

"My *great*-grandma. Then she got sick and had to be put in the rest home, so Dad came and got me. I talk to her on the phone sometimes when she's feeling better."

Brett wanted to ask Jesse where his mom was, but he was afraid of the answer. No sense grilling the poor kid.

"Dad didn't know a lot about being a dad,

because Grandma always took care of me, but he's learning."

Brett forced the corners of his mouth up. "That's good."

"Yeah." Jesse suddenly ran ahead and grabbed a rope hanging from the apple tree. He kicked off from the ground and lifted his feet, swinging out in a big arc.

"There used to be a tire on this rope. Maybe I can find another."

"That'd be cool," Jesse said, kicking up a cloud of dust as he skidded to a stop.

"Easier on the hands, too. I'll see what I can do."

ASHLEY'S ATTITUDE WAS just a bit too self-satisfied for Claire's comfort the next day. She exchanged so many secret glances with Dylan and Toni that Claire made it a point to check for tacks on her chair.

For journal that day, Jesse wrote about his cat, Sarina, and how fat she was getting living at Brett's house. He ended with the observation, "I'm glad she's there, so the dogs don't get her and she gets lots to eat. Sometimes I'd cook her eggs when Dad forgot to buy cat food."

Claire stamped the page with a shamrock

twice—once to indicate she'd read it, and a second time for good measure. Jesse had written a lot more than usual. At the beginning of the school year, she'd had to struggle to get two sentences out of him. Here, he'd written over half a page about his cat. Progress like that was worth getting choked up about. The lump in her throat had nothing to do with a young boy trying to feed a pet on his own.

THE STALLION JERKED his head again, out of reach. Brett calmly put his hand on the horse's poll and applied light pressure. The horse dropped his head slightly and Brett immediately released. He continued until the animal was once again dropping his head as Brett had taught him, but as soon as the bit came close to his mouth the head snapped back up.

Brett continued the exercise until he was able to slip a finger in the horse's mouth, in the gap between the front and back teeth, and massage the gum without the horse going bonkers. He rubbed the bit over the animal's mouth. Opened the mouth and slipped it in and out. Small steps.

It took an hour before he could put the bit in the horse's mouth and slip the bridle over his head without provoking a reaction. Brett had just finished the lesson and released the horse when Phil came ambling out with a gangly black-and-white pup on a leather leash.

Phil frowned when he saw that the stud wasn't bridled. "I thought you were working with him."

Brett looped the reins over the bridle. "Have *you* been working with him?"

"A little here and there." Phil leaned down to scoop up the pup, who'd settled his behind on his boot.

"If you want me to train the animal, then you have to stop working with him."

Phil opened his mouth, probably to say that it was his horse and he'd do what he damn well wanted to, but Brett cut him off. "It confuses the horse. We use two different methods." *And your method sucks.*

Phil-the-Boss struggled with Phil-the-Cowboy. "I guess I can see that."

The pup squirmed, trying to get out of Phil's arms so he could investigate the interesting smells in the corral.

"Where'd you get him?" Brett asked.

"The pound in Wesley. He needed a home."

And that summed up Phil. He was a guy who didn't know jack about the expensive horses he bought, but rescued pound puppies.

His heart was in the right place; it was his refusal to listen and his lack of animal sense that did him in.

"After I get the stud settled, I can work with the two of you together," Brett suggested. "My way's not the only way, but consistency will speed the training process." And it'd keep the horse from being ruined, and Phil from getting injured.

"Sounds reasonable," he agreed. "Let me know when you're ready." He glanced over at the pens on the other side of the barn. "Maybe I'll take Bella out for a ride."

"That would be a great idea," Brett agreed. Because Bella was bombproof.

Phil put the pup back on the ground. "That new teacher. She's related to you, right?"

He felt instantly wary. "By marriage. Her sister is married to my brother."

Phil smiled as if he'd just discovered an important clue in a treasure hunt. "What can you tell me about her?"

"Not a lot."

The other man regarded him for a moment. "Am I stepping on your toes here?"

"No." The abrupt answer sounded like a lie.

"You sure?"

"Positive."

"All right." Phil started toward the barn. "You don't know her favorite wine or flower or anything?"

"Nope." Brett tried to make the word sound light as he handed Phil the bridle. "Wish I could help you, but I don't know her all that well myself. I gotta get back to my place and feed."

CLAIRE HAD BARELY STARTED her morning grading when Bertie came into her classroom holding the wireless phone.

"Mr. Rupert." It was obvious from her expression that this was not a happy call.

"Good morning, Mr. Rupert," Claire said as she put the phone to her ear.

"Good morning. We have a parent problem."

Claire quickly flashed through all the possible problem scenarios. As far as she knew she hadn't ruffled any feathers over the past few days, but she took a guess anyway. "The Landaus?"

"Yes. Apparently you had their daughter involved in some kind of school maintenance?"

"What?"

"That's what I said," Rupert said. "I thought you had her mopping floors for detention, but apparently you had her using power equipment without proper safety gear."

Claire closed her eyes. "You mean, the cordless drill."

"Yes."

"Guilty," Claire said. "I had the class putting up the whiteboards."

"What whiteboards?"

"The ones I use on a daily basis to improve their math skills." She told him the story, procurement procedure and all, ending with how the math homework scores had already improved—now that she could send the students to the board to work, and correct errors as they happened. The whole class was getting involved. Finally.

"I see."

"So what happens now?"

"What happens now is that I scramble. The Landaus wrote a letter to the board. They wrote a letter to me. For all I know they wrote a letter to the governor. I don't think the Landaus realize how hard it is to get a teacher to move to Barlow," Rupert finished with a growl.

"So…"

"So I'll do what I can to fix things. You may end up with a reprimand in your file."

"That probably won't be good for future employment."

"I'll word it as nicely as I can. It only stays

for two years. If there's no more trouble during that time, the letter gets trashed."

"But *I'm* not staying for two years."

"Hey, maybe that's something for you to consider."

"I don't think so. But thank you for helping."

"I'll keep you posted."

CLAIRE EXITED the mercantile a half hour later, a bit winded after her usual skirmish with Anne, just as Phil pulled to a stop in front of the store. He got out of his truck, and a young black-and-white dog jumped out after him, making an eager beeline for Claire.

"What's his name?" She knelt to ruffle the animal's fuzzy coat and was bombarded with enthusiastic doggy kisses. She laughed as she fended him off. He was obviously a dog of dubious ancestry, which surprised her. She would have pegged Phil as a purebred kind of guy.

"Toby."

"Toby," Claire repeated, and the pup's ears perked up. "Oh, you know your name?"

"He should. He hears it enough. *Toby, no. Toby, down. Toby, off the couch.*" Phil grinned as the pup cocked his head and stared at him, obviously trying to figure out what his dad wanted. Claire gave the pup a final pat before straightening up again.

Phil reached down to snap a leash onto Toby's collar. "Hey, I know it's a ways off, but would you like to hear the folksinger who's coming to town over Thanksgiving? She's a Wesley girl and she's supposed to be good."

"You mean, spend an evening not grading or planning or doing teacher stuff? I don't know…."

"I've heard that I'm slightly better company than a red pen," Phil said with his confident, crooked smile.

"All right, you've convinced me. I'll mark my calendar. It's the Wednesday before Turkey Day, right?"

The pup squirmed as a car drove by, and Phil lifted a hand in greeting. "Right."

"I should be going," Claire said, recognizing two of her fifth graders in the car. "I'll see you then."

"Can I pick you up?"

Claire shook her head. "I'll meet you there." That way if things didn't go well, she had an easy means of escape.

THERE WEREN'T AS MANY women at the quilting session as usual, but other than that, everything was the same. Anne was crotchety and Deirdre was cold, giving no outward indication that she had lodged an official complaint against Claire. And everyone else, including the other PTO moms, was friendly enough. Claire wondered how they were going to feel after the report card meeting the following week.

"Those squares are pretty," Trini commented as Claire pulled out her two completed quilt blocks and smoothed them on the table. She'd worked an abstract design of oddly shaped pieces she could cut with the rotary cutter, and the wild colors suited the pattern well.

"Thank you. I'm working on developing my free-form side," she added facetiously.

Anne gave a snort. "Maybe you should work on your seam allowances instead." She had a point. Claire's seam allowances tended to narrow or swell from the prescribed quarter inch. Even so, with some tugging and creative pressing, her squares came out...well, almost square.

She raised her eyes to see several of the other women watching her, and Trini seemed to be holding her breath as she waited for her response. Claire gave a small conspiratorial smile and then refocused her attention on her sewing. Anne went right back on the offensive.

"Saw Brett Bishop hanging around your place the other day."

"He's working on my furnace."

"Oh." Anne seemed disappointed.

"If you watch, you might see Phil Ryker hanging around, too," Claire added helpfully. "He asked me to go hear the folksinger with him."

Claire heard a rapidly suppressed chuckle.

"You're going out with him?" Anne sounded disgusted.

"Hey. I like Phil," Gloria interjected. "Money and good looks. What's not to like?"

"He lacks substance," Anne said.

"How do you know?" Gloria demanded. "He looks like he has substance to me."

"Well, what he's lacking in substance, he makes up for in the way he wears his jeans," Trini added. "Have you seen how they…" She shut her mouth suddenly, as laughter erupted. "Hey. It's just an observation."

The rest of the meeting was devoted to an analysis of various men—celebrities and community members. No one was safe, and Claire's stomach ached from laughing by the time she packed her tote bag. A breakthrough with the quilting club.

"Nothing gets to you, does it?" Trini asked her, as she and Claire were leaving the meeting.

"What do you mean?" Claire was still focused on their candid dissection of men.

"Anne keeps jabbing at you every meeting, and you never flinch. I'd be in tears if she was doing that to me."

"But she's not, which just proves she has a heart. She only jabs people who can take it."

"You're nuts," Trini said with a laugh.

"That goes without saying. I'm teaching in Barlow Ridge."

And liking it.

CHAPTER SEVEN

DEIRDRE LANDAU HAD SIGNED up for the very first report-card conference, and as soon as the kids cleared out of the classroom at three o'clock, she sailed in with the air of an overly busy woman who wanted to get a mere technicality out of the way. Just give her daughter a few compliments, hand over the report card and she'd be off.

Claire bit her lip as she gathered her grade book and seated herself across the table. Something seemed odd here.

After exchanging a few pleasantries, Claire showed Deirdre her daughter's report card, making the point that Ashley should be making better grades than C's and that perhaps together they could work out some kind of a strategy.

Deirdre frowned, checked the name at the top of the card and then traced a manicured fingernail down the column of C's, making Claire wonder just who had been signing Ashley's weekly progress reports. She was about to ask, when Deirdre's eyes locked on hers.

"Ashley had straight A's until this year."

"She's not doing A work now."

"Because you're not doing A-level teaching."

Claire drew back. She knew from years of sparring with Arlene that meeting an assault with an assault was not always the best strategy. Quickly debating tactics, she decided that data collection was the safest track.

"Ashley's been at this school for…"

"This is her third year."

"And before that…"

"She attended school in Boise. Where she was also a straight-A student." Deirdre's chin rose self-righteously.

"She *is* capable of straight A's," Claire agreed.

"Then she should have straight A's, shouldn't she?"

"Yes."

Deirdre's expression hardened as she leaned toward Claire. "Then why doesn't she have the grades she should have?"

"Because she's not doing the work she should do."

Her mother straightened. "She knows the material."

"Yes." Most of it anyway, though her understanding was slipping in a few areas. But Ashley was bright, and much of the time, she could keep up by simply listening in class.

"Then…?"

"Part of the grade is for participation, which includes homework and class discussions. Ashley doesn't do homework and she's not a…helpful participant in class discussions."

"You should grade her on what she knows."

"I'm trying, Mrs. Landau. But Ashley doesn't know how to fulfill obligations. Homework is an obligation, and so is class participation."

"I don't think *obligations* should carry so much weight." Deirdre ground out the word. "The grade should be based on what the student *knows*."

"Mrs. Landau," Claire said gently, "the world is not going to change for Ashley, depending on what she does or doesn't want to do. If she grows up and doesn't feel like doing her taxes, the IRS isn't going to let her off the hook because she knows how to do them but chooses not to."

"That's a ridiculous comparison."

"Work ethic and self-discipline are important." Claire knew from firsthand experience.

"I'm trying to help Ashley become a better student."

"By giving her C's."

"It's what she earned. She knew the parameters going in. I explained to the students—"

Deirdre raised a hand, cutting Claire off as she suddenly rose. "I've heard enough for now. I'm bringing my husband the next time we meet. And I think Mr. Rupert will be here, too, and then we'll see about your grading practices." She turned and marched out of the room, leaving the report card sitting on the table.

"Mrs. Landau—"

But the outer door clanged shut. Claire let out a breath. Short of chasing the woman and tackling her in the parking lot, there wasn't much she could do.

She straightened the chair that Deirdre had pushed aside, then went to the door. Mrs. Hernandez, who spoke very little English, was waiting, her eyes wide as she stared at the door Deirdre had just slammed behind her.

"Buenas tardes," Claire said pleasantly.

Mrs. Hernandez nodded, her expression cautious. Claire smiled, searched for the proper Spanish to explain what had just occurred. *"Una equivocación pequeña."* She held her thumb and forefinger millimeters apart, to emphasize how small the misunderstanding had been. "It's nice to see you. Come in." When the woman hesitated, Claire added, *"Venir, por favor, adentro,"* and gestured to her classroom.

Mrs. Hernandez followed Claire inside and perched on the edge of her chair, obviously wondering if she, too, was about to be involved in a loud and unpleasant misunderstanding. Fortunately, the meeting went well and Claire's Spanish, though rusty after a few years on the shelf, came back fast. The Hernandez kids were working hard, their grades were improving and they were making up for lost time. Mrs. Hernandez was beaming by the end of meeting.

Toni's mom, Marla, was waiting in the hall, glancing at her watch, when Claire ushered Mrs. Hernandez out. Claire was actually running ahead of schedule, thanks to Deirdre Landau's abbreviated meeting, and that seemed to be a good thing, since Marla was obviously in a hurry.

"Deke is expecting me home pretty soon," she said in a husky voice that came from breathing too much cigarette smoke in her working environment.

"This shouldn't take long," Claire said, pushing Toni's report card across the table. "As you can see, there is room for improvement, but Toni has made some good progress since that first weekly report I sent home."

"What weekly report?"

"The weekly progress reports?" *You know, the ones you sign...or supposedly sign?*

The woman frowned. "Toni's in charge of her own grades. I've got enough on my hands with Deke and the bar."

"Do you sign the reports she brings home?"

"Toni's better at my signature than I am."

Claire leaned forward, intrigued. "Doesn't that bother you?"

Marla shook her head. "I trust Toni. I have to. My only concern is that she behaves. You called that one time and I'm guessing there wasn't any more trouble after that?"

"No trouble."

"Great. Well, thanks a lot. Toni seems to like you okay, so you must be doing something right."

"Thank you," Claire said. She rose from her chair, feeling amazingly gratified. *Toni liked her? Wow.*

So much for being good at reading the kids. *And so much for signed weekly progress reports,* she thought after escorting Marla to the door. Apparently it wasn't the parents who were doing the signing.

Her final meeting of the evening was with Tom Lane, Jesse's dad, and she was slightly surprised that the guy showed up. Jesse waited in the hall.

Tom was a quiet man who didn't meet Claire's eyes very often, but he seemed concerned about his son, and pleased with the straight B's and C's Jesse had earned. Claire told him how much she enjoyed Jesse, and tentatively offered to drive the boy home after school if he ever needed a ride. The father hesitated, then declined, telling her his dogs were unpredictable with strangers and he didn't want his son home alone. The fact that Jesse was sitting out in the hall at that moment underscored the point.

Claire thanked Tom Lane for coming and saw him out, waving at Jesse before disappearing back into her room. The meetings were over. She'd survived. All she had to do now was get her quilting supplies, which Brett had once again picked up from Regan in Wesley, and then she could settle into a hot bath.

BRETT HAD A FEELING he wasn't going to be a college graduate—at least not in the foreseeable future.

Algebra was kicking his butt.

He should have learned this stuff back when he was younger and his brain worked better. He hit the X at the top corner of the computer screen and brought his world back to normal. A half hour later he was laying floor when he heard a knock on the kitchen door.

It was Claire, there to pick up the stuff Regan had sent back with him on his last trip to Wesley. He'd meant to drop the things off while she was at school, but he hadn't gotten around to it.

"Hi," he said. "The box is right here. It's light."

"It should be. All it has is quilt batting and thread in it." She patted the top, then nodded at the carpenter knee pads he was wearing. "Home repairs?"

"Yeah. It's time." It was past time, in fact. The old flooring was worn-through linoleum, circa 1970.

"I thought you leased this place," Claire said as she walked past him to peek into the living room, where he had about half the new floor down.

"I've optioned to buy, so my lease payments will turn into mortgage payments."

"I was wondering why you were my landlord instead of Phil."

"All pastures and rentals go with the lease, so I'd be your landlord regardless."

Sarina chose that moment to saunter out of Brett's bedroom and pick her way across the new flooring. She stopped at Claire's feet, her yellow eyes inquisitive.

"How's the roommate?" Claire asked, leaning down to stroke the cat.

"She's working out."

Sarina suddenly rolled over onto her back and stretched, showing off her white belly. Claire tickled the animal, who gave a playful kick with her hind legs, then jumped to her feet and strutted away.

"Jesse writes about her in his journal, and I can see why. She's a character." Claire shifted her attention back to Brett. "He also writes about you, you know."

No, Brett didn't know, and it kind of embarrassed him to have Jesse writing about him. "Maybe I'm a character, too."

Claire nodded, humoring him. "He likes coming here."

"I like having him around," Brett admitted.

"It must get lonely here sometimes," she said, tilting her head inquisitively.

"Not really."

"But you spend so much time alone. You live alone. You work alone."

"I'm used to it."

"I'm not." Claire blew out a sigh. "I don't mind living alone, but when I hit a rough spot in life I like companionship. You're not like that, are you?"

No. The last thing Brett wanted, when times got rough, was companionship. Every tough spot in his life he'd gotten through alone—except for the time he'd gotten the shit beat out of him trying to stop the theft of some livestock. Then, Will had camped in the hospital until Brett had come around. He'd refused to see his older brother, so technically, he'd gotten through that spot on his own, too, but it had helped knowing that Will was there.

"No. I'm not like that," he said, getting back to her question. And that was when he realized Claire wasn't as animated as usual. He'd been so focused on protecting himself, he hadn't noticed. "Are you having a rough spot?"

"No. Just exhausted from parent meetings."

She lifted the box into her arms, gesturing toward the door with her head. "I should get going. I can't believe how much paperwork ten students can generate, and I didn't get anything done at school tonight because of parent report-card meetings."

Brett walked with her, opened the door.

"How did they go?" he asked.

"Some were great. Some were…not so great."

"How so?" He leaned a forearm on the door frame.

"I can't really talk about parent meetings," she said.

He cocked his head. "How many good meetings and how many bad?"

"Do you ever get tired of asking personal questions?" she asked, mimicking the same words he had once said to her.

"No. But I respect your right not to answer."

"Thank heaven for small favors." She smiled, and he couldn't help smiling back.

"Do you want some company, Claire?" he asked softly. It was almost nine o'clock. He'd done enough work for the night. He could listen if she wanted to talk. He just didn't want to answer questions about himself.

She shook her head. "No. I think I need a glass of wine and a bath."

He had a feeling she was lying. "All right. Just don't pass out in the tub."

She smiled again. "I'll try, but no promises."

"I'll see you, Claire."

He did want to see her, which was something that surprised him, and he didn't want her to be lonely. He knew how painful a bad case of loneliness could be.

BRETT HAD TO MAKE a trip to Elko the next morning, and he spent most of the next day running errands and buying supplies—feed, flooring, food—he couldn't get in Wesley. He ate dinner alone before starting home, only to put a nail through one of his new tires about twenty miles out of Wesley, in an area with no phone service. He spent a ridiculous amount of time trying to loosen overly tight lug nuts before he finally managed to free them and replace the ruined tire with his spare.

It was almost eleven o'clock, a half hour before closing time, when he pulled into the Wesley grocery-store parking lot to pick up the two things he'd forgotten in Elko, coffee and toilet paper. Both kind of essential to life. A group of kids were hanging out next to the door, laughing and pushing one another.

And he recognized one of them.

"Kylie!"

The laughter faded from Kylie's face as she heard her name called out in an authoritative tone. The guy who'd had his arm around her stepped back a bit. She glanced up at him, then walked over to Brett.

"What are you doing?" he asked, eying the

group of kids. They didn't look like criminals, but it was hard to tell these days.

"Hanging around. We're about to play fugitive." She spoke breezily.

He was familiar with fugitive—a game where kids ran around town, usually after curfew, trying to find one another. It was a teenage version of hide-and-seek, often played with cars.

"Are you sure that's a good idea?"

Her expression shifted as she realized that he wasn't making conversation; he was getting parental. "Hey, my dad knows about it."

"He knows you're going to be out running around town after curfew?"

Kylie's eyes narrowed ever so slightly, making him wonder if Will did indeed know all the facts. "Yes," she said stonily. Brett could see that she was very close to telling him to mind his own business. "And he knows I'm staying with Sadie tonight."

"So if I call and ask him, you're all right with that?"

She drew a deep breath through her nose, then bluffed. "You can call him."

"I will." Brett reached in his pocket for his phone.

Fifteen minutes later he was dropping a

pissed-off Kylie at her house. She'd been embarassed when he'd ordered her into his truck in front of her friends, so he thought she would probably storm back *out* of the truck without a word as soon as he got her home. He'd been mistaken. Instead she gave him a long, cold look.

"You had no right to do this."

"You were lying to me."

"I don't see why you have the right to interrogate me to begin with," she muttered. "You're barely part of the family." And that was when she got out of the truck and stomped away.

Will stepped onto the porch as Kylie marched up the steps, her back ramrod straight. He raised a hand to Brett, who nodded back before putting the truck in Reverse. Will already had the story. No sense hanging around, getting in the way, and no sense dwelling on something an angry kid had said to just hurt his feelings.

"MISS FLYNN…" Mr. Rupert drew in a deep breath, clearly audible over the phone line. "Don't get me wrong. I'm thrilled to have you teaching at Barlow Ridge. But what is going on between you and the Landau family?"

"Another complaint?"

"Mmm, hmm."

"Grades?"

"Mmm, hmm."

Claire rolled her eyes and studied the ceiling. "Do you want me to change them?"

There was a long pause, which told her how tempted the principal was to say yes. "I want you to stick to your standards," he said at last. "But if you can come up with any way to placate this woman, or better yet get her on your side, please do it."

"I will, when the opportunity arises."

"The opportunity is here. We're having a meeting. The three of us."

"When?"

"Tomorrow. Three o'clock."

"I'm sorry about this."

"It isn't your fault," he said with the air of someone used to dealing with such situations. "I'll see you then."

CLAIRE HAD A HARD TIME concentrating on her sewing during the quilting session that afternoon. As usual, Deirdre gave no indication she was actively stirring up professional trouble for Claire.

The quilters were packing up after the

meeting when Claire strolled over to Deirdre's end of the table. She waited until the other woman glanced up from her beautifully pieced square.

"I thought you'd like to know that I'm changing all of Ashley's grades to A's," Claire said.

There was a beat of silence before Deirdre said, "You are?" Suspicion hung heavy in her voice.

"Yep." Claire slung her tote over her shoulder and headed for the door. Deirdre caught up with her at her car.

"I don't understand this."

"It's what you wanted, right? A's for Ashley? Well, now she has them."

Deirdre pursed her lips, uncertain as to whether she'd won or not. Claire thought that maybe she wasn't even certain of what she wanted at this point.

"I'll see you tomorrow," Claire said, and then she got into her car, leaving Deirdre staring at her through the windshield before she turned and walked back into the community hall.

Claire honestly didn't know if Deirdre would blink, but she got her answer later that evening when there was a knock on her door.

"You don't seem to have a phone number," Deirdre said by way of greeting.

"I have my cell," Claire said. "I saw no reason to pay two phone bills."

"Yes. Well." The woman drew herself up. "I'd like to talk to you about Ashley's grades."

"Please come in." Claire stepped back, wondering if Deirdre had ever been in an honest-to-goodness trailer before. Indeed, she crossed over the threshold cautiously, then she blinked in surprise. Claire had made the place habitable with overstuffed furniture and afghans in pale blues, greens and purples, plus pillows and candles in the same tones. She was a big believer in the importance of environment.

"Have a seat." Claire waved at the sofa, which she'd wrapped in a huge plum throw in order to disguise what lay beneath.

"Thank you, I'll stand." Deirdre briefly pressed her lips together. "Why did you change Ashley's grades?" she asked quietly.

"Before I answer, may I ask if you honestly believe I don't know what I'm doing?"

"This is your first year teaching."

"After about five years of college plus half a year of student teaching and half a year of long-term substitute work." Claire was almost grateful, now, that she'd changed majors three times.

"Ashley's grades were perfect until this year."

"If a teacher gives all A's and B's, then usually no one takes a closer look at what they're doing…or *not* doing."

Deirdre fixed Claire with a unsmiling gaze. "You were serious about these kids having holes in their education, weren't you?"

She nodded. "I was surprised."

"I do think you are too hard on Ashley. I mean, putting her in the hall and embarrassing her."

"I'm not doing that to embarrass her. I'm trying to do what's best for the entire class and, frankly, Ashley has an attitude. And it spreads to the younger kids. If they think there are no consequences, then…" Claire spread her hands.

Deirdre set her jaw. "You'd honestly leave her grades as A's."

"I can give her an A on everything, whether she turns in homework or not. But I don't think you want me to do that."

"No," Deirdre said softly. "That's not what I want." She paced a few steps. "I want to know what's going on. I want to know what Ashley's doing and where the trouble spots are."

Claire smiled weakly. "That was what the progress reports were supposed to be for."

"I still haven't seen one."

"I hand them out every Monday. Ask for it. Also, you can stop by anytime. And I'll contact you if there's anything you need to know about." Claire paused. "I am on Ashley's side, you know," she added gently.

Deirdre took a step toward the door. "I'll call Mr. Rupert tomorrow and cancel the meeting, but I would like to meet with you and go over Ashley's grades again. Her real grades."

"That would be good. I think Mr. Rupert will appreciate not having to make that drive," Claire said.

"And you and I will talk more often."

Claire kept a straight face as she said, "I look forward to that."

THERE WAS NO GETTING OUT of the community Thanksgiving celebration that was held the Friday before the actual holiday. Everyone came to the event—even confirmed hermits.

As soon as Brett walked into the community hall, Jesse waved him over to where he was sitting with Claire, Trini and her husband and a couple of younger kids.

"Hi, Brett." Jesse stood up. He was smiling widely, expectantly, practically vibrating with excitement. For the life of him, Brett couldn't figure out why.

"Hi, Jess." He offered a tentative smile, buying time. What was he supposed to do?

The kid's expression started to shift toward disappointment when Claire caught Brett's eye and gave the fabric of her blouse a discreet tug. Brett felt a rush of relief.

"That's a nice shirt, Jesse. Hey, new jeans, too." The kid beamed and held up one foot. He was wearing cowboy boots. Quite possibly vinyl, from the look of them. Brett smiled. "Somebody went shopping."

"I told you I was going to spend my payday money wisely."

Brett felt his heart twist. He'd assumed *wisely* meant saving some and spending the rest on a CD or a video game or something. He'd never dreamed the kid was going to buy himself clothes.

But Claire had known. He could see it in her face.

"Can you sit with us?" Jesse asked.

"You bet, if Miss Flynn can make room."

"Oh, I can make room," she said. Then something across the hall caught her eye and she smiled. Brett glanced toward the door and saw that Phil Ryker had just walked in. He headed straight for her.

"Hey, pard."

Brett forced a smile. "Hi, Phil."

To make room for Phil, Claire slid closer to Brett, momentarily bringing her thigh up against his. Brett didn't budge. Phil eased onto the bench on her other side, and she slid away from Brett, who wondered if her thigh was now pressed against Phil's. He scooted a few inches closer to Jesse, giving Claire room that she didn't take advantage of.

Not that it mattered.

"I still have some money left, so I can make my cat-food payment," Jesse was saying.

Phil leaned forward to look at Brett, who was trying hard not to notice his boss staring at him.

"You make this boy pay for cat food?"

"He boards my cat," Jesse stated proudly.

"It's kind of a sideline," Brett said.

"I thought you weren't able to make the celebration," Claire said to Phil, drawing his attention away from Brett, who wondered if she'd done it purposefully. If so, he was grateful.

"I changed my plans," Phil said, in a way that made Brett grit his teeth harder than *"pard"* did

"Look," Jesse said excitedly. "The line's starting. Wanna get our food now? And there's Ramon. He must have just got here. I'm spending the night with him."

"Let's go," Brett agreed. He was on his feet before Jesse was. He wanted to get away from Phil and Claire.

Much to Jesse's disappointment, Brett steered him to another table after they'd filled their plates, but Ramon plopped down a few minutes later, along with his sister, and Jesse was happy.

The rest of the evening went well. Jesse was pleased that Brett stayed with him, and Brett enjoyed listening to the kids jabbering away on the same topics that he and his friends had talked about at the same age—the fort they wanted to build in the willows, the best kind of four-wheeler, the upcoming basketball season. Claire and Phil were at their original table, and talked throughout the meal. Claire seemed to find Phil quite amusing.

The pastor from Wesley gave a sermon, and everyone in the room took a moment to count their blessings and give thanks. Jesse was smiling when they raised their heads, and Brett had a feeling the boy was thankful for his new clothes and a place to keep his cat.

People began gathering plates and washing dishes. Brett offered to help, but he was shooed away, so decided to take the hint and go.

"Are you leaving?" Jesse asked with a touch of disappointment.

"Important math lesson," he answered, using an excuse he figured Jesse could understand. "Due tomorrow. I need to get working."

"You shouldn't leave it to the last minute. Hey, have you talked to Miss Flynn yet?"

"About what?" Claire asked. She was gathering plates at the next table, but had been close enough to hear her name. Brett decided to come clean before Jesse made a public announcement.

"I'm taking a math class online."

"What kind of math are you studying?"

"Algebra 1," Jesse declared, beaming with pride.

"Algebra 1?" Claire did not seem impressed. Brett couldn't really blame her. She'd probably had math courses he'd never even heard of, and here he was relearning the stuff they taught in eighth grade.

"Differential Equations was full," he muttered, glad that Phil wasn't close enough to hear the conversation. "I'm saving that for next semester. Now—" he smiled at Jesse "—it's been great, but I've got to go."

"See ya, Brett." Jesse always said his name proudly, as if he was claiming him as his own.

"Bye, Jess. Have fun at Ramon's house."

Brett nodded at Claire and then made his escape.

The icy November air enveloped him as he stepped outside, chilling him and making him realize just how much he'd been sweating. And it wasn't due to the overheated room. It was due to Claire Flynn looking at him as if he was an idiot because he was just now learning algebra.

CHAPTER EIGHT

CLAIRE'S SMALL CAR was gone all day Saturday, and Brett took advantage of the fact to install a new thermocouple on the water heater without her being there, distracting him. He really wished things would stop falling apart in the trailer so that he wouldn't have to keep going in, because while he was there, he thought about her. A lot. They weren't exactly G-rated thoughts, either.

Of course, after the community Thanksgiving, she probably thought he was too stupid to mess around with, so he was safe to fantasize to his heart's content. His theory was shaken that evening, however, when Claire came calling. The teakettle whistled as he answered the door. He couldn't ignore it, so he motioned for her to come inside. "You want a cup of coffee?"

"Sure."

"It's instant," he warned.

"That's fine."

Claire took the cup from him a few minutes later. She was wearing pale pink nail polish and small silver rings that emphasized the daintiness of her hands—hands more suited for delicate china than the heavy mug she'd just been given.

"Was I supposed to bring something back from Wesley yesterday?" he asked.

"Nope," Claire said briskly. "I came to see if you need help with your algebra class. Rumor has it that you're not doing your homework until the last minute."

Brett took a big swallow of hot coffee. "Been talking to Jesse?"

"He's concerned." Her green eyes held an amused light. "I mean, you *are* old, you know."

"Old doesn't mean stupid."

"It does if you're ten. And he told me you were afraid to ask for help."

Brett's mouth flattened. Jesse was an astute kid, even if he had confused fear with stubbornness. "I don't need help."

"I honestly don't mind. It would give me something to do."

"Oh, you mean, besides grading papers and getting all that stuff ready to teach?" He attempted an offhand smile, but had a feeling it wasn't all that convincing. "I'm doing all right on my own."

Claire took a slow sip, watching him over the top of her cup, and Brett had to force himself not to stare at her mouth. "Does it come back fast? The math, I mean?"

He thought about continuing to fake it, but decided to come clean. It would save time. "Hard for it to come back when it was never there in the first place."

"*Never* there?"

"They didn't have exit proficiency exams when I was in high school," Brett explained. "I pretty much cheated my way through math and got away with it."

He almost laughed at how shocked she looked. So Claire wasn't a total rebel.

"Hey, I'm doing my penance." In fact, penance could be his middle name.

"I guess you are." She picked up a copy of *Moby Dick* lying on the sideboard, and made a face.

"I'm taking humanities, too."

"There is nothing humane about having to read *Moby Dick*." She set down the book. "Did you graduate high school?"

"Barely. I was more interested in roping and riding than in studying government or solving for X."

Claire took the information matter-of-factly. "So you have holes in your education."

"Holes you could drive a Mack truck through." He took another swig of coffee. It was almost gone, and soon he wouldn't have anything to focus on except her.

"You'd never know it," she commented. "Maybe…" She frowned and shook her head.

"Maybe what?"

"Maybe if you're having trouble with algebra, it's because you don't have the necessary base to build on."

"Algebra is eighth-grade math."

"Which you haven't seen in what? Over twenty years?"

"Maybe."

"I could help you out."

He shook his head. That was the last thing he wanted. He couldn't say why, but it was important to him that he conquer this on his own. "You want more coffee?"

"I'm good." Her cup was almost full. She smiled wryly. "Trying to sidetrack me?"

"Why would I want to do that?" He took his time measuring coffee crystals and then adding hot water.

"It's kind of funny," she said as she watched

him. "Will's a coffee-brewing fanatic and you make instant."

"Will and I are different in a lot of ways."

"So I gathered." He gave her a quick look, but there didn't seem to be any underlying meaning to her words. She further exonerated herself by saying, "Regan and I are different, too."

"Yes," he agreed. He and Regan had gone out a time or two before she'd hooked up with his brother for good.

"Are you going to Will and Regan's for Thanksgiving dinner?"

Brett shook his head. Claire didn't look surprised.

"Then I guess there's no sense asking if you want to share a ride."

"Sorry."

She looked as if she wanted to ask him what the deal was, why he avoided family get-togethers. But she didn't.

She glanced at the kitchen clock. "I have to get going. I'm meeting Phil at seven."

"Phil?"

"Yes. We're going to the bar to hear that folksinger from Wesley." She must have noticed his expression. "You don't care if I go out with your boss, do you?"

"It's none of my business."

"If you say so," she said as she set her cup aside.

"What does that mean?"

She looked him square in the eye. "It means that I get vibes from you."

"Vibes?" He didn't like the sound of that.

She continued to regard him steadily. "Yes. You know. The kind of vibes you feel when someone is interested in you? Even if he doesn't want to admit it and won't let you help him with his math?"

"Claire…"

"Don't," she said, taking a step closer to lay her palm flat against the front of his shirt. "There's no need to say anything." She patted him lightly and then headed for the door. "I'll see you later. And if you ever do need help with your *math*—" she smiled in a way that made his groin tighten "—you know where to find me."

PHIL RYKER WAS VERY SURE of himself. He was rich, handsome, charming, and he knew it. Claire had a strong suspicion that if they'd been anywhere else, he would have been making some serious moves on her, but Barlow Ridge was a tiny town that didn't see a lot of entertainment, so he was being careful. He had to be, with so many people casting speculative looks their way.

Claire settled back in her chair when the music started, enjoying the performance and ignoring the curious glances, thinking it was a good thing she wasn't self-conscious, because if she were, she'd have her jacket over her head by now. Phil seemed to enjoy the attention.

The singer, a local girl who toured the country with a bluegrass group, was surprisingly good. Many of those in the audience knew her, and after she'd finished her hourlong show she was surrounded by people.

Phil turned his attention to Claire. "I liked her," he said, a note of surprise in his voice.

"Me, too."

"Let me get you another drink." He took her glass and went to the bar without waiting for an answer.

Claire was getting tired of Phil-in-command. She watched as Marla flirted with him a little, stopping when Deke, her boyfriend, ambled through the door scratching his chest.

Phil returned a few seconds later with a Manhattan and a glass of wine. "Where were we before the music started?"

"You were telling me about your horse." And

trying to wow Claire with a lot of names she'd never heard before.

"But you weren't really all that interested in my horse, were you?"

Claire gave the wine a slow swirl. It wasn't so much lack of interest as not being impressed by the idea of owning a zillion-dollar horse for the sole purpose of bragging about its pedigree. She was much more impressed by Toby, the mutt, which was why she was giving Phil the benefit of the doubt. A guy who picked a dog out of the pound had to have some redeeming qualities. She just wished he'd get over trying to impress her, so she could discover what those redeeming qualities were.

"I don't know a lot about animals," she confessed over the top of her glass. "My sister is the horse nut."

Phil shifted in his chair, letting one arm drop over the back, affecting a relaxed pose. "How is it that one sister's a horse nut and the other knows nothing about animals?"

"I wanted to be an actress. Regan wanted to ride on the Olympic equestrian team. We both followed our own dreams."

"You don't seem to be acting," he pointed out.

"Are you sure?" Claire asked with a half smile.

It took Phil a moment to catch her meaning. He smiled in turn, but it didn't reach his eyes. Claire could see that he didn't like to be played with. She could also see that she represented a challenge to him. Apparently, women didn't normally toy with Phil Ryker.

"I'm not acting," she said gently, "but I've never been able to let a straight line go by."

"I'll have to be more careful around you." He tried to sound as if he was kidding, but Claire had the feeling he wasn't.

"Always a wise strategy." She toasted him with the glass of wine Marla had drawn her from a box with a plastic spigot. Phil answered her salute and sipped his drink, studying her in a way that made her think he was planning his strategy.

"Where do you live when you're not at your ranch?" she asked.

"I have a place near the home office in California. The folks own land in Nevada, Oregon and Idaho, but we manage most of it from San Luis."

"So you live here part of the year and in California the rest?"

"I like to get away," he said, with sincerity, and Claire realized she was finally getting a glimpse of the real Phil. "I like the slower pace of life here. I like the animals. Ranch life appeals to me."

"What is it about ranch life, exactly, that you like?"

He grinned. "It's hard to say. Maybe I watched too many westerns as a kid, but I like the independence and I like fighting the elements. I like being my own boss."

"I thought you *were* your own boss," Claire pointed out.

"I'm on Dad's payroll."

"Ah." She traced a finger around the edge of her wineglass—which was exactly like Brett's oversize shot glasses. "So will you be the big boss of the family company someday?"

"No. I think my sister will be the big boss. Frankly, I'd kind of like to settle on the ranch, try to raise some cows or horses. Just lead the simple life."

"You aren't afraid of getting bored?"

He shook his head. "I'll find things to do. I want to show my horses, and I was thinking of joining the volunteer fire department."

"The fire department?"

"Yeah," he said, the charmingly crooked smile once more making an appearance. "I always wanted to be a fireman."

"This world needs more firemen," Claire agreed.

Phil slid his hand across the table and

touched the large square stone in her ring. She arched an eyebrow and he pulled his hand back, letting it settle on the edge of the table.

"You're no pushover, are you, Claire?"

"Did you think I was?"

He shook his head. "No. I think you are a damn intelligent woman."

"But you were hoping I'd also be easy?"

He laughed. "Maybe."

"Well, I'm not."

It was his turn to smile evilly. "Not even after another drink?"

"Not even then," she said, pleased that he could tease.

"You can't blame me for trying."

"I don't blame you one bit. And I have to tell you, I like you better when you're just…Phil." She spoke gently, watching his reaction. He frowned, and she thought he was going to profess ignorance, but instead he said, "I've never had anyone tell me that."

"I prefer honesty to flash. I can't help it."

"Okay. I'll tone down the flash."

Claire finished the last drops of her box wine. "I really should be getting home." Especially now that things were going well between them. "I'm driving to Wesley early tomorrow for Thanksgiving."

He walked her to her car, and when they got there she offered her hand, which was probably not the way he'd intended to end the evening. "It's been fun."

"Yeah." There was a touch of irony in his voice.

Claire laughed and kissed his cheek. "I'll see you, Phil. Thanks for asking me out."

THANKSGIVING DINNER at the Bishop house was a low-key affair. With only four people, and none of them football fans, it could hardly have been anything else. The homemade rolls turned out well, the pies Claire had baked that morning were much appreciated and the turkey was roasted exactly on time.

After dinner was over Will and an uncharacteristically quiet Kylie headed out to feed, and Claire was able to ask Regan a question that had been bothering her for quite a while.

"What's the deal with Will and Brett?" she asked.

Regan handed her the dish of mashed potatoes. "Deal?"

"You know what I mean. Brothers living less than a hundred miles apart and one of them chooses to spend Thanksgiving alone."

"They were never close," Regan said,

carrying the empty turkey platter to the sink and dumping it into the soapy water.

"And that's it?"

"What more do you want?"

"I want to know why," Claire said, stretching plastic wrap over the potatoes. "The whole situation strikes me as odd. I mean, Brett goes to all the public family events, but none of the private ones. Why?"

"Sometimes it's hard to pin down the why," Regan said vaguely, lifting a dish out of the draining rack and wiping it dry.

And sometimes it's not. Regan had information she didn't want to share.

Claire debated as she gathered cutlery off the table and transferred it to the dishwater. Yes, she was curious about Brett, but it was none of her business. She decided to take the high road. If Regan didn't want to tell her the story, fine. Brett was part of Regan's family, not part of Claire's.

But the whole situation was driving her crazy.

"Kylie said that her first basketball game is coming up soon."

"Yes," Regan confirmed more cheerfully. "We have a schedule printed out for you."

"She seemed kind of quiet at dinner."

"Yeah." Regan continued to wipe the already dry plate. "She broke curfew the other night and Brett brought her home. She's not happy with any of us right now. Brett embarrassed her in front of her new boyfriend and then we grounded her."

"Brett brought her home?"

"Total fluke. He happened to see her out late and realized it was a little *too* late. And then, because we grounded her she didn't get to go to the Harvest Dance. Her boyfriend took someone else, and now *those* two are a couple and Kylie's left out in the cold. She's hurt and furious, and guess who's she's blaming?"

"Everyone except herself?" Claire remembered those days well. "Parenthood is hard, isn't it?" And Regan had pretty much been tossed into the deep end when she'd married Will. Will's first wife had left when Kylie was only an infant, so Regan was, in essence, the first mother the girl had ever known.

"Yes. You know what's best for the kid, and you know what it feels like to be a kid." Regan blew out a breath as Claire gently pried the dry dish from her hands and replaced it with a wet one. Regan automatically began to wipe again.

"Speaking of parents, what do you think Mom's doing in San Diego right now?"

"I hope she's having dinner with Stephen."

"Think they'll work it out? I mean, do you think Mom will ever change?"

"I could make all kinds of comments about pigs flying and hell freezing over but…" Regan glanced at her sister conspiratorially "…I don't think there really is a conference in San Diego. I think she's gone there to patch things up."

"And she's covering herself, in case she fails." Claire nodded appreciatively. "Smart woman."

BRETT GOT PAID TWICE a month, and his payday became Jesse's payday, as well. He made certain that he had enough cash on hand to pay the boy on the fifteenth and the thirtieth. "Are you going to buy more clothes?" he asked on the payday immediately following Thanksgiving—which was in itself a cause for thanksgiving. Phil hadn't mentioned riding the stud again, and he hadn't fired Brett, either.

Jesse nodded.

"Saving money to buy clothes is a mature thing to do," Brett said. "I'm impressed. But don't you think maybe you should spend a little on something more… fun?"

The look of pride faded from Jesse's face. "Dad couldn't afford school clothes this year, and I'm tired of wearing stuff that doesn't fit," he said stiffly.

Brett felt that twisting sensation in his gut again, and he attempted damage control. "Sounds like you know what you're doing. I never was any good at managing my money." He tucked his wallet back in his jeans pocket. "Maybe you could give me some pointers."

Jesse slowly smiled. "I didn't only get clothes, you know. I got a better backpack, and a web belt with a cowboy buckle."

"Sounds cool."

"I'll show you the belt tomorrow."

"Can't wait."

Brett set out a couple of cookies and a soda pop—not exactly health food, but there was a place for indulgence food, too. He leaned against the door frame when Jesse left, watching as the boy happily trotted down the drive, wearing his new finery.

Shit. If he'd known the kid didn't have decent clothes, he would have bought him some.

Brett zipped his coat against the cold November air and went to his truck. It was feeding time at Phil's, and he wanted to get done early so he could work on his math and get another chapter of *Moby Dick* under his belt. He pulled open the door and there, sitting on the driver's seat, was a book. A textbook, to be exact. *Pre-algebra.*

Damn. Claire had left him a present. He pushed the book aside and got into the truck, but while he waited for the glow plugs to heat before turning on the ignition, he picked up the text and flipped through it. Then he stopped. Read a little. He frowned and then turned back a page. He read some more, studied the example, closed the book and put it on the seat beside him.

Okay, maybe Claire was right. Maybe he had to brush up on some basics before proceeding, and maybe this book would help. Even though he'd made it clear he didn't want help, and she'd dropped the damn book off, anyway.

She's a teacher. She probably couldn't help herself.

He turned the key and the engine chugged to life.

Either that or she recognized a guy in trouble who was too stubborn for his own good.

IT WASN'T UNTIL the pep band started playing the national anthem and the crowd rose that

Claire managed to spot Brett on the opposite side of the gymnasium at Kylie's first home game. She turned her attention back to the basketball court as the referee prepared for the tip-off.

Wesley's first game of the season was against the town's arch rival, the team that had taken the state championship from them the previous season by two points. Emotions were running high on both sides. Thirty seconds into play the whistle blew for the first foul.

"I hope this doesn't set the tone for the game," Regan muttered, as the ref held up fingers to indicate Kylie's number.

It did. By the end of the first half a technical had been called and two players, one on each team, had fouled out. Kylie was close to being the next player benched, with four fouls of her own.

"Play nice," Will said under his breath as the second half began. But Kylie played for only a matter of minutes before the coach took her out, too.

"Good," Regan said. "She needs to settle down and focus on her play."

"Since when did you become a basketball expert?" Claire asked. Claire had been the one who'd played basketball in high school for two years. Regan had been too busy at the stables to participate in high-school athletics.

"Since I became a mom," Regan said, her attention on the game. She flinched as one of the Wesley players missed an easy layup. "She needs some time to regroup. She's taking too many chances, and she's letting that Spartan girl get to her."

Claire knew exactly which girl Regan was talking about. Number 12. She was about Kylie's size, with long blond braids and an aggressive attitude. She had three fouls—all against Kylie. And two of Kylie's fouls were against her.

"Kylie does get her dander up."

Will and Regan nodded in unison, their eyes on the game. Claire glanced across the court at Brett. Even at a distance she could see that he was scowling. Apparently, the entire family took basketball seriously.

Kylie went out on the floor again at the start of the fourth quarter. And she did seem more focused. Her play was calmer, more methodical. The Spartan girl, on the other hand, was starting to get frustrated. The Wesley team was winning by four points, and number 12 was doing everything she could to turn that around.

She attempted to steal the ball from Kylie

again, who neatly sidestepped her. The girl overreached and lost her balance, tumbling onto the floor. Another player tripped over her and the whistle blew. Kylie handed the ball off to the ref and calmly waited for play to resume.

The girl got to her feet and walked by Kylie, muttering something as she passed that made Kylie snap to attention. She said something back and the girl stopped short, turned and made an aggressive move toward her.

The Spartan coach shouted at his player and she grudgingly turned back to the court. Kylie walked to her position and the game resumed. Kylie got the ball almost immediately and headed down the court, maneuvering neatly around several opponents. She had just squeezed through a small gap when number 12 made a diving grab for the ball and crashed sideways into her. The crowd gasped as Kylie went down, her head smacking the floor hard. And then she lay still.

Regan and Will were instantly on their feet and moving, Claire close behind. They made it to the far side of the court just as the crowd surrounding Kylie parted, and she sat up with the help of the trainer, hugging her arm to her body. Brett was kneeling next to her, his expression taut. He stood and moved to the sideline, almost bumping into Will as the trainer helped Kylie to her feet and escorted her off the court.

Will pushed through the players to catch up with them, with Regan, Brett and Claire following behind. He glanced over his shoulder at Regan as they approached the training room.

"You go," she said. "It's a small room," she explained after the door closed. She reached out to touch Brett's arm, drawing his attention. "Are you all right?"

"I'm good." But he didn't look good. "It's just…the sound her head made…" He seemed to be speaking more to himself than Regan, who ran her hand up and down his arm in a gesture of acknowledgment and empathy. Claire stood by, watching, the odd man out. There were undercurrents between Brett and Regan that she didn't understand, undercurrents that made her vaguely uncomfortable.

The door opened several minutes later and Will came out.

"They're icing her arm and the bump on her head," he said, "and I have a list of instructions on how to monitor for a concussion." He smiled weakly at his wife. "I didn't tell them how much experience I had with that in the rodeo."

"What about her arm?" Brett asked.

"We have to wait until Monday and then get it x-rayed."

"Other than that, she's fine?"

"For the most part. She's mad she's missing the end of the game."

A huge cheer from the crowd nearly drowned out his words.

Brett shifted his weight, his body language radiating discomfort. "Well, if she's okay, I'll think I'll get going. I'll call later, to find out the prognosis."

Will nodded, but Regan looked uncertain. "Brett—" she began, but he shook his head.

"I need to go." A few seconds later he was striding down the narrow strip of floor between the basketball court and the bleachers. The crowd was on its feet, screaming as the score was tied, but Brett didn't even seem to notice.

Regan let out a breath. "I'll bet she said something to him."

"You think?" Claire asked.

"I wouldn't be surprised."

BRETT'S TRUCK WAS PARKED in the supermarket lot when Claire pulled in to do her weekly shopping before heading home. It wasn't uncommon to meet Barlow Ridge residents in the Wesley grocery store, since living in

Barlow meant a person had to stock up whenever he managed to get to a store of any size. But somehow Claire didn't think Brett was going to believe this meeting was accidental.

She counted to ten before entering, and then decided to let fate take over. If she ran into him, she did, if she didn't, she didn't.

Fate led her straight to the produce department, where she found him dropping potatoes into a plastic bag. He looked up before she could get her cart turned around.

"So what's the secret of choosing a good potato?" she asked with a half smile as she wheeled her cart closer. Brett did not smile. "Sorry," she said. "And I'm not stalking you. I just need to pick up a few things before heading home."

"Yeah, I figured." He tied a knot in the top of his plastic bag and dropped it in the cart. "I suppose you're wondering why I tore out of the game like that?"

"Of course," she said softly, "but I don't need to know."

"It's no big deal. Kylie and I haven't been getting on so well since the night I found her out late and made her go home. I thought she'd be happier if I wasn't there."

But there was more to the story than that.

Claire sensed it, and wondered if Kylie really had said something when Brett was kneeling next to her. Kylie tended to speak her mind.

"Kids can be cruel, Brett. A lot of times they don't realize adults have feelings, too."

"Yeah. Come to think of it, I remember thinking like that myself." His features relaxed some, making Claire even more aware of his attractiveness. Making her want to spend some time with him.

"I didn't get to eat anything at the game," she said. "I don't suppose…" A shift in Brett's expression stopped her from finishing the invitation. "Of course not. We have long drives ahead of us."

Even though she thought they would both benefit from a shared meal. It would help him relax, put things into perspective, and it would save her from having to eat pretzels out of a bag on the drive home.

"Actually…" Brett's quiet voice stopped her. "I wouldn't mind having a bite to eat with you, but I have to make another stop before I go home."

"Well, maybe some other time?"

"Yeah. Maybe." He surprised her by reaching out to brush her cheek briefly with his fingertips. "Thanks, Claire."

And then he wheeled his cart away.

She resisted the urge to touch where his hand had been, but she could still feel the warmth of the simple caress. She automatically started moving toward the organic section, a little amazed that a brief encounter in the produce department could give her so much to think about.

CHAPTER NINE

"LET ME GET THIS STRAIGHT. I have to find a guy to wear the Santa suit?"

Fifteen heads nodded in unison. Claire was beginning to dread PTO meetings. "Why me?"

"It's your turn. We've all done it."

"I take it this isn't easy."

"We have a list of everyone who's already been Santa," Trini said helpfully.

"I need a list of the guys who *haven't* done it so far." Claire took the printed list and quickly scanned it. Brett wasn't on it. Well, he would be next year.

"Do you think any of these guys would be up for another Santa stint?"

"Maybe. It's not that bad," Bertie said in the kind of voice a mother might use if she was trying to convince a child that going to the dentist would be fun.

"Oh, all right," Claire said, pretending she

had a say in the matter. She had two weeks to find a Santa and, she'd start working on it tonight.

BRETT WONDERED WHAT HIS life would be like when he no longer had a beautiful blonde showing up on his doorstep whenever she got the whim.

"Hi. I brought you something. A bribe, actually." Claire pushed by him into the kitchen and deposited a wicker basket on the table. It was bread. Fresh out of the oven.

"You cook?"

"Of course I cook. It's just chemistry."

"And I suppose you're good at chemistry."

"Yes, I am."

He lifted the corner of the cloth that covered the bread. "Looks good."

"It is."

"Is there anything you're not good at?"

"No," she said lightly, wondering if he was making a double entendre, or if it was just wishful thinking on her part.

"So why are you bringing bribes?"

"I need someone to dress up as Santa at the Christmas play."

"And you want me to help you find…" His

voice suddenly trailed off as realization set in. *"No."*

"Please?"

He shook his head, and then had a flash of brilliance. "Ask Phil."

"He won't be here."

Brett hated that she already knew that and he didn't.

"It's really hard to get someone to do this because practically everyone in Barlow has been Santa at least once already, and since I'm the new teacher they're making me do it, and… Please, Brett?"

"No." He continued to shake his head. "I'm not that kind of guy."

"What kind of guy?"

"A Santa kind of guy," he said gruffly.

"Oh, I don't know." She nodded at Sarina, who was studying them from under one of the kitchen chairs.

"That's different." He paced to the sink and put some dishes in the water he'd run just before Claire knocked. "Have you asked anyone else?"

She pulled a list out of her jacket pocket and showed it to him. "These are the people who won't do it. Can you think of anyone who isn't on it?"

No one suitable. Deke would probably be

drunk. Little Manny Fernandez—he was maybe half a Santa.

"The kids need a Santa, Brett."

Brett wondered briefly if a kid like Jesse still believed in Santa—even a little—and then he had an idea.

"What?" Claire asked softly, sensing his shift in attitude.

"If you can find out what Jesse wants for Christmas, I'll do it."

"That's all?"

"I want to get him something kind of special. And I have to figure out how to give it to him so it doesn't look like charity."

She smiled slowly, watching him fight not to smile in return. "All right, Scrooge, I'll see what I can do."

"Then I'll wear the stupid suit," he said with a scowl.

"And now I'm going to do something I've wanted to do since the wedding." She rose up on her toes and, taking his face between her palms and pressing her body lightly along the length of his, she kissed him. Softly. Warmly. A friendly thank-you kiss that shouldn't have given him an instant hard-on. He worked to keep frowning as she pulled away.

"Oh, come on, Brett, you didn't mind, did you?"

"I think it's obvious that I didn't." His anatomy was sending out all the proper signals.

"No," she said softly, raising her fingers to gently tap his forehead. "I mean, up here."

He caught her hand, held on for a moment. He didn't have a straight answer. No, he didn't mind. Yes, he did mind. They were both the truth. If she were anyone else, related to anyone else, he'd probably already have been actively working toward getting her in the sack.

"Thank you for agreeing to be Santa." She squeezed his fingers and slipped her hand free, taking a backward step to put some space between them.

"Just find out what Jesse wants, okay?"

"I'll do my best."

A few seconds later, he was alone and wondering what he was doing. With Claire. With Jesse.

He didn't know.

Jesse needed someone to take an interest in him, and Brett found himself stepping into that position more and more. And liking it. But the big question was why? Was he helping Jesse, or filling an empty hole in his own life?

Brett was still smarting from what Kylie had said to him at the game, when she'd opened her eyes and seen him hovering over her. *"I want you to leave me alone."* And she'd meant it.

He tried to tell himself Kylie was just angry about being caught in a lie and having to pay the consequences, that she'd get over it. But it bothered him. A lot.

As PROMISED, Claire discovered what Jesse wanted for Christmas from a writing assignment, and after that she managed to wheedle Brett into going shopping in Elko with her.

Brett pulled into her driveway at 5:00 a.m. one Saturday morning. Claire wrapped her mulberry scarf around her neck, grabbed her purse and let herself out into the frigid predawn air.

Brett was not smiling when she slid into the passenger seat.

"Stop looking like you're not going to enjoy this," she said sternly before burrowing down into her coat. The truck was cold, even though the heater was blowing, and she was beginning to wish she'd brought along a cup of coffee. Brett granted her wish by indicating the extra travel cup in the holder between them.

"You're a good man," she said with a sigh as she picked up the cup closer to her.

"How many kids are we shopping for?"

"Ten."

"Ten?"

Claire looked at him out of the corner of her eye. "It started as six, but since it wouldn't be right for some kids to get a gift and others not to, Bertie approached the PTO for financing. We're going to get something for every kid. I'm responsible for my class. Bertie's responsible for her class."

"Ten presents." Brett took a moment to digest the new plan of action. "What does Jesse want?"

"Well, he wants a bike, but that's kind of pricey, so you might consider a winter coat. His is pathetic. A hooded sweatshirt under a light-weight fall coat. And he did mention a coat in his journals."

"Yeah. I guess that'd be good."

But when they got to Wal-Mart, Brett went straight to the bikes.

"I thought—"

"I'll get him both."

Claire sucked in a breath. "Brett…" He sent her a frowning glance. "That's a lot of money. More than the other kids are getting."

"I know." He ran his hand over the curved handlebars of the floor model. "But I'm thinking, what the hell. I'm entitled to give my best employee a Christmas bonus, aren't I? Santa can give him the coat."

"I still—"

Brett turned toward Claire then and put his hands on her shoulders, stopping her midsentence.

"I want to give Jesse a bike." He squeezed lightly and then let go. Claire turned back to the bikes, still feeling the phantom pressure of his grip.

She had to clear her throat before saying, "Well, which one is the Christmas bonus?"

"None of these. We're going to the bike shop downtown."

"If you say so." Claire perused her list again. "But we're going to need a cart for this other stuff."

Jesse ended up with an awesome bike. Claire had a feeling it was exactly the bike Brett would have bought himself. It had all the necessary extras to allow Jesse to ride to school in style and to also tear up the trails.

Brett was really pleased with the purchase. He made certain, after that, that Claire didn't pick out a geeky coat, nixing a red one in favor of dark blue, and he added a knit hat with a popular insignia and gloves.

"How are you giving out the other presents?"

he asked after they'd ordered lunch at a small downtown café.

"Mrs. Presley is going to pretend Santa left some stuff at the post office. She's going to have her husband deliver the gifts on Christmas Eve."

"That's nice."

"I don't know what we're going to do about Jesse's gift, though."

"Why?"

"When I talked to his dad at the parent meeting—"

"The guy actually came to the parent meeting?"

"Yes, he did."

"He came to something that involved his kid?"

"I believe I established that." Brett took the hint and shut up. "He has not been a dad for long, by the way."

"Jesse said something about that."

"Yes. He paid his child support all along, but he had minimal contact with Jesse until his grandmother got too sick to take care him." Claire did not like the stormy expression on Brett's face. "He was only eighteen when Jesse was born," she explained.

"That may seem like an excuse to him, but it isn't."

Brett spoke with a quiet intensity that startled Claire. She leaned back as the waiter delivered their sandwiches, but her eyes stayed locked on his.

"Why do you say that?"

Brett shook his head. "Why do you think it might be hard to deliver Jesse's present?"

"I told Tom—that's the father—that I'd be happy to drive Jesse home on the nights when he was working late, and he was adamant that he didn't want Jesse home alone."

"He prefers him freezing his ass off in a school playground."

"And he also said that his dogs were unpredictable and that it wasn't safe for strangers to come to his place unless he was there."

"Oh, yeah. That's a good environment for a kid." Brett looked a little sick as he pushed his plate away.

"Hey." Claire reached out and placed her fingers over his. "He does seem to care about Jesse. And he said that the dogs love him."

"If he cares about Jesse, then why doesn't he take care of him?"

"Maybe he doesn't know how to?"

"I know how to, and I'm...not a father."

Claire squeezed his fingers, surprised he hadn't pulled them away. "One thing I learned from my stint student teaching is that there are always kids we want to take home with us, to save. But we can't."

Brett held her gaze, the expression in his dark eyes very, very serious. "I don't know if I can play by those rules," he said quietly.

He slipped his hand out from under hers and picked up his sandwich, taking a bite. Finally he said, "I'll do my best, but no promises."

JESSE LANE WAS A SUPERB actor, or so it seemed to Brett, who spent most of his Christmas pageant audience time smiling as he watched his protégé chew the scenery in the role of a forgetful elf who was delaying Christmas.

Brett sat near the back of the room, sandwiched between the Moreno clan and old Grandpa Meyers, who always traveled out from Wesley to watch his great-grandkids perform. Brett made sure that Jesse saw him, and then, after the first play ended, he slipped out the side exit. Reentering through the front door, he stepped quietly into the darkened office before anyone noticed him.

Santa. He couldn't believe he was doing this. He'd missed Kylie's Santa years, and although he was now able to get her something for her birthday and Christmas, in the role of an uncle, it all felt so inadequate. A small part of him acknowledged that his indulgence of Jesse was a compensatory move. A larger part of him knew he cared for Jesse, plain and simple. The boy had weaseled his way into Brett's heart.

And where the hell was Jesse's father? His kid was in a play and he couldn't take time out of his busy schedule to show up. Jesse had probably bummed a ride from the Hernandezes.

Well, Brett would take him home if he needed a ride, whether his dad had rules about it or not. Brett wasn't concerned about unpredictable dogs. He wanted to make sure the boy wasn't staying alone, that the dad wasn't out on his sales route. Jesse was amazingly reticent about his home life, considering how willingly he poured out everything else.

Brett locked the office door and peeled off his jacket and boots. He pulled on the velvety red pants over his jeans and tied the drawstring. Next the jacket. He buttoned it halfway, then shoved the homemade stuffed belly into the front. He glanced down. He looked more pregnant than fat. Oh, well. Closing the jacket, he buckled on the black belt, slipped his feet into his cowboy boots and tucked the pant legs into the tops. Next, a white wig.

His head was instantly hot.

And now the beard. He grimaced as he held up a mass of silvery curls. How many guys had breathed into this thing? During cold-and-flu season?

It's for the kids.

Fastening the beard in place, he slapped the Santa cap on his head. *Ho, ho, ho.*

He opened the office door, peeking out just as Bertie appeared at the stage door. She held up five fingers, indicating five minutes, then pointed to the door he would use to enter the gym and begin spreading Christmas joy.

He still couldn't believe he was doing this.

THE LINE OF KIDS wound around the gym. Parents snapped pictures and waited for their little ones to confide to Brett what they wanted for Christmas. And damned if he didn't have a real desire to fulfill all their wishes.

Next year, maybe he'd go shopping after the Santa stint.

What on earth was he thinking? He wasn't doing this twice.

But…it really wasn't that bad. Except for the damn beard. He couldn't wait to get that off.

Even the older kids sat on Santa's lap. It was part of what he appreciated about small towns—that older kids stayed kids for a while and they set an example for the younger ones. For the most part, anyway.

Jesse obviously recognized him. He had a conspiratorial gleam in his eye as he asked for a 4x4 pickup truck. A Dodge diesel crew cab, if Santa could swing it. Brett told him he'd do what he could.

Toni was next and she sat on the edge of his knee, barely making contact. She looked into his eyes, obviously trying to guess his identity. Brett gamely asked what she wanted for Christmas.

"Honest?" she asked with a touch of grim irony.

"Yes," he answered, surprised at her response.

"I want a real place to live. Just me and my mom."

Brett didn't know what to say. He handed her a candy cane and she got up, and then Ashley made a big show of sitting on Santa's lap, giggling as she wrapped her arms around his neck, leaning her cheek against his in a cheesy way and smiling as her stepdad took a picture. Once the photo shoot was over, she jumped up and went to join Toni, without saying a word to Brett.

Nice kid. He had a feeling that if Ashley lived anywhere except for Barlow, she wouldn't have a thing to do with Toni.

Funny. He'd never thought about kid dynamics much until Claire came breezing into his life. And speaking of which, his eyes strayed over to where she was talking to a couple of parents—who were actually listening to what she had to say. She was making inroads. And looking good while she did it, in a long black skirt and a sparkly green top.

She always looked good. And he wasn't the only guy who seemed to be noticing. Several guys, single and otherwise, seemed to be ogling her.

"Santa?"

Elena Moreno got his attention before she took her turn on his rapidly numbing knee. He smiled through the beard and she took her seat.

BRETT HAD JUST FINISHED his duties and was talking to a small boy when the gym door opened and Jesse's dad came in. Claire had to fight to keep her mouth from popping open. One side of the man's face was burned bright scarlet. The wound was obviously fairly new, just starting to scab over. Maybe he'd actually had a legitimate reason for missing Jesse's performance, because he wasn't looking well.

She glanced at Brett, who was now working his way through the crowd with a determined look on his face. Claire went into action. It wouldn't do to have Santa assault a man in front of an audience.

"Santa, may I have a word?"

She spoke firmly, and Brett slowed down. Jesse appeared out of the crowd then and walked over to his father, handing him his goodie bag and costume. The guy took it, laid a hand on his son's shoulder, more as a steering mechanism than out of affection, and pushed the door open. A second later the two Lanes disappeared out into the night.

Claire did not say a word, but took Brett's hand and pressed her classroom key into it. He understood. He couldn't exactly get into his truck and drive away wearing the Santa suit— at least not without disillusioning any small child who might see him. And since his clothing was still locked in the office, he had no choice but to disappear.

He pretended to be heading back to the stage, but instead slipped into Claire's dark room and managed to fumble his way past the student desks to her chair without hurting himself. He pulled off the hat and let out a long breath.

He couldn't shake the image in his mind of Jesse's dad steering him out that door. What in the hell had happened to the guy, and why hadn't Jesse mentioned that his dad had been hurt?

Brett was still mulling the matter over when Claire opened the door and snapped on the lights.

"Are they gone?" he asked, blinking as his eyes adjusted.

"Every one of them."

He yanked off the wig and beard, rubbing a hand over his head and ruffling his hair. "I was afraid to take the damn thing off, in case some kid came in. I should have put my clothes somewhere more accessible."

"Should have," Claire agreed, holding up a big bag that held his jeans and shirt. "You want to come to my place and have a celebratory drink after you change?"

"I just want to go home."

"You are really chipping away at my confidence," she said as she strolled closer, swinging the bag on one finger.

Brett stood. "I don't think anything shakes your confidence."

She stepped even closer, near enough for him to smell her perfume. Something with a spicy cinnamon base that made him want to pull her onto his lap, press his face into her neck and inhale deeply—before he did some even better stuff.

"Just a nightcap. As a thank-you." She ran a finger down the front of the soft red suit. "And you can start the furnace, because it went off just before I left and the reset button isn't working."

"All right." He couldn't exactly leave her without heat. Brett reached out and took the bag. "I'll change in the office."

THE FUEL LINE on the furnace was plugged. Brett blew it clear and pushed the button. The furnace hesitated, then gave a shudder and started to hum. A minute later the blower came on and warm air wafted out through the vents. Claire went to stand over one of the grates, letting the warm air flutter the hem of her silky skirt.

"The tank must have been low when they filled it. Sometimes debris gets into the line."

"I do seem to use a lot of fuel," Claire agreed. "I like to be warm."

"Do you miss the Vegas heat?"

"Not as much as I thought I would. I won't mind going back, but I do like it here. Even if it does get cold."

"I'm surprised."

"I bet you are," she said. "You thought I was a hothouse flower, didn't you?"

"You are more...adaptable than I'd first thought." In fact, she was a hell of a lot tougher than he'd imagined she'd be. Definitely tougher than Mr. Nelson, and a lot less whiny.

The trailer was warming up fast. It had its problems, but poor insulation wasn't one of them. Claire eventually shrugged out of her coat and went into the kitchen. "What do you want? I have wine or wine."

"I'll take wine."

She brought two glasses—with stems. One was filled with red and one with white. "I remembered that you prefer red." She raised her glass. "To Santa."

"To Santa."

"Sit down," she said, after their first sip. "Relax. You've earned it."

She settled on the plum-colored sofa, stretching out her legs to rest her heels on the coffee table. "What do you think happened to Jesse's dad?" she asked conversationally.

"It looked like a flash burn."

Claire frowned. "Jesse hasn't said a word about it."

"Have you noticed that he doesn't talk about his dad much?"

"Maybe because they haven't been together that long."

Claire crossed her ankles, making the sparkles on her less-than-sensible shoes catch the light. "It's good that you're there for him. Kids need someone to talk to."

"Yeah," Brett agreed, feeling slightly ill at ease. He wasn't used to being the good guy.

A silence followed. Claire seemed totally comfortable with it—more comfortable than Brett was, anyway. He felt aware. Hyperaware.

"What are you doing for Christmas?" he finally asked.

"I think I'll go to Las Vegas and spar with my mother."

"Sounds like fun."

"It's more fun than it used to be, now that she's finally seeing me as an adult."

"She didn't before?"

"It was my own fault. I was blissfully flaky,

and then Regan moved and my world came crashing down."

"Why?"

"I was on my own. Decisions that I would have automatically asked Regan for advice on, I had to make myself, since I felt dumb calling her all the time. I had to handle Mom on my own. I had to grow up." Claire reached out to take his half-empty wineglass, and placed it on the end table next to her own, then smiled languidly at him. "It was awful."

He knew exactly what was coming next, and he didn't resist when she curled her hand around his neck and pulled his lips down to hers.

Her mouth was as inviting as he remembered. No, it was better. As was the feel of her body snuggled up against his. He let his hand skim over her. Lightly, while reminding himself that this was just a thank-you kiss, like the one in his kitchen. A mistletoe-type Happy Holiday kiss.

Who was he trying to kid? This was a toe-curling, groin-hardening kiss.

"Are you much of a fighter?" Claire asked, when she finally came up for air.

"What?" he asked huskily. He brushed the hair away from her temples with his fingertips, wanting to go on touching her.

She suddenly rolled on top of him, smiling down into his eyes. "As I continue my assault on your virtue, will be you be putting up a struggle?" He wanted to smile, but managed not to.

"Yes." Or so his mind said. Although his body had different ideas.

And it seemed to be winning.

She cupped his face in her hands and kissed him deeply. His mind was losing. When she came up for air once more, he tried again.

"Clai—" She cut him off with another hot kiss. "You may as well surrender."

"No." But his hands were at her waist, traveling over her hips, then cupping her butt to press her into his erection.

"You'll have to be more convincing than that," she commented wryly. "I know all the arguments, but…" She brushed her lips over his. "I also know that you shouldn't spend your life alone."

"I can have company, if I choose."

"But you're not choosing."

"So I'm going to have company thrust upon me?"

"It's for your own good."

Now he did laugh. "You're doing this to help me out?"

"I think you're a good man who needs companionship." She raised her eyebrows suggestively.

"You might be surprised about the 'good man' part."

"But I'm not wrong about the companion-ship part," she said, unfazed, "and I think we could be good together."

"I'm not denying that." But there was more to life than momentary pleasure. There were long-term consequences, and if there was one subject he was familiar with, it was long-term consequences. "I'm tempted," he said truthfully.

"But not quite ready to make the big leap." She eased away from him, and he immediately missed her warmth, her softness. Her scent. "No hard feelings?"

She reached for her glass and drained the last few drops. In spite of her such-is-life attitude, he wondered if he'd hurt her feelings. He reached out to touch her face.

"I like you, Claire, but there are some issues here that:…" He paused, trying to figure out how much he wanted to say. How much he could say.

"Hey, it's fine, Brett. Honest. If I wasn't ready for rejection, I wouldn't have come on to you. I *am* tougher than I look."

As he stepped out into the cold night a few minutes later, however, he had a feeling that Claire was not quite as bulletproof as she pre-tended.

CHAPTER TEN

THE KIDS OF BARLOW RIDGE had a happy
Christmas, thanks to Claire. Brett discovered
this not from Claire, who'd kept her distance
during the week preceding Christmas vacation,
but from Anne McKirk, when he stopped by
her store the day after a rather lonely Christmas.

"So you stayed here for Christmas, did
ya?" she asked.

"I did."

Regan had called and invited him to dinner,
as she always did, but he'd told her he'd see
them all at Kylie's game a few days later. Claire
was in Las Vegas and Phil was in California.
Jesse was supposed to be in Carson City
visiting his great-grandmother.

Brett was totally alone. It wasn't a new state
of affairs, but this year it felt different.

"Do you know anything about this Lane guy?"
he asked Anne as he paid for his groceries.

"Hard to know anything about a guy you never see."

"But, Anne, you know everything."

She pretended to be insulted, but she wasn't. "Not this time. The only thing I do know is that he's living in that place rent-free because it belongs to his ex-mother-in-law."

Or perhaps Jesse's grandma. "Is she local?"

"Nope. She and her husband bought the place as an investment years ago, and then the husband passed away."

"I wonder why she hasn't sold."

"Hernandez offered to buy it from her once, but she didn't sell because she's leaving it to her grandson."

So Jesse had a legacy, too. Five acres and a trailer house. Not bad for a ten-year-old who didn't have a decent winter coat. Brett wondered if Jesse was aware of his inheritance.

"That clears some stuff up, Anne. Thanks."

"No problem." She walked him to the door, glancing out at his truck. "Where're you going with that bike?"

"Christmas bonus that I need to deliver."

Anne smiled briefly, in spite of herself.

THERE WERE TWO TRAILERS on the Lane place, one behind the other, and two nasty-looking dogs. No wonder Sarina seemed so happy living with Brett. She could relax.

The dogs charged the truck as Brett drove in. He put the rig in Neutral, and watched as the animals took aggressive stances within easy attack range, teeth bared, the hair on their backs bristling straight up. So these were the dogs that loved Jesse. Damn, Brett hoped so.

He let out a breath and put the truck in Reverse. The dogs took deliberate strides forward in unison, their teeth still bared as he swung the truck around. He would not be leaving the bike as a surprise. Instead, he'd have Anne give him a heads-up when the Lanes returned, and then he'd deliver the bike.

As it turned out, though, Brett didn't have to deliver it. Jesse showed up at his place the next day, wearing his new Christmas coat and hat, worried because he'd missed chores without telling Brett, but thrilled that he'd gotten to spend Christmas with his great-grandmother.

"Dad had friends to go see, so I spent the whole day with her and the other old people until it was their bedtime." He smiled sadly. "Old guys have bedtimes. Isn't that weird?"

"Totally," Brett agreed. "Hey, speaking of chores, I have something to tell you." Instantly, Jesse looked worried. "Something good," Brett amended. "Come on. I'll show you instead of telling you."

He led the way to the enclosed side porch and opened the door. The bike was leaning against a saddle rack. Jesse's eyes grew as big as saucers.

"No way," he said softly.

Brett smiled. "You've worked hard. This is your Christmas bonus."

"A Christmas bonus? For real?"

"For real."

Jesse slowly approached the bike. He ran a hand over the handlebars, just as Brett had done in the store, and then grinned at him over his shoulder.

"Too bad there's so much snow, or you could try it out."

"This is an all-terrain bike. I *can* use it in the snow."

Brett had his doubts, but he was not going to spoil the boy's fun. "Well, let's go see what you can do."

CLAIRE LEANED AGAINST her sink and watched Brett and Jesse playing in the snow. The bike was eventually abandoned for snowballs, and then, after a pelting that must have soaked both of them clear through, Brett lifted the bike and carried it back into the house, Jesse following close behind.

Claire turned away from the window. It was awful being jealous of a kid—especially one she liked—but why couldn't *she* get any kind of response out of Brett other than one that was physical and obviously quite resistible?

And why was it bugging her so much? Rejection was part of the game and had never bothered her before. Was this her contrary nature, wanting what it couldn't have? Or something more?

She knew which one it felt like, and it wasn't the one that would make Brett a happy man.

PHIL RYKER HAD DECIDED to become a full-time rancher. Brett listened numbly in silence as Phil explained over the phone that he was moving the base of operations for his other businesses to the ranch, and since he'd be living there full-time, he'd decided he might as well run the ranch, too. He could hire an hourly worker for about two-thirds of Brett's salary, so as of June 1, there was a good chance he would no longer need Brett's managerial services, except on a consulting basis.

Brett set the phone on the counter when Phil was done explaining, his stomach pulled into a tight knot.

Now what was he going to do? He didn't have a way to make a living in Barlow unless he managed a ranch—the only work he'd ever done besides rodeo riding in his entire life. And he knew that even if he got a regular job somewhere else, he wouldn't be able to swing mortgage payments for the homestead along with rent for a place in his new locale.

He leaned on the counter and stared into space, wondering how the hell this was all going to play out. Phil would run the ranch into the ground in no time, but what did that matter when a guy had tons of money and didn't care if the place paid for itself? Maybe that was the problem. Maybe Brett had been too efficient. The ranch finances had been easing closer toward the black every month. Maybe Brett should have made more of an effort to provide Phil with a nice fat tax write-off.

Brett had hoped he'd have a plan before anyone found out about his predicament, but it didn't work out that way. His brother called early the next day.

"I heard that Phil's taking over the ranch." Will sounded concerned, which always made Brett feel defensive. Will had no business being concerned about him.

"Word travels fast. I just found out myself yesterday."

"What now?"

"I wait and see if he can handle it. If he can't, I imagine he'll take me back on. If he can, well, I go looking for employment elsewhere. I don't have much of a choice."

"What about the homestead?"

Brett had known the question was coming, but it still irritated him to hear it spoken aloud. "I don't know."

"Maybe I could help with the finances, if things don't work out with Phil, so you don't lose the place."

Yeah. As if Will was swimming in money. "No," Brett said curtly.

"You could at least hear me out. We could form a partnership."

"No."

"You could pay me back."

"No."

"You aren't a stubborn son of a bitch or anything, are you?" Will challenged.

"I don't want help."

"That's not always a positive," his brother said. And then he hung up.

Brett put his own phone down. Way to go. Alienating the rest of his family again. But he wasn't going to take charity in the form of a partnership. Especially from Will. He already owed his brother a bigger debt than he could ever repay. He wasn't going to add to it.

LATER THAT AFTERNOON, Claire came tramping across the field, following the trail Jesse had made with his bike.

Brett didn't know if he was strong enough to handle another outpouring of sympathy. But at least she wasn't carrying a bottle of wine, which made him think that maybe she didn't know. Maybe she had a problem of her own. Snake, cooler, furnace. Yeah. It could be something she needed help with.

That hope was put to rest as soon as he opened the kitchen door.

"I heard about Phil," she said, in place of "hello."

He silently stepped back to allow her entry. He knew better than to try and stop her.

"What are you going to do?"

"I don't know." He was tired of the question. Tired of hearing it, tired of mulling it over. And it had only been a day since Phil had called. Brett was beginning to think maybe he should simply drop his option, throw his bedroll into the back of his truck and hit the road—which was the way he'd handled all difficulties in his life up until now.

But if he did that, who was going to take care of Sarina?

The answer—Claire—was in front of him, watching him with a steady, matter-of-fact gaze.

Okay, then who'd look out for Jesse? And was Brett willing to blow out of Kylie's life again? No. Even if she was angry with him, he still wanted to be there. He didn't know whether he was motivated by paternity or penance—maybe a combination of the two—but he needed to be part of her life.

"Is this a done deal?" Claire asked, boosting herself up on the counter. So much for an outpouring of sympathy.

"Not yet."

"How hard is it to run a ranch? I mean, could Phil do it?"

"Maybe."

Her mouth twisted ironically, and Brett told her the truth.

"With no practical experience. It's hard. It takes more than general business savvy."

"He said he was hiring an hourly guy."

"Who will only be as good as the directions Phil gives him, unless he's a pretty out-of-the-ordinary hourly guy, and those kind of people don't work for what Phil plans on paying."

"So the real problem is how, once he figures out he can't run the ranch, to ease things back to the current situation with his ego intact."

Brett nodded slowly. "Yeah. I guess that is the real problem."

"Do you want to keep working for him?"

"Right now, it's the only way I can buy the homestead. I'm not in a position to work elsewhere and make payments on this place, plus pay rent wherever I'm working." As it was, most of what Phil paid Brett went to living expenses. He was fortunate that his small herd of cows not only paid for themselves but usually gave him a bit of profit—enough to invest in home repairs occasionally, although not enough to live on. If he had to rent another place, he'd have to make nearly double what he was making now. Not likely, in his chosen profession.

"Why are you taking college courses?"

The sudden shift of topic threw him. He shook his head.

"Are you doing it in order to get a degree you can use in some profession? Are you doing it for personal satisfaction?"

"A little of both," he answered cautiously.

"If you got your degree, would it be one that you could use here in Barlow?"

He didn't answer. Claire slid off the counter and crossed to where he stood. "Brett, you can talk to me. I won't tell anyone."

But he'd made a career of not talking, at least about things that mattered.

"What do you think you'll do with a degree?"

"I think…" He looked down into her eyes and promptly lost his train of thought as he remembered the other evening in her trailer.

"You think…?"

"If I can get a degree in business management, or maybe agricultural economics, I could combine it with my practical experience and get a real job. Even if it's with a government agency, I'd make more than I make now. Under those circumstances, I'd probably be able to work elsewhere and still make payments on this place, if I live frugally." A condition for which ranch management had prepared him well. "Eventually, I'd either retire here or turn it into a money-making proposition, depending on the market."

"That's a good plan."

"If I hadn't been thirty-three when I started, it might have been a good plan."

Claire smiled that secret smile of hers, making him wonder what she was thinking. She stepped back, giving him the space he thought he wanted, until he began fighting the urge to close the gap between them again. But if he'd learned nothing else in his screwed-up life, he'd at least learned self-discipline. The hard way, of course.

"I'm curious, Brett. And probably out of line, but why is this homestead so important to you?"

"It's a family thing." Even if he hadn't gotten along so well with his father, he had adored his grandfather, who'd once worked this same land.

"So family is important to you?"

He'd blundered into the trap, probably because he was thinking about how good she looked.

"Because if it is, well, I gotta tell you, I don't understand why you're so standoffish with your own family."

It was a legitimate question. And one he couldn't answer, because there were more people involved in the answer than just him.

"If I told anyone, it would probably be you, but…"

"You've kept it quiet for so long, you can't imagine sharing."

"Yes." Not the full truth, but close enough. And it seemed to satisfy her. She really hadn't expected him to share.

"I'd much rather be told to mind my own business than be lied to." She went back over to the counter, but this time simply leaned against it.

"Have you been lied to?" Brett latched on to the change of topic.

"Who hasn't?"

"By someone you trusted?"

She wrinkled her nose. "One of my college boyfriends turned out to be a real snake. It was quite the learning experience." Brett was glad to see a wry smile playing on her lips, telling him she was well over whatever had happened. "I thought he was wonderful—trustworthy, honest and brave. A veritable Eagle Scout. But then I found out he'd been lying to me for practically our entire relationship. Not an easy pill to swallow for someone who fancies herself a student of human nature."

"Anyone can make a mistake."

"I lent him money."

"Ouch."

"Yes." She looked out the window, feigning interest in the scenery as she spoke. "As near as I can figure, he spent it on his other girlfriend. She was more demanding than I was."

"How could anyone be more demanding than you?"

She shifted her attention to him and a slow smile curved her lips. He had a feeling he'd made another mistake. He was further convinced when she raised her forefinger in a beckoning motion.

He held his ground. Her eyebrows went up.

"What good is it being demanding if no one acquiesces?"

"Acquiesces?"

"Gives in. Agrees. Plays ball."

Oh, he'd like to play ball.

He shook his head, but he couldn't keep from smiling at her audacity.

"I like it when you smile," she said. "You don't do it enough."

"Maybe I've never had that much to smile about."

"Maybe you need someone to bring a little joy into your life."

"Claire, you make my life difficult."

"Hey." She spread her hands. "I'm only trying to help."

"And don't think I don't appreciate it. I hope I won't insult you if I shoo you on your way, so I can get some work done."

"No. You've done so before. In fact…" she thought for a moment "…I don't think I've *ever* come over without you shooing me away."

"You're exaggerating."

"No, I'm not," she said sincerely.

He thought about it. Maybe she was on the mark there. "If I don't shoo you away, what are you going to do?"

"Avoid my grading by helping you with your floor."

"My floor's done."

"There's always your math."

"It's coming easier." And it was, thanks to Claire and her pre-algebra textbook with the answers in the back. If he passed the final in a week, he'd pass the course, which had seemed impossible when he'd started the class in September. He cleared his throat. "I never did thank you for the book."

"No need," Claire said lightly. "But we could continue to talk about your future. Over a drink, maybe."

"You really do want to avoid that grading, don't you?"

"Or maybe I just want to spend time with you."

"I don't know that anything will come of that, Claire."

"But it might."

He did not respond, hoping she'd take the hint. If she'd been anyone else, related to anyone else, he would have been pulling glasses out of the cupboard and uncorking the wine.

As it was, he was still tempted. They were both adults, responsible for their own decisions.

Claire sighed, her expression resigned as she sauntered up to him and placed her hands on the planes of his cheeks. Her palms were firm and cool as they gently stroked the rough stubble.

"There are so many things about you that I wish I understood. But…" She leaned toward him, and then, just when he thought she was going to kiss him again, she dropped her hands to her sides and took a half step back. "I'm going to give you a break and leave you in peace."

He reached out and stopped her before she could turn away.

"Claire." He had no idea what he wanted to say. "You…" *Deserve better?* Too hokey. Even if he did believe it. "You need to understand that this isn't easy for me."

"Then maybe you should give in to temptation."

"You deserve better." *Shit*. He'd said it. Obvious proof that, thanks to her, his brain was turning to mush. To his surprise, Claire laughed.

"Are you kidding? I drive my mother crazy. I depend far too much on my sister. And I pick on little kids for a living." She arched her brows. "Think about it."

And he did, long after she'd let herself out the kitchen door and started across the field for home. She might do all those things, but she still deserved better.

Jesse was unusually quiet when he came to do chores on Monday after school. Brett knew that sometimes a guy needed to be left alone when he was like that, and other times he needed to be drawn out. This felt like one of the latter times.

"What's up?" Brett asked, deciding on the direct approach.

Jesse cast him a sidelong look. "Just some stuff."

"Home stuff or school stuff?"

"School."

"Grades?"

"No. It's just some stuff that's been goin' on for a while." He kicked a rock with enough force that Brett knew it had to be something serious—to Jesse, anyway.

"Have you talked to your dad?"

"He's been busy lately."

The boy's voice was defensive enough that Brett decided not to push. After all, whether Brett approved of Tom Lane or not, he was Jesse's dad.

"So what's bugging you?"

"Ashley." Jesse said the name in a low, disgusted voice.

"How so?"

"She makes fun of me."

"She's a bully."

Jesse looked shocked. "She's a girl."

"Hey. Girls can be bullies. I've been pushed around by a woman or two."

"You have?" Jesse asked, sounding dubious.

"Oh, yeah."

Jesse climbed into the tire, now encrusted with frost, that Brett had attached to the rope in the apple tree just after Thanksgiving. "Like who?"

"Nobody you'd know." Brett watched as Jesse spun idly in a slow circle.

"You know, lots of times when people treat you bad, it's because they're insecure or afraid."

"I don't think Ashley is afraid of anything."

Brett shrugged. "Maybe she needs to pick on people to reassure herself that she's the best."

"Or maybe she's just mean."

Brett gave up on psychology. "Maybe she *is* just mean." He leaned against the fence. "What do you do when Ashley makes fun of you?"

"Sometimes I walk away like Grandma taught me. And sometimes I say things back."

"Which one works the best?"

Jesse thought for a moment. "Neither one seems to work too great, 'cause she keeps doing it."

"I guess you're going to have to change tactics."

"How?"

"Well, when you're working with a horse, you make it hard for him to do the thing you don't want him to do, and easy to do the thing you *do* want him to do. You can do the same with people." Sometimes. It didn't seem to work with Claire.

Jesse frowned. "All right," he said uncertainly, obviously at a loss as to how he could do that with Ashley.

"So, how could you make it harder for Ashley to pick on you?"

"Not go to school?"

"That'd work," Brett agreed with a slight smile, "but I don't think Miss Flynn or your dad would approve."

Jesse grinned. "Stay away from her, I guess, but that's kinda hard when we're in the same room."

"Maybe you could be nice to her?"

"Huh?" It was the second time Brett had shocked the kid in the space of five minutes.

"Think about it. If you said something nice to Ashley before she had a chance to say something rotten to you, what would happen?"

"She'd probably say the rotten thing, anyway."

"Yeah, but how's she going to look to other people?"

Jesse considered for a moment. "Like a jerk?"

"Probably."

The boy screwed up his face. "I'm not going to like being nice to her."

"I know."

"But I'll try."

CLAIRE WAS PULLING a cardboard box out of the trunk of her car in front of the community hall when Brett stopped at the post office on his way out of town. She waved at him and he crossed the street, wondering what she'd say if she knew she'd been the subject of his thoughts for most of the day.

"I hear you've been plotting strategy with Jesse concerning Ashley," she said as Brett took the box so she could close her trunk.

"I told him to be nice to her," he said, surprised. "What happened?"

"It worked."

"It did?"

"Yep." Claire reached for the carton, and he handed it to her. "He was nice, Ashley was not, and Toni and Dylan finally came down hard on her for picking on a younger kid for no reason. It startled the heck out of her."

Brett couldn't say he was overly concerned about Ashley, and was about to say so, when two cars pulled in close to Claire's. Claire smiled at Trini, who nodded as she walked by, also carrying a cardboard box. Deirdre was carrying two fancy leather tote bags when she entered the hall a few seconds later, without looking at either Brett or Claire.

"So what happened?"

"We had a life lesson in class about doing unto others, which most of the kids seemed to understand—except Ashley, of course." Claire started toward the community hall. "Jesse told me that you were the one who suggested that he be nice to her instead of fighting back."

"She was making fun of him, so I told him to use reverse psychology to try to get her to stop. You know, make it hard to do the wrong thing and easy to do the right thing."

Claire gave him an odd look. "Will you be using that reverse psychology thing on Phil? You know, make it easy for him to leave, hard to stay?"

"Not a bad idea." And actually, it wasn't, except for the fact that if things got hard, Phil would simply hire someone temporarily to make them easy again.

"Well, I'd better get in there," Claire said.

"Yeah." Brett opened the door, but neither of them moved, until Anne started across the street from her store, toting her own box.

"I think we need to get together and…talk," Claire said in a low voice.

"Probably," Brett conceded. It seemed almost inevitable.

BRETT KNEW HE WAS IN trouble when he spent more time thinking about Claire than about his shaky job situation as he drove to Wesley to pick up parts for Phil's flatbed the next day. He wasn't deluding himself into believing Claire wanted a future with him. She wasn't the type to settle on a ranch, he wasn't the type to settle elsewhere, and they were both aware of those facts. No, Claire wanted a challenge, and he was that challenge. And he kind of felt like letting her win.

As long as they were honest. That was the important part. That was the part that had come back to bite him in the ass once before. He never would have hooked up with Des all those years ago if she had been honest with him and told him she was only taking a break from her marriage to Will, not ending it. He might have had issues with Will at the time, but he wouldn't have slept with Des if he'd known she was only using him to get back at her husband.

Claire was different, and now that he knew her, he believed that when things fizzled they'd be capable of maintaining Flynn-Bishop family dynamics in an adult way.

Hell, he was barely part of the family dynamics, anyway.

He was smiling by the time he pulled into Wesley.

CHAPTER ELEVEN

"YOU'LL BE DONE in time for the quilt show."

Claire, who'd been arranging her finished squares on the worktable, looked up in amazement at Gloria's statement. She had just assumed that she'd be excused from the show.

"Oh, I don't think so," she said. The workmanship of her early squares was noticeably amateurish, which was fine with her because it allowed her to see her progress, but that didn't mean she wanted to share it with everyone else in the community.

"You don't have to sell your quilt," Trini pointed out.

"I don't want to display it, either."

"Why not?" Anne demanded.

"I think it's obvious."

"With colors like that, no one will be looking at the craftsmanship, and even if they do, so what?"

Claire took her seat without replying, picked

up her work and ran a few stitches onto her needle. She had never in her life publicly displayed anything that was less than her best effort. It was one of the small survival tactics she'd adopted to keep her mother off her back, and by now it was deeply ingrained.

The group fell silent. Claire sewed for a few more minutes, her head down until the silence became overwhelming.

"Oh, all right," she said. "*If* I get done, I'll display." But Arlene would not be getting an invitation.

The session broke up late that evening. As they were approaching the date of the show, these quilting nights were lasting longer. Claire wasn't complaining. She enjoyed her time away from the trailer, which seemed to be getting smaller every day. Still, she had only four more months of trailer life and then she'd be able to walk in more than two directions again.

But although she wouldn't miss her compact home, and she was looking forward to more convenient shopping, she knew she was going to miss her job. Teaching a small class—even one that required a prodigious amount of prep work—was so much more intimate and rewarding than her student teaching had been. And as far as professional freedom went, she was her own boss. She decided how, what, where, when and why. With no one else collecting lesson-plan books, asking for justification, questioning strategy.

On the other hand, she was solely responsible for the achievement scores, so if the kids bombed there was no question about who was to blame. The previous three teachers at Barlow Ridge Elementary hadn't cared. But Claire did. And she hoped with all of her heart that the person who took the job after she left would care, as well.

The school was dark when Claire stopped by on her way home to pick up her grade book so she could work on attendance tallies. They were due the next morning, and she'd completely forgotten, due to the day's impromptu lesson on the Golden Rule. She left her headlights on so she could see to mount the steps, then froze as something moved in the shadows.

"It's just me, Miss Flynn," Toni said as she stepped into the light, her hands shoved deep in her pockets.

"Toni, what are you doing here?"

"I was just out walking. Sometimes I stop and sit on the swings. Like Jesse."

At nine o'clock in cold weather, when other kids were curled up with their video games, televisions and iPods. Yeah.

"Does your mom know where you are?"

"She doesn't care, as long as I'm back before Deke takes off for his shift."

"Which is…?"

"Soon. I'd better get going."

"Toni, is everything all right? At home, I mean?"

The girl didn't answer immediately. "Things have been better."

"Is there anything you need help with?"

"I don't think there's anything that can be helped. I don't like Deke and my mom does."

"What don't you like about him?" Claire asked carefully, wondering if she had a situation on her hands.

Toni gave her a shrewd look, guessing the exact direction of Claire's thoughts. "He's not being creepy or anything—he's just an ass." Her eyes suddenly widened, as she realized what she'd just said to a teacher. "What I mean," she said quickly, "is that he only thinks about himself. Nobody else. And he wants my mom to do the same thing."

"Which doesn't leave a lot of time for you?"

"I don't need a lot of time."

But she needed some.

"I had a stepfather once who wanted all of my mom's attention," Claire told her. He hadn't lasted long. Arlene was not a woman who put her husband ahead of her business.

Toni looked interested. "You had a stepfather?"

"Two of them. I really like the one I have now, but the other…" Claire wrinkled her nose.

"So what did you do?"

"I focused on everything else in my life. Like my *schoolwork*," she added with mock sternness. Toni grudgingly smiled. "I closed my bedroom door a lot." She raised her eyebrows before saying gently, "I did *not* go walking around by myself after dark." Even if it was Barlow Ridge, Toni shouldn't be out in the cold alone.

"I should get back," she agreed.

"I'll walk with you."

The girl shook her head. "You don't have to. I'm going straight home. Honest."

Claire believed her. "You can come see me anytime, you know."

"Or I can close my bedroom door and pretend not to hear them fight." Toni smiled slightly, then turned and headed down the empty street.

KYLIE REMINDED CLAIRE a little of Toni and a lot of herself. They thought alike, and had similar tastes, which made it all the more difficult to bypass the purple fabric in favor of black for her quilt border.

"The other quilters said to buy black border fabric."

"I know it'd look cool with black," Kylie said, "but the deep, dark purple is so pretty, and it matches the flowers."

"We'll buy some purple for your quilt."

"You're going to make me a quilt?" Kylie asked happily.

"I'm going to teach you to quilt."

Kylie made a face. "Wouldn't it be easier on both of us if you just *made* me a quilt?"

"Nope."

Kylie huffed dramatically and then pulled the purple bolt from the rack. "How much will I need?"

"I just happen to have the list I followed for my quilt." Claire pulled a sheet of paper from her purse. "And we'll need to pick a few more colors."

"ARE YOU READY for the next game?" Claire asked later, as they piled bolts of fabric on the cutting counter and gave the clerk the list of yardages.

"Very ready," Kylie said. "We play the Spartans again."

"That should be fun," Claire said ironically. Kylie had missed two games after the previous Spartan game because of her injured wrist.

"Yeah. And I have a horse clinic with Dad on the same day, so I'll be busy."

"Kylie, I've got to tell you, horses and basketball are a weird combination."

Kylie tilted her head. "No, they're not. I know lots of kids who do both. Basketball is the only sport we can work into the rodeo schedule."

"Okay, maybe it's not weird here, but everywhere else in the world it is."

"Everywhere else in the world is dumb, then," Kylie said. "So, are you coming to the clinic?"

Claire almost said, *"Yeah, right."* Horses and dust were still not her favorite things. If Kylie wasn't performing, she probably wouldn't be there. "I'll come to the game."

"Phil wanted us to use his stud as a demonstration horse, but Dad won't do it."

"Really. I didn't know your dad knew Phil."

"He's been talking to Dad about training and

buying horses and stuff. Dad's hoping Phil'll get smart and sell the stud before it hurts someone."

"I think Brett is hoping the same thing."

Kylie gave Claire a sly look. "Phil's kind of cute, even though he doesn't have a lot of horse sense."

Claire nodded. "Yes. I agree he's on the hunky side." There was no use denying the obvious.

"And Regan thinks he likes you."

"Is that a fact?"

"So, are you…you know."

"What?" Claire asked innocently.

"Are you going to do anything about it?" Kylie asked with a touch of impatience.

"Probably not."

"Why?"

"Because he just doesn't do it for me."

Kylie's mouth dropped open. "Nuh-uh."

"How many cute guys do you know?" Claire asked patiently.

"A lot."

"How many would you date?"

"A lot," Kylie responded with a sassy smile.

"Are there any who are cute but aren't dating material?"

"Yeah."

"Phil's one of those. Cute guy, but I'm not feeling the chemistry."

"But don't you get lonely out there in Barlow?"

"I was when I first moved there, but now…" Claire cocked her head. "It's kind of funny, but I'm not so lonely anymore."

"Regan thought you'd be climbing the walls."

"Is that a direct quote?"

"Mmm, hmm."

"Well, it's different than where I used to live, that's for sure. And I won't mind going back to a city. But I have to admit that there are some things I've found in Barlow that I haven't found elsewhere."

"Like what?"

Like Brett. She couldn't get the guy out of her head, and what's more, she didn't particularly *want* to.

"I've never lived in a place with a strong sense of community before," Claire said, coming up with a truthful answer she could share with her niece.

"Regan says it's like working in a fishbowl. Everyone is watching what you do."

Claire gathered up the neat stack of fabrics the clerk had pushed across the counter toward her. "Am I the topic of many conversations at your house?" she asked her niece mildly.

"A few."

"Good or bad?"

"I plead the fifth."

Claire rolled her eyes, since she'd been the one who'd taught Kylie the phrase during another boyfriend interrogation.

"Do you see Uncle Brett very often?" Kylie asked the question with studied casualness.

"Every now and then. I'll probably see him at your last game."

"I don't think so," Kylie said.

"What makes you think I won't?"

"I, uh, said some things to him when I was angry, and he hasn't been to a game since."

"How bad?" Claire asked flatly, remembering Regan's guess that Kylie had done just that.

"Bad enough, I guess."

"Phil has been keeping him busy," Claire hedged, even though she knew that wasn't exactly true. Phil had been trying to handle things alone. "You might try apologizing."

"Yeah. I've been thinking about that."

They were almost to the car when Kylie said casually, "I got asked to the prom, you know."

"No, I didn't know. Why didn't you tell me sooner?"

Kylie gave her a cheeky grin. "Because it happened about twenty minutes ago, while you were in the fitting room. He called my cell."

"Very classy," Claire said. "Who is it?"

"New guy in school." Kylie swung her shopping bag. "His family comes from Wesley, but he was born in Colorado. Now they've moved back. His dad used to know my dad when they were kids."

"That's cool."

"I thought so." Kylie waited while Claire unlocked the car. "If I apologize to Uncle Brett, will you go prom-dress shopping with me?"

"I promise you, Kylie, there is nothing I like better than prom-dress shopping. But maybe, for safety's sake, we'll bring Regan along this time."

Kylie grinned, clearly remembering her parents' horror at the modestly cut, yet outrageously sequined black dress the two of them had picked out the previous spring. "Yeah. I think that might be good."

ONCE HE'D DECIDED to take up residence in Barlow Ridge, Phil Ryker wasted no time in becoming an active member of the community. He joined the volunteer fire department, having no idea that the local boys didn't particularly want him as a member. He attended the quarterly community board meeting and volunteered for the Chili Feed committee. He showed up at community dinners, ate lunch at the town bar. And in his spare time he ran the ranch—which wasn't all that time-consuming in January—especially since Brett still did all the feeding. Come February, though, when calving started, he'd probably have less free time on his hands, since Brett had every intention of letting Phil share in the responsibilities, all in the name of teaching him what he could expect once he was on his own. The one place Brett didn't want him sharing responsibility was in the round pen.

The headstrong stud was making progress now that Phil had stopped working with him on the sly, but Brett didn't believe a man with Phil's limited abilities had any business bringing such an unpredictable horse into the show ring. Brett was beginning to think that Phil was getting the picture after the stud shied once and slammed him into the arena rails. Phil had been muttering something about the horse being replaceable as he'd limped away.

A few hours later, Brett found out just how serious his boss had been. Phil pulled into the drive with his dog, Toby, sitting in the seat behind him. The dog had a red bandanna tied around his neck. Brett tried not to notice.

"I'm going to be taking off for a few days this Friday," his boss said.

"All right."

"Got a new show prospect."

Brett avoided saying *It's about time,* mainly because there was always a chance that this prospect would be worse than the last one had been. "If you want, I'll take a look at him for you," he offered.

Phil flashed his superior smile. "No need. This one's well broke. He's a cutter."

"Are you taking up cutting?" The rich man's arena event.

"I'm considering it. Anyway, I'll be back on Sunday night."

ABOUT THE LAST THING Claire expected after an exhausting day at school was to find Phil Ryker waiting outside, next to her car. His truck was parked across the street, the engine idling. Toby sat in the backseat with a cute bandanna tied around his neck.

"Rough day?" Phil asked as Claire approached.

"Does it show?"

"You're not smiling."

"Not so much rough as exhausting. We're getting ready for achievement tests." And Claire was determined that her kids were going to do themselves proud.

"So what would you think of getting away for a weekend?"

"How so?" she asked cautiously. She and Phil had seen each other a few times after their folksinger date, but to Claire's relief, he'd shown no interest in pursuing anything but a friendship with her. Until now.

"Well, I'm heading over to California to look at a horse." His smile exuded confident charm. "I can offer warm weather, no students, and my parents have a nice guest cottage you could have all to yourself." His expression became more serious. "I know this is last-minute, but I'd like to have company, and you look as if you could use a weekend away. Just friends."

Claire couldn't help but appreciate the offer, even if she had no intention of taking him up on it. "Phil, I can't."

"Are you sure?"

"Yes, I'm sure," she said with a note of apology in her voice, but without an explanation. Explanations led to debate, and Claire wanted to keep her relationship with Phil exactly as it was now. He might be saying "just friends," but weekends away were not usually "just friends" situations. "Thanks for asking, though."

Phil hesitated, as though contemplating tactics, before giving in gracefully. "All right. If you change your mind, I'm not leaving until tomorrow night."

"I'll keep that in mind," Claire said gently. *Now, please...just give it up.* If she spent a weekend with anyone, it was not going to be Phil.

BRETT BOOTED UP the computer Friday morning after tending to Phil's animals. The e-mail he'd been both anticipating and dreading was waiting for him. He pulled in a ragged breath, double clicked the icon and then waited for what seemed like two years for the screen to open.

He'd passed algebra.

A foolish grin spread across his face.

He'd passed algebra with a fairly respectable C. And he'd gotten a B+ in humanities—*Moby Dick, Beowulf* and all.

But he didn't really care about humanities. He'd conquered algebra—and he even understood it. He'd been terrified that it had been a case of too little, too late, and that he'd be ponying up several hundred more dollars in order to take the class again.

Now he could sign up for other classes and torture himself for another semester. He logged onto the site and started perusing the catalog, feeling a hell of a lot more confident than he had the time before.

He signed up for two more classes and logged off, leaning back in his chair and staring at the computer desktop until the screensaver finally popped up.

He owed Claire a thank-you. If she hadn't dropped off the pre-algebra book, hadn't given him a firm push in the right direction, he might still be trying to figure things out. But what kind of thank-you was appropriate?

One from the heart. Claire had had him running scared for most of their short acquaintance, but it was time to admit that, yeah, there was an attraction there and, yeah, maybe he should do something about it. Instead of expecting the worst to happen, as usual, maybe he needed to have some faith in the two of them and their ability to handle things in a civilized way.

Claire liked wine and she liked conversation. He'd start there.

CLAIRE HAD ATTACHED black borders to all her squares and was ready to begin the quilting process, but, regardless of what her fellow quilters said, she knew her masterpiece wouldn't be done in time for the show. And she made the mistake of saying so.

"We're going to get out the frame for you," Anne said grimly.

Claire's head snapped up. "The frame? Is that like a torture device for people who don't get their quilts done in time?"

Trini giggled. "It's a quilting frame. Instead of lap quilting, you'll piece your entire top, then we'll baste it to the batting and backing, put it in the big frame and we'll work together to quilt it."

"But then it won't be all mine."

"No," Gloria said. "It'll be a collaboration of friends."

It was hard to argue with that, so Claire didn't even try. And she liked the warm feeling the simple words brought.

When the women finished for the evening, they decided it was high time for a post-quilting libation, so they locked the community hall, loaded their supplies in their various cars, then walked the two blocks down the street to the saloon.

Marla was alone at the bar. She looked up

from a magazine she was reading as the quilters entered the nearly empty establishment and headed, as a group, to the sofas near the propane fire. Claire dropped her coat on a chair and went to order the first round of drinks. It was the least she could do for her fellow quilters, who were going to see to it that her quilt didn't end up as a pile of squares stuffed in a linen closet somewhere. She smiled at Marla and leaned her elbows on the bar.

Marla did not smile back. "You have some nerve coming in here after telling my kid that Deke was no good," the woman hissed.

Claire instinctively recoiled, lifting her elbows back off the bar. Marla had to be talking to someone else, but there *was* no one else. The venomous accusation was aimed at her.

"I never said anything about Deke."

Marla gave her a disbelieving look with narrowed eyes. "Then what did you say?"

"Nothing." Claire was so astounded that she almost stuttered. She could handle confrontation just fine, when she was expecting it, but this was coming out of nowhere.

Marla stepped from behind the bar then, moving to stand directly in front of Claire, her heavily made up eyes fixed on her face. "I don't believe you." She thrust her jaw forward. "Toni wouldn't make up stuff like that, because she knows she'd be in deep shit if she did."

"I don't think Toni made anything up, but I think there's been a misinterpretation." Claire had had enough backpedaling. "Maybe we should talk to Toni?"

"She's doing her homework, and I think you've said enough already. And you'd better damn well watch what you say at school, too, or I'll be filing a harassment claim."

Anne's hand settled firmly on Claire's forearm, startling her, since she hadn't heard the older woman approach. "Come on," she said, her focus on Marla. "We're taking our business elsewhere."

"I want to—" Claire pressed her lips together instead of finishing her sentence. As much as she wanted to straighten out the situation, Marla was not in a mood to listen to reason, and Claire didn't want to get Toni into more trouble. Or give Toni the opportunity to get *her* into more trouble. Claire needed facts before she could proceed. "I think you're right," she said to Anne.

The other quilters had already gathered their purses and coats. Trini handed Claire her belongings, then the other women closed ranks behind her as she and Anne made their way out of the bar into the frigid night air.

"Don't take it personal." Anne muttered the words that Claire had come to think of as the motto of Barlow Ridge as they walked across the street to their cars. "She picks bad boyfriends, then defends them to the death."

"Is he abusive?" Claire asked.

"Deke?" Trini snorted, making Claire feel slightly better. "He's too lazy to be abusive. If Marla kicked him out, he'd starve."

"But he has a job."

"Only because she pushes him out the door at the right time every day, and he doesn't want his pickup repossessed," Deirdre explained. And that was when Claire realized Deirdre had been one of her supporters just now. Either that or she hadn't wanted to be left alone in the bar.

Anne settled a hand on Claire's shoulder. "Marla's a flake, Deke's a lazy bum, and that's just the way things are. There's not a damn thing you can do about it, so don't waste your energy worrying about it."

"What about Toni?"

"Toni will be fine," Trini said. "Honest. She just has to put up with the headache of living with two morons. She's smarter than both of them. Gets it from her real father."

"You're sure?"

"Positive."

But even if Toni was fine, Claire still felt depressed by the confrontation. She didn't know if Toni had lied or Marla had misinterpreted. All she knew was that, once again, she had a situation on her hands—as well as a potential harassment claim and probably a whole lot of rumors.

But at least this time her situation didn't involve the Landaus. It was always good to change things up.

CHAPTER TWELVE

CLAIRE DIDN'T GET HOME at eight…or nine. Brett was wondering what was taking so long at quilting when he saw headlights turn off Main Street and head down their road. He grabbed the bottle of wine and started across the field to meet her, arriving at the trailer just as she pulled into the drive.

Claire got out of the car. "Brett? Is something wrong?" There was a note of alarm in her voice.

"No. I, uh, just came to see you." Maybe he should have called first. "What happened to you?" Because it was obvious from her distracted demeanor that something had.

"Parent meeting," she said ironically, as she trudged up the stairs.

"Can't get enough of those, can you?" He followed her, planning to deliver his gift and find out what was wrong.

"Apparently not." She concentrated on fitting

the key into the lock. "And I think I'm banned from the bar."

Okay.

She tried to turn the key, but it refused to give. She tried again, then rattled the knob in frustration before Brett gently moved her hand, took the key out of the door, turned it over and reinserted it. The lock popped open with one twist.

"Thank goodness for the Y chromosome," she murmured as she pushed the door and preceded him inside. The furnace clicked on as the cold air swirled in after them.

Claire adjusted the thermostat. "It'll warm up fast in here. It's the one great thing about living in a tin can—it's cozy." She hugged her coat around her in a self-protective way.

"Yeah. Cozy." Brett reached out to push wisps of blond hair away from her cheek, feeling protective, wanting to make things better for her. Thinking that he'd like to know what the hell was going on. "You want to tell me what happened tonight?"

"Marla thinks I bad-mouthed Deke to Toni, and she kicked me out of the bar." Claire shrugged out of her coat and draped it over the back of the sofa. "It bothers me, because I wouldn't do something that unprofessional. But word travels fast in a small town, so I'm probably as good as guilty. And Marla also threatened to file a harassment claim. Mr. Rupert is going to love that."

"I don't think she'll file a claim. It takes too much energy."

"You think?" Claire moistened her lips.

"I'm pretty damn certain."

"Then I'm glad you picked tonight to come calling. Otherwise, I probably wouldn't have slept much." And then she noticed he'd not only come calling, he'd come bearing a gift. All that was missing was the wilted bouquet of daisies. "You brought wine."

"Yes."

"*You* brought wine," she repeated.

He couldn't help smiling. "Yes."

"I already feel better," she said dryly. Then she cocked her head. "*Why* have you brought wine?"

"To thank you." The smile was still plastered on his face, albeit a little self-consciously. "I passed the algebra class."

There was a long beat of silence, as if she couldn't quite grasp what he was saying, and then she smiled for real. A Claire smile. "I knew you would."

"At least one of us did."

"Would you like to open that bottle?" Claire

asked, stepping out of her shoes. "I could use a glass. Or two."

"Sure."

She walked into the kitchen in her stocking feet and pulled a fancy contraption out of a drawer. Brett gave it a skeptical look. "Do you need to have a license to run that thing?"

"I'll do it." She reached for the wine, but he stopped her, his hand covering hers as he gently eased the bottle away.

"I can figure it out. That Y chromosome, you know." He proved his point by flipping the corkscrew into working position over the bottle.

Claire edged past him in the tiny kitchen and opened a cupboard. "So what now?" she asked as she stretched up on her toes to pull two wineglasses down from the second shelf.

"I signed up for another math class, before I forget everything, and biology 1. It's going to take about ten years to get a degree this way, but at least I'm chipping away at it."

"Hey," she said softly, "you have a goal. You're working toward it. That's commendable." She set the glasses on the counter as he eased the handles of the corkscrew together, pulling the cork smoothly out of the bottle. He poured a healthy quantity of wine for each of them.

Claire raised her glass to touch his with a musical clink. "I'm glad you're here. On many levels."

"I'm glad I'm here, too." It felt good. Natural.

And it still felt natural when she took him by the hand and led him out of the kitchen to the sofa, pulling him down to sit beside her. "Sorry about the rant," she said as they settled in.

"You're entitled. Marla is kind of a nut, you know."

"Kind of?"

"And the people here like you."

"Most of them," she agreed. She touched her glass to his again, and then they sat in silence, shoulders and thighs touching as they sipped wine and stared at the faded wood paneling on the opposite wall.

"I'm kind of picturing a crackling fireplace over there," Claire murmured after several minutes. "What are you picturing?"

"Waves on the beach." He stretched his arm out along the back of the sofa and she let her head rest against it.

"So what's changed?" she asked softly. "You're here and all of your barriers are down. I barely recognize you."

He didn't feign ignorance. The vibes

humming between them were too strong. "I'm ready to admit we're consenting adults."

"You've finally quit worrying about Will beating the snot out of you if you hurt my feelings?"

Brett smiled, not altogether surprised she'd figured that one out. "That, too."

She set her wineglass on the end table and shifted position, pulling one foot up under her. "So you just suddenly came to this realization?"

"I lied before. I do get lonely." He reached for her hand and interlocked his fingers with hers.

"We all get lonely," Claire said, leaning closer, her lips grazing his cheek and then the corner of his mouth. "It's just that some of us do something about it."

"That's what I'm doing now," he said, turning his head to gently nip her full lower lip. She touched her forehead to his.

"May I say, it's about time?"

CLAIRE BEGAN UNBUTTONING Brett's shirt, half expecting him to come to his senses and stop her, but when her fingers fumbled, he set his wine on the end table and undid the remaining buttons himself.

Okay, this is a good sign.

And he was a beautiful man, lean yet well muscled.

She smoothed her palms over his chest, pushing the fabric of his shirt away from his shoulders. His stomach muscles contracted with the action. They were rock hard, as were other parts of him. She pressed a kiss to his pectorals, circled his nipple with her tongue. His hand buried itself in her hair as she circled the other nipple. He caught his breath, then eased her away from him, kissing her deeply while trying to undo the square pearl buttons on her sweater with one hand. He got the first one undone, awkwardly, and then another, more smoothly this time. Finally, the third and fourth buttons popped open, revealing the swell of her breasts. He traced the tips of his fingers over her exposed flesh as he continued to kiss her.

"You're beautiful."

"So are you," she whispered.

He smiled at her as he pulled back, but then his expression grew serious. "I don't have anything to offer you."

She couldn't repress a small surprised laugh. "Like what?" she asked. No one had ever made a qualifying speech to her before making love. Especially an old-fashioned one about offering things.

"Like anything."

"Maybe I don't want anything." And maybe she did. She wasn't sure, but time would tell. "If you're trying to say this is a no-strings deal that does not involve our siblings and will *never* involve them, trust me, I understand and agree."

She took hold of his belt buckle with both hands, letting her fingers slide between metal and muscle as she whispered, "So please, just shut up and make love to me."

She didn't have to ask twice.

Claire had never been touched so reverently before, had never felt such a shared sense of lust and tenderness.

When he entered her, it hurt a little, because it had been a long time since she'd made love. But he stilled and waited for her to adjust, without asking if she wanted to stop. He could probably read the answer to that question in her eyes.

She wrapped her arms around him, cupping his head with her palm and smoothing the fingers of her other hand over his spine, and then he began to move.

They made love silently, lost in each other. It was over far too soon.

Afterward, Brett lay on his back, his arm around her as she curled against his side. She'd known it would be this good, but she wondered if Brett had been prepared. From the way he was focused on the ceiling tile above them, a frown drawing his brows together, she had the feeling he hadn't been.

She stirred, and his arm tightened protectively, pulling her closer, but she wasn't fooled. He might want to protect her, but he wasn't comfortable to have her so near. He was already shutting down.

Maybe he'd been solitary for too long, or maybe there was some other reason he had trouble letting himself get close to someone else. Whatever it was, she eased away from him, allowing him his retreat, knowing it was the only thing she could do.

A moment later he sat up and swung his legs around so that he was sitting on the edge of the bed. Claire resisted the urge to reach out and run a hand over the corded muscles of his back. Instead, she tucked an arm under her head and waited for the farewell speech she knew he was working on. But Brett remained silent. He sat, gripping the mattress on either side of his thighs, staring out the darkened window, and Claire decided that she might as well be the one to set the wheels in motion. She knew this was not the time for analysis or a speech. They both needed a little space, a little time to figure out where they wanted this thing to go.

She got out of bed, pulled her kimono off the brass hook on the back of the bedroom door and slipped it on, cinching the waist. Then she picked up Brett's jeans and held them out to him, her finger through a single belt loop.

"It's late," she said, "and we both need some thinking time."

He looked both surprised and relieved.

He took the jeans without a word, dressing quickly, his movements precise. She walked out to the living room with him and waited while he put on his shirt and coat.

He turned toward her, looked as if he wanted to say something, but Claire was having none of that. The less said, the better for now. It was best that things be left unspoken than to say something that would be regretted later. She cupped his face, gave him a quick, soft kiss, then put a hand on his back and propelled him to the door. He went quietly.

"Are you—"

She put her fingertips to his lips, effectively shushing him.

"Don't ruin things, Brett. I'm fine."
And I hope you are, too.

BRETT'S live-for-the-moment evening had not gone as planned.

During the chilly walk home, he told himself repeatedly that this was no different than any other time he'd gone to bed with a willing woman. Except for her connection to his brother.

But everything about it felt different.

Maybe if they hadn't been so good together, maybe if he hadn't realized just how tenderly he felt toward her, he wouldn't feel so damned guilty. But he did. He was lying to her, lying to himself and lying to the world.

His gut told him that if he and Claire continued on this track, things could get serious, and then he would owe her the truth. But how fair would it be to Will to tell yet another person the secret? As it was, only Regan knew the truth. On the other hand, how fair was it to Claire to continue as they were without telling her? Was it not entirely possible that what he was feeling was one-sided? Claire was attracted to him, yes, but that didn't mean she wanted anything serious. In fact, she'd pretty much indicated the opposite.

He stomped the snow from his feet before stepping into his kitchen. Sarina opened her yellow eyes and blinked at him before narrowing them again, feigning sleep as she laid her chin on her front paws.

Brett crossed over to the fridge and pulled out a beer, suddenly glad that Claire had handed him his pants and sent him on his way. He could not remember another time in his life—other than his disastrous experience with Des—when sleeping with a woman had given him so damn much to think about.

And he really hoped he was overreacting.

CLAIRE DROVE TO WESLEY on Sunday just to get out of the house, clear her head. Brett had been right about one thing—having her sister married to his brother was a bit of a complication. So she wouldn't be discussing Brett with Regan. But there were a host of other things, like Marla, that she could talk about. And besides that, she just wanted to spend time with her sister. It had been awhile.

"Have you heard from Mom?" Regan asked as soon as she answered Claire's knock.

"Not since last Saturday." Claire stopped just inside the door. "You've been painting." Regan had been slowly refurbishing Will's old ranch house, and the kitchen walls, once a boring off-white, were now a warm apricot.

"I'm making curtains next."

"When the homemaking bug bit you, it bit hard," Claire commented, taking the cup of tea Regan had brewed for her.

"Look who's talking—the queen of quilting."

Claire laughed. "If you could see my quilt, you'd demand my crown back. The colors are good, but some of the squares look like I did my sewing in the dark. The other women helped me put it together yesterday, and we've started quilting it." And it had been fun working around the big frame—almost like an Amish quilting bee, except that the conversation had been a bit on the raunchy side. Another good thing had come out of the quilting session, too. Claire now knew that her fellow quilters believed she hadn't bad-mouthed Deke. If rumors circulated, they'd do their part to set them straight.

"I can't wait to see this quilt." Regan set a plate of shortbread in the middle of the table, then took a seat opposite her sister.

"It'll be on display at the show," Claire said fatalistically.

"But I might miss it. There's a conference

in Las Vegas at about that time, and I'm going to go visit Mom. In person. There's something going on."

Claire took a bite of shortbread. "Like…?"

"I tried to call her at work this week, when I couldn't get her at home. Her associate said she wouldn't be in for several days."

"Mom, shirking her duty?"

"I knew we should have insisted on a medical checkup," Regan said, before stirring sugar into her tea.

"Do you think she's working on reconciling with Stephen?"

Regan shook her head and set the spoon on a saucer. "I finally got a hold of her at home. She said she was taking a few days off, but when I asked some questions she said she didn't have to clear her decisions with us."

Claire snorted. "I remember saying the same thing to her once and getting grounded."

"I asked about Stephen, thinking that maybe they were working things out, but she told me he's still in San Diego and has no intention of moving back to Las Vegas."

Claire brushed the crumbs off her fingertips, frowning in concern. "You don't think Mom is home nursing a broken heart, do you?"

Regan debated for a moment. "I didn't get

that impression. But she was definitely sidestepping."

"Maybe a health crisis she's not telling us about?"

"She swore she wouldn't keep anything like that secret."

Claire pushed her plate aside and reached for her teacup. "Maybe now that we've been such major disappointments, Mom's gone off the deep end?"

"That's closer to what I was afraid of, but…" Regan's mouth tightened. "I called Stephen. Damned if he isn't being as evasive as she is."

"So, it's over, but he's covering for her?"

"As weird as it sounds, that's what I think."

"Maybe they don't need our help, Reg."

"I just hope they aren't doing anything illegal."

Claire laughed. "Hey, not to change the subject, but I'm supposed to firm up a prom-dress shopping date with Kylie, and I was thinking about the first Saturday in March." She got up to pour more hot water into her cup. She lifted the pot in Regan's direction, but her sister shook her head. "You're coming along, aren't you?"

"After last time, yes."

"There was nothing wrong with that dress,"

Claire said defensively. "It was practically a turtleneck."

"I think it was the sequins and the way it fit," Regan remarked dryly. "And the first Saturday in March works fine for me. We'll have fun."

"So, does Will approve of *this* boy?" Claire asked, dunking her tea bag. Kylie had yet to have a boyfriend Will wholeheartedly approved of. Even that cute Shane kid hadn't received full marks.

"Will grew up with this one's dad, but I haven't figured out if that's helping or hindering. I guess they dated some of the same girls in high school and competed against each other in rodeo."

"Montagues and Capulets?" Claire asked.

Regan grinned. "Not quite. Honestly, I think the only thing Will has against the kid is that he's another boy interested in his daughter."

"I guess that's a dad's job," Claire said. "Which is why I was so glad that Mom was between husbands while I was in high school."

"Weren't you lucky?" Regan asked sarcastically.

"Very," Claire said with an air of self-satisfaction. "And when I wasn't, I had you to help bail me out." She reached across the table to pat her sister's hand. "Thanks."

JESSE'S DAD WAS SITTING alone at a table in the corner of the bar when Brett dropped by to pick up a sandwich on his way home from Wesley. He ordered his lunch, debated for a moment, then ambled over. "Hi," he said to the wary-looking man. "You're Jesse's dad, right?"

"Right."

Brett stayed planted where he was, close to the table, until the seated man took the hint.

"You wanna sit down?"

"Yeah." Brett pulled out a chair.

"I'm Tom," the man said. "But you probably know that."

Brett didn't know how he would have known, since *Tom* had never spoken to him before.

"Brett Bishop."

"I know." Tom studied his hands for a moment. They were beaten up, red and covered in a rash. Not exactly a salesman's hands. "Jesse likes working for you. Thanks for letting him do that."

"I like Jesse."

The man's eyes flashed at Brett's tone, which was more pointed than he'd intended. But now that he thought about it, the guy deserved to be challenged. He had never taken the time to meet or find out anything about the man his son was spending so much time with. For all he knew, Brett could be some kind of a deviant.

"I like him, too," Tom muttered defensively.

"You're his father."

"Yeah." Tom pushed his drink in a small circle, leaving a trail of moisture on the table. "But he's only been with me for about a year. It's a learning curve."

"Divorce?"

"We were never married. Jesse's mom left me while she was pregnant, and moved in with her grandmother. Then she moved on altogether and her grandmother raised Jesse on her own."

"So you didn't have contact?"

"Not much, and I'm not exactly proud of that." Tom frowned as he focused on the drink again. "But I wasn't living a kid-oriented life, either."

Sometimes you change your life when you have a kid....

But Brett hadn't, so he was in no position to cast stones. He'd run away from fatherhood, too.

"I know what you're thinking," Tom continued in a low voice, talking more to the table than to Brett. He looked tired. "Before Jesse was born I was a chemistry major, but then I lost my scholarships and quit school. I had some problems." He twisted his mouth. "I had some problems with depression and I couldn't focus. I kinda gave up."

"You never went back to school?"

He shook his head. "I kicked around from job to job. Didn't really matter, since it was just me. Then Jesse's grandma went into the rest home and suddenly I'm responsible for a kid. And I wasn't exactly rolling in dough."

"So you came here?"

"Free place to live. I have my sales route and I've been working to expand it. I'm kinda piecing a life together."

"That's good," Brett said. He was surprised the man was letting go with so much information—until it dawned on him that maybe Tom still wasn't over his depression. Or maybe he felt another one coming on, which could explain why he looked so tired.

Maybe he was trying to set things up so there'd be someone to look out for Jesse, if that happened.

"You know," Brett said, "I'd be happy to let Jesse stay with me for a while, if you ever had an extended route or anything."

Tom Lane's jaw shifted sideways as he

studied Brett. "Yeah. I'll keep that in mind." He pushed his chair back. "I'd better be going. School's out soon and I'm not usually here this early. Don't want to miss the kid."

Tom went to the bar and paid his tab, counting out the exact amount and not leaving a tip, giving Brett the feeling that he didn't have a lot of money to waste on a drink in the afternoon.

Maybe Brett should have picked up the tab—for Jesse's sake.

IT WAS NEARLY TEN O'CLOCK when the phone rang, and Brett caught it on the second ring, hoping it was Claire. He wanted to talk to her, even if he hadn't worked out what to say.

But it wasn't Claire—it was Phil, sounding panicked. "I need some help."

"Calving?" What else, this time of year? But then, with Phil, it could be as minor as a stopped-up drain.

No such luck.

"The cow's having some kind of problem."

"Be right there."

Five minutes later Brett pulled open the barn door. The cow was down, obviously in distress. Phil was staring at her from the wrong side of the pen.

"How long has she been straining like this?"

Brett asked, grabbing the disinfectant off the shelf before he climbed over the rails and dropped to the other side. The cow didn't even roll an eye his way.

"I don't know."

Brett started applying the disinfectant to both himself and the business end of the exhausted cow. "What do you mean, you don't know? You put her in the barn when she went into labor." Just as Brett had told him to do with the heifers. "Haven't you been checking on her?"

"I didn't think she'd have any problems. She's in a warm, dry place and she's out of the weather."

A heifer having her first calf out of a big bull. And Phil didn't think there'd be any problems that a warm, dry place wouldn't solve. Ignorance was bliss—unless you were a heifer in trouble. Brett set aside the disinfectant and slowly eased his hand in to analyze the situation.

"Were you home?" he asked as he came into contact with a nose and a bent back front leg, which he gently worked into a better position.

"Close."

"What in the hell does that mean?"

"I was at Claire's place."

"And did you think the damn cow was going to call you if she had trouble?" Brett snapped, forcing himself to ignore the surge of jealousy that had just shot through him. "Get the chains," he said through gritted teeth. The heifer was obviously too exhausted to finish delivering this big baby on her own.

"The chains?"

"There." He pointed to the smooth stainless steel chains that hung near the pen. "Get them and get in here." A few minutes later he had a chain slipped over each fetlock, just above the calf's hooves. He handed the top one to Phil. "First, I pull, and when I get the bottom shoulder through the pelvis, I'll hold that leg in place and then you pull. But remember, we work *with* the cow, not against her."

Phil turned pale.

By the time the calf was delivered—alive, but barely—and the afterbirth had followed, Phil looked as if he might puke. Brett wanted to ask him how the hell he thought baby calves came into the world, and how he was going to handle his first prolapsed uterus, but he was too tired and angry to waste the time. He rubbed the calf with a towel and waited for the cow to recover.

Eventually the mother heaved herself to her feet and started showing interest in her weak little offspring, first sniffing and then licking it.

"I think we'd better tube the baby," Brett said. "Make sure it gets its colostrum."

"You mean, stick a tube…"

"Down its throat and into its stomach." Brett tilted his cap back. "How are you at milking?"

As it turned out, Phil wasn't all that great at milking, but the mama was cooperative, so Brett made him do it, anyway. Once the calf was tubed and showing signs of life, Brett zipped up his coat and started for the door. "You should probably check the other heifers before you go to bed. And keep an eye on this calf. We'll probably tube him again tomorrow, unless he's up and sucking."

"Yeah."

"Hey, this is one of sixty," Brett said, and then he headed for his truck.

It was only nine-thirty, but it felt like midnight. Brett was tired, mentally and physically.

And he still wanted to talk to Claire.

BRETT DID NOT RUN INTO Claire by accident, and they both knew it. She was coming out of the post office with a letter in her hand when he emerged from the bar, where he'd been waiting for her.

"I hear Phil experienced his first birth," she said when she realized he was heading directly for her and not the post office.

"Yes. He's probably an old hand at cow obstetrics by now," Brett said, thinking word had gotten to Claire mighty fast.

She smiled distantly, so he got to the point.

"I'd like to talk about…us." It felt so strange to say that word.

"Are you sure?" She tapped the letter against her leg.

"Yes," he said with a touch of impatience. He did. "I would have talked the other night, but you kicked me out."

"I kicked you out because you didn't want to be there."

"That isn't true," he said, even though he knew it was. He'd been uncertain as to his next move, and escape had seemed a reasonable option.

"Then next time you can stay," Claire said in that maddeningly calm way she had.

"Hey, Brett! Miss Flynn!"

They both turned as Jesse came pedaling up on his bike, Ramon balancing on the rear pegs.

"Brett, can Ramon come over and help with chores today?"

"Sure. Maybe I can even find a few extra chores for another guy, if he wanted to earn some cash."

Ramon smiled broadly and gave a big nod.

"We can go right now, if you want," Jesse said.

"I'll meet you there in a few minutes." He waited until the boys had pedaled away before looking at Claire.

"Can I come by tonight?"

"Sure," she said. "Any time you want." She gave him a brief smile, then turned and started walking back down the street to the school.

THE LETTER WAS WRINKLED. Claire had clutched it too tightly when she'd been talking to Brett, and now she smoothed it out on her kitchen table and read it again.

Apparently her decision to get real-world experience was going to pay off, because due to that experience she had been invited to take part in a two-year research project in conjunction with her graduate studies.

She'd originally planned to write a thesis on combined-classroom education in an urban setting, collecting data from the few schools that were experimenting with the idea, but she'd now be involved in a major study researching the same topic, working under one of her former professors who'd just received grant funding. She'd be helping to make decisions concerning class setups, age combinations, curriculum. It was an academic dream come true.

So why wasn't she more excited?

Because she was tired? Because she'd been away from college for a while and liked her job? Because she was falling in love with Brett Bishop?

All of the above?

She carefully folded the letter and put it back into the envelope.

All of the above.

CHAPTER THIRTEEN

BRETT DID NOT GET a chance to talk to Claire. Phil made certain of that by calling with two more heifer emergencies. After the second young cow delivered on her own and was protectively tending to her calf, Brett looked at his watch. Twelve-thirty. Even if Claire was still up, he was too tired to have a decent discussion.

"There's more to this than I thought," Phil said, sluicing his hands in a bucket of cold water.

"Yeah." Brett fixed his tired eyes on his boss's face. "Wait until your first C-section."

"How do you know when you have to…?"

"Experience," Brett said quietly. "Unfortunately, you can kill cows and calves getting it." And Phil had expensive registered cows.

Phil nodded and leaned on the fence.

"You know," Brett said, "I'm going to have to get a job elsewhere." Wesley, if he could swing it. Elko, if he had to. Maybe one of the mines, even though he had no experience with heavy equipment. He was determined to stay in the area until Kylie graduated. He might not be able to claim her, but he was going to watch her finish growing up—from a distance, if necessary. "I can't get by on half a paycheck and still make payments on the homestead." And there were no other jobs in Barlow to supplement his income. Nothing dependable, anyway.

Phil hooked his fingers over the top rail of the fence, focusing on the first calf born that night, which was now vigorously punching its mother's udder with its nose. "I hate to lose you, but it doesn't make sense to have two of us running the place."

"Nope. Not at all," Brett agreed, his heart somewhere near the top of his boots.

Phil turned to him, once again the businessman instead of the cowboy. "You are staying until June 1, aren't you?"

"I told you I would."

"I'll give you full pay until then. After that…" Phil's eyes went back to the cow and calf. "I'll have a better idea as to what I plan to do."

Brett nodded and headed for the door.

He had a feeling Phil was going to keep him

on, that he was already figuring out that running a small ranch took a lot of work and there was a sharp learning curve. But nothing was ever certain with Phil, so Brett was going to have to live with an *un*certain future for another three and a half months, which was nothing new. It was the cowboy way of life.

SO WHERE WAS BRETT? Did he think pulling a no-show was going to change things, make her start to think he wasn't worth wasting time over?

No, Claire thought, as she turned off the kitchen light before padding down the narrow trailer hallway to her bedroom, hurrying her steps just a little as she passed the washer in the dark. He wasn't the kind of guy to play games like that. Probably another calving problem and he was too busy to call. Phil's barn lights were on, so the theory made sense.

And she didn't mind that Brett hadn't stopped by, since she knew his mission. He was going to distance himself. Claire was still debating about how she was going to handle the situation. Should she let him go quietly or put up a tussle? She'd never dealt with a matter like this before—one where a man was walking away before she was done with him.

Claire Flynn, who'd never been able to settle on anything—career, hobby or man—felt as if she might have found a guy she wanted to stick with.

Now it was just a matter of convincing him it was a good idea.

BRETT WAS MAKING COFFEE the next morning, debating about his future and wondering if he should discuss the matter with Will at Kylie's game that day, when a rap sounded at his kitchen door. The top of Jesse's blond head was just visible through the window, and Brett immediately crossed the room to pull the door open. The Christmas bike lay carelessly abandoned on its side near the front porch.

"What's wrong?" Brett instantly asked. Jesse never dropped his bike.

"What happens if I can't come and do chores for Sarina's cat food anymore?" The boy blurted the question, his face close to crumpling, and Brett's heart gave an uneven thump.

"Why wouldn't you be able to do that?"

"I think we're going to move."

Another unpleasant jolt shot through Brett's chest. "You're moving?" Damn it, he didn't want Jesse to move.

"Yeah. And I can't bring Sarina."

"I'll keep her," Brett said automatically. "Where're you moving to?"

"Dunno. Some valley. Smoky Valley?"

"That's a ways away." And sparsely populated.

"I don't want to go."

"Are you moving because of your dad's job?" Although Brett didn't see how, unless Tom Lane had hired on at a remote mine site.

"I don't know. My dad don't talk much anymore." Jesse pulled in a shaky breath. "And he didn't come home last night. I wasn't afraid to be alone, because of the dogs, but I was afraid that something had happened to him. And then when he came home early this morning, he said we were moving."

The kid was on the verge of tears. Brett had no idea what to do, so he went with his gut and knelt down, holding Jesse the way he wished his own dad would have held him after his mom had died. Finally Jesse stepped back, brushing his cheeks with the backs of his hands and then wiping his nose on his sleeve.

"The next time your dad doesn't come home, you call me, okay?"

"But I don't want to get him in trouble."

"I won't get him in trouble, Jess. I'll just come and stay with you or bring you here so you won't be alone. Okay?" Brett brushed the remaining tears from under the boy's eyes with the pad of his thumb. "Promise?"

Tears clung to Jesse's pale lashes. "Promise," he said solemnly. "I'm sorry I cried."

"What's wrong with crying?" Brett asked gruffly. "Everybody cries."

"Really?" he asked softly.

"Really," Brett said. "So what do you say we skip chores today and go over to the ranch. Phil needs some help with his calves."

"All right," Jesse said, wiping the back of his hand over his cheek again.

Even though he was supposed to go to the basketball finals that afternoon and watch Kylie play, Brett couldn't bring himself to abandon Jesse, so he stayed home and let Jesse help him first with chores and then with his biology homework. The boy tried to put on a brave face, but he was still upset about leaving, anxious about his cat and worried about being alone.

Finally, in the late afternoon, he told Brett his dad wanted him home by dinner. Brett refrained from asking Jesse who did the cooking. He had a feeling he knew the answer. He offered a ride home, but Jesse refused, and

Brett's heart squeezed tight as he stood on the porch and watched him ride away.

If the kid moved, it was going to leave a big hole in Brett's life—which startled him, considering the fact that Jesse had only been *in* his life for all of five or six months. And he hated the idea of him living somewhere faraway, with no one there if his nut job of a father decided not to come home.

But there was absolutely nothing he could do about it.

LATELY, CLAIRE SEEMED to be spending most of her daytime hours at the school, and if the quilt display racks didn't start going together any faster, she'd probably be spending her nights there, too. But at least it gave her something to think about other than Brett.

The quilt show was being held over the long President's Day weekend. In addition to the display at the school, there was a barbeque dinner at the community hall, and the Wesley antique car club was putting on a small rally in spite of the fact that there was still snow on the ground.

"Something for everyone," Bertie said as she and Claire worked to assemble the wooden frames. "The campground is completely booked with RVs and lots of people will drive out just for the quilt raffle and the rally." She smiled wryly as she finished twisting a wing nut onto a screw. "We're quaint out here, you know, so people come for the day."

"Are they honestly going to get the lights hooked up over the quilts?" she asked. The school gym was dim, but Anne had promised light and rarely failed to deliver.

"The volunteer firemen are going to do it for us. Oh, look," Bertie added, "here comes the chief now."

But it wasn't the chief who walked into the gym, exuding charm and confidence. It was Phil, totally unaware that people were poking fun at him for cluelessly insinuating himself into an organization that was known for closing its ranks to outsiders. The firemen had no choice but to accept him, since he was landlord to many of them, but that didn't mean they liked it. Phil was oblivious.

"Hi, Phil," Claire called. She had a soft spot for the man, in spite of his self-importance. He simply didn't understand how the people in this town thought. In fact, he'd have been appalled if he knew *what* they thought of him. "Are you here to solve our light problem?"

"I'm here to take a look," he answered with a wink.

The man who'd come in with him rolled his eyes but said nothing.

"'Bout time," Anne grumbled, easing herself down off the stage. "Here. I've drawn up a plan."

Bertie took Claire's screwdriver out of her hand as the two men approached Anne. "We're going home," she said in a low voice. "It's late." She gestured toward the exit. "Quick. Before Anne sees us."

CLAIRE DID NOT GO HOME. Instead, she went to Brett's house. It was time.

He didn't answer the knock on the door, but she heard noises coming from the barn, and she found him there, moving items around in the tack room. He turned, holding a saddle in one hand, looking every inch the hot cowboy and causing Claire's stomach to fill with butterflies as she remembered just *how* hot he'd been a few nights ago.

He'd been an amazing lover, tender and giving, yet demanding enough to bring an edge to things. And she knew he'd been surprised by his own response to her, which was part of the reason he'd shut down that night. They'd both gotten more than they'd expected.

He carried the saddle across the room and settled it on a wall-mounted rack, pushing it into place.

"I'm sorry I didn't make it over like I promised," he said.

"No problem." She wanted to step closer, touch him, but his body language made it clear that wouldn't be welcome. She ran her hand down the reins of a bridle hanging next to her, barely feeling the leather as it slipped between her fingers.

"The other night felt like more than just a one-time occurrence, didn't it?" she murmured.

"Yes."

"Does that bother you?"

"It raises issues," Brett said truthfully.

Claire studied him for a moment, trying to read the expression in his dark eyes before she said, "This is new territory for me, too. I'm more of a hit-and-run girl, but…I'm not ready to run yet."

She hoped she was imagining the color draining from his face, and she did her best to make things right. "It takes two, Brett, and if this isn't what you want then I'd like to stay friends."

He rubbed the tips of his fingers over his

forehead. "I don't think we should sleep together—at least not until I work through a few things. That's what I wanted to tell you when I asked to come over."

"All right."

He gave a brief smile. "You could at least do my ego some good and fight me a little."

She took a step closer. "That's a mixed message, Brett. Very ineffective communication."

"I've never been all that good at communication, which is why I'm usually in so much trouble." She was close enough for him to reach out, touch her, but he didn't.

"I think you have some talents in that area that you may be underrating."

"And I think if I spend a lot of time with you, I'm never going to work through anything." He folded his arms. "Before we slept together, I thought we could fill a few evenings, have some fun. Go on with our lives, you know?"

She knew. She'd thought the same thing.

"I thought we'd just be two lonely people helping each other out."

"I think we were more like two horny people, helping each other out."

He laughed and it was a good sound, even if

it was gone too soon. Claire's smile faded. "So what you're saying is that things have the potential to get more serious than you intended, and you need some time."

"That's what I'm saying."

"Okay. I can live with that."

Brett tipped his hat back. "Did you know Jesse was moving?"

"Actually, that's part of the reason I came over. He told me today."

Brett pushed another saddle farther back on its rack. "I worry about him. I met his dad at the bar, and I think I see a problem there." He quickly filled her in on the meeting.

"Unfortunately, there's nothing you can do about it."

"I know."

"You've been good for Jesse."

"I'll miss him." Brett swallowed, and Claire realized that Jesse's departure was going to be even harder on him than she'd imagined.

"You know," she said, "nothing in Barlow Ridge has turned out the way I thought it would."

"Amen to that," he muttered.

"But," she continued, as she took a few steps toward the door, "it still turned out right. Sometimes you just have to have faith."

BRETT SPENT A LOT OF TIME thinking about Claire that evening, amazed how when he was with her he could almost believe that maybe, magically, things could work out. Until he tried to come up with the words to tell her what he'd done so many years ago.

There was no way to sugarcoat the situation, and no way to continue seeing Claire, with whom he was halfway in love, without explaining. If he was serious about her, he'd have to come clean, but before he confessed to anything, he was going to get Will's permission. And for all he knew, his brother might not give it—not when it involved Kylie's peace of mind.

So what to do?

Brett was no closer to an answer the following day, when he drove to Wesley to stock up. He had just left the shopping center late that afternoon with about a month's worth of groceries when his phone rang. It crackled when he answered it, but he recognized Regan's voice.

"Great, I got you," she said. "Anne McKirk called, and she has a list of lighting supplies and general hardware she needs. Some quilt-show emergency, and she knew you were in town. Do you have a pencil?"

Brett glanced around the truck. No. And he

didn't have anything to write on, except a cereal box. "Do you have a list?"

"Boy, do I."

"How about I swing by your place and get it."

"Meet you there in ten minutes. Will just picked me up at school."

Brett was at the place in five. He'd intended to cool his heels on the porch and wait, but Kylie was home. She pushed the door open.

"I thought you were coming to the game," she said without a hello.

"Something came up."

Her eyes, so like his own, were hooded as she studied him, one hand still on the screen door.

"You want to come in?" It sounded like a dare.

"No," he said, spotting Will's truck down the road. "I'll be leaving in a second."

"You always do."

"Do what?" he asked.

"Leave. Either that or you don't show up." Her tone was more scathing than he'd ever heard—even after the big curfew incident. She sounded almost hateful.

"Maybe there's a reason I leave," he said, trying to think on his feet.

"You might have a reason *now*." Kylie emphasized the last word coldly. "But what I don't understand is why you left me in the first place. Didn't feel like having a kid?"

Brett's mouth went dry. She knew. He'd always wondered, but now he had the answer.

"Is that why you abandoned me and my mom? Left my dad to marry her and take over?"

She must have pieced the story together herself, since she didn't have the whole truth. Damn, he didn't want her to have the whole truth.

What a mucked-up mess.

He swallowed dryly. "You need to talk to your dad," he said, as the truck turned into the long drive. It felt like the coward's way out, but Brett owed it to Will to allow him to tell Kylie the truth in the way he thought best.

"No," she said adamantly. "I am not going to hurt him by doing that. I just wanted to tell you that I *know* what you did."

"You may not know everything."

"I know enough." She pressed her lips together, but her eyes never left his. "My boyfriend's parents used to rodeo with you."

"And…?" Brett prompted grimly.

"His sister heard them talking. About you

and Dad and my mother. It wasn't a very nice story, but she thought I should know."

"Why would you believe it?" Brett asked softly.

"Because the facts fit," Kylie said bluntly, as Will pulled his truck to a stop next to Brett's rig. "And don't you dare talk to my dad about this." She stepped back into the house, letting the screen door bang before turning to speak through the screen. "And you know what? I kinda wish you'd quit hanging around, *Uncle* Brett. I really liked it better when you were gone." The wooden door closed in his face.

"I'm glad we caught you," Regan said seconds later as she came up the steps, looking so much like Claire it almost hurt to see her. "Anne says to put it on her account."

Brett squinted at the list, trying not to appear shell-shocked. "This'll take some time."

"Is something wrong?" Regan asked.

He glanced up, attempting to act normal. As if he'd ever feel normal again. "No. Just the usual stuff with Phil."

"What's going on with Phil?" Will asked, putting a hand on his wife's shoulder.

"He's trying to handle calving on his own, which means I spend most of my time rushing over there and saving the day. I think *he* thinks he's handling it alone." Brett held up the list. "He's in charge of lighting, too."

Brett had no idea how the words kept coming out in such a normal tone.

Regan laughed. "I wish I could attend the big weekend."

"You aren't?"

"I'm going to Las Vegas for a meeting that Saturday, and I'm going to try to pin down my mother while I'm there. Will and Kylie may drive out, though."

Somehow, Brett doubted that.

"I don't suppose you have time to come in for a minute?" Regan asked. Brett answered with a shake of his head, and she disappeared inside.

"You need to talk to Kylie," he said as soon as the door closed. "Her boyfriend's sister found out the truth about me and told Kylie, but she doesn't have all the facts right." He forced himself to hold his brother's gaze, wishing he had some way to make the situation right, because, damn it, Will didn't deserve this. "I'm sorry this happened," Brett finished lamely, halfway wishing his brother would take a swing at him, although that would have been too easy. Instead, he had to watch as Will's face went blank, the way it did whenever he was dealing with something that hurt.

It took a few seconds before he said, "Any idea what the kid told her?"

"That I abandoned Des when she got pregnant and then you stepped in to marry her."

Which was halfway true. Des had actually left Brett and gone back to Will as soon as she'd discovered she was pregnant. Brett had been well out of the picture by the time Kylie was born, and he'd stayed out of the picture.

Brett lifted his chin. "It's okay if she keeps on believing that."

"I'll talk to her," Will said in a detached voice, and Brett took it as his cue to leave. He started down the steps without another word, and was almost to his truck when Will said his name. He looked back, but his brother only shook his head, giving up on whatever he'd been about to say.

Brett sucked in a breath, got into his truck and drove away, leaving his brother to deal with a situation he had not created.

BRETT'S HEAD WAS POUNDING by the time he drove into his yard. Leave or stay? Shit, he didn't know. The only thing he was certain of was that he wasn't going to cause his family any more grief. He was through forcing himself into Kylie and Will's lives, through trying to be part of something he had no right to be part of.

He knew it would be easier on everyone if he left, including himself. Which was exactly why he was hesitant to make that decision. He was done being easy on himself.

The phone was ringing when he walked in the door, and he knew he had to answer it, just in case it was Will.

"I have some thoughts about our situation," Claire announced without even saying hello. "I'm coming over."

"Don't—"

But she'd already hung up. Her approach was like a blitzkrieg.

"What's wrong?" she immediately asked when he answered her knock.

"I tried to tell you not to come." Brett knew he had to look like hell.

"Why?"

"Because damn it, Claire, this isn't going to work."

She blinked at him. "Will you at least let me come in for a minute?"

"I think you'd *better* come in." It was time to set the record straight and end things once and for all. Otherwise, she would just continue to hammer away at him, and there was no way now he was going to have Claire tying him closer to his family.

"Have a seat," he said, waving at the kitchen chairs. "Do you want something to drink?"

"Will I need a drink?" She remained standing, watching him.

"Probably," Brett said grimly. "The reason I don't want to get involved is because of Kylie."

"Kylie?"

"She's my daughter."

Claire sat down abruptly. "Kylie is *your* daughter?" She looked up at him, seeking a denial to the scenario her mind was obviously piecing together. "So you and…"

"I had an affair with my brother's wife. She got pregnant."

Claire shifted her gaze to stare straight ahead. "Then why does Will have anything to do with you?"

Hell, Brett didn't know, but he made a guess. "Because I'm Kylie's biological father. In the age of DNA, I could always push for parental rights."

"Would you do that?"

"No. But I don't think Will is taking any chances. I haven't been the most trustworthy of brothers."

Claire stared at him.

"I'm sorry."

"So am I." Claire swallowed hard. "I need to go."

CLAIRE HAD NEVER BEEN afraid to cry, and she indulged herself freely that day. She felt like a fool. Regan had known. Will. Brett. Everyone in the equation had known but her. She'd sensed the weird undercurrents, but she'd chosen to ignore them. After all, if there was anything she needed to know, her sister would have clued her in. Right?

Wrong.

And the bitch of the matter was that she couldn't even blame Regan. This was a sensitive issue.

But they were sisters. And Regan obviously knew that Claire was getting seriously interested in Brett. Yet she hadn't said one word. Why?

Probably because Claire had never stuck with anything except teaching for more than six months. Regan probably figured she would have her fun with Brett, move on and no harm would be done. The secret of Kylie's paternity would be safe. Regan hadn't counted on Claire falling in love.

Claire hadn't counted on falling in love.

And now the big question was who had she fallen in love with? The real Brett Bishop, or some man she'd invented in her mind?

CLAIRE SPENT THE DAY numbly doing all the mundane tasks she usually put off until the very last minute, including her taxes. She sealed the IRS envelope, then walked the half mile to town to mail it. She needed to move, to breathe, to do anything but think.

She was standing in line behind two other people at the post office, willing them not to talk to her, when the bell on the door signaled yet another customer.

It was Marla. She stalked straight toward Claire. Claire drew herself up, ready to blast her out of the water if need be, but then her jaw dropped when the woman said, "I'm sorry," in a voice loud enough for the postmistress and the two patrons at the counter to hear. "What I did and said the other night was wrong."

Claire frowned, wondering if she'd heard correctly. It sounded like an apology.

"Toni told me that you didn't say anything about Deke, that you just told her to go home. I misunderstood. I hope there won't be any hard feelings." And then Marla held out her hand. Claire took it, shook and released. Marla glanced over at the postmistress, as if to say, *"There, I did it… Happy?"* Then she exited, as quickly as she'd arrived.

Bemused, Claire watched her go.

"Marla's business has fallen off some," the postmistress explained, when Claire stepped up to the counter.

"But she's the only game in town."

"Yes, but people aren't going to the bar quite as often as they used to. They're afraid that you might leave because of what she did. It's kind of a show of support, you know?"

"I'm going to leave, anyway."

"Yes." The postmistress smiled. "But people were kind of hoping… Well, you know."

Claire gave a slow nod. "I appreciate the support," she said. And she did. Now, if she could just shove Brett Bishop out of her mind, she'd be a happy woman.

"Uh, Miss Flynn."

Claire turned, marker in hand. "Yes?"

"You did that wrong."

"What?"

"You made a mistake in the equation."

Claire took a step back. Dylan was right. In her hurry to get through the problem, she had missed the decimal place.

She held out the marker. Dylan got out of his seat, took it and corrected her error.

"Thank you, Dylan." She spoke dryly, as she always did when the kids corrected her, but she felt a deep sense of satisfaction. The students were with her, paying attention, taking an active role in their education. Finally.

And as much as she would have liked to take all the credit, she knew that it was more a matter of consistency and expectations than any special ability—other than dedication— on her part. Any teacher could have achieved the same result. The trick was to actually work at teaching, unlike Mr. Nelson, and not to leave midyear as the two previous teachers had done. Kids could do amazing things, with some consistency and guidance. And they could fall to pieces fast without it.

"Hey, uh, Miss Flynn…?"

"Yes?" She looked up several minutes after taking her seat. Her desk was surrounded by her female students.

"Are you all right?" Ashley spoke, but Elena, Lexi, Rachel and Toni stood with her. "You seem kind of, I don't know. Weird?"

Claire couldn't help but smile. "Weird?" she asked, raising her eyebrows.

"Yes," Elena said seriously. "We think something's not right."

"I'm just tired."

She wasn't fooling these girls, who exchanged dissatisfied glances as they filed back to their desks. Not much she could do about it but continue to stonewall. She idly peeled the pink sticky note from the cover of her grade book, the one reminding her to e-mail the graduate school admissions department at UNLV. She had to confirm her acceptance of their offer so they could send her the paperwork required to complete the arrangements.

She rolled the note between her fingers as she looked out over her own combined classroom, the members of which were now silently working on the science problems she'd assigned. What could she possibly research in graduate school that she hadn't already discovered through direct experience?

What would she achieve by leaving?

She was too honest not to admit that Brett Bishop factored heavily into the equation—it was very tempting to do the easy thing and hightail it away from this community because of him. But personal issues aside, she hated to leave these kids, hated to see their education handed off to someone who would probably take the position for a year in order to get into the Wesley school system and then transfer to town. Or worse yet, someone who was in Barlow Ridge because he couldn't get a job elsewhere—or who was being involuntarily transferred here, as Mr. Nelson had been. These kids deserved better than that.

These kids deserved her.

CHAPTER FOURTEEN

CLAIRE WAS A BIG BELIEVER in getting to the heart of a matter rather than edging around the periphery. She needed to make a decision, and in order to do that, she needed information, so she drove to Wesley Friday after school, when she knew Regan was on her way to Las Vegas.

Will was at the pasture gate, a halter and rope in his hand, when she drove in. "Hi," Claire said as she approached, thinking that was probably the last nonchalant thing she'd be saying in this conversation.

Will seemed to sense the same thing. He pushed his hat back. "What's on your mind?"

"Brett."

"What about him?" But a look of dawning comprehension had already crossed his features.

"Yes, he told me," Claire said quietly.

Will unlatched the gate and held it open. "I have to catch a horse. Come on."

They walked across the pasture toward the small herd in the far corner. "Regan knows, doesn't she?"

Will nodded. "You can see why she didn't tell you."

"Yes." And she didn't blame her sister. Not much, anyway. "How about Kylie?"

"She knows now. Her boyfriend's bitch of a sister told her an almost-true story she got from her parents. Kylie blindsided Brett two days ago."

Claire hadn't realized it had been that recent.

"It's been a rugged couple days for us here, but Regan's pretty good at this kind of stuff."

"She had a lot of practice with me," Claire muttered. "So Kylie's doing all right?"

"If she wasn't, Regan wouldn't have left. Kylie's pissed at Brett, and we're all pissed at the girl who told the story, but I think Kylie's doing better now that she's aware of the whole truth."

"She's lucky to have a strong family. How are *you* doing?"

"I always suspected this day was coming, and in a way I guess I'm glad it has, so we can deal with it." Claire nodded, and then Will amazed her by saying, "You know, this is harder on Brett than it is on me."

"How so?" she asked incredulously.

"I have Kylie. Brett has guilt."

"He probably should have." Claire couldn't quite erase the bitterness from her voice.

"There are circumstances." Will pulled a tall weed and bent it between his fingers as he walked. "Did he tell you?"

"No."

"Well, to begin with, our dad would never have won any father-of-the-year awards. He kept me and Brett in competition for most of our lives. He picked at Brett and doted on me. It wasn't the kind of environment where brotherhood thrived."

"Did you like each other?"

"I would have killed anyone who messed with my brother, but… We didn't exactly get along face-to-face. I used to try to talk to Brett about what the old man was doing, but he had a hard time listening."

"Regan and I were always close. Maybe too close. I depended on her for everything."

"That wasn't the case with us. And then Des and I got married. We traveled on the rodeo circuit, and we had troubles." Will kept his eyes on the horizon. "Which wasn't that surprising for two kids still in their teens who'd had no home life to speak of. I wanted to settle down, get a real job and start building a future. Des wanted to party while we were young." He tossed the weed aside. "Then I got hurt and had to come home for a while, which made both sets of goals difficult."

"She didn't come home with you?" Claire guessed.

"Nope. She stayed on the circuit, angry that I wasn't there with her, spending money we didn't have. Brett was doing rodeo, too. She told him we were separated, and he believed her. She came on to him, and he finally had a way to be better than his brother."

"But still…"

"There are lots of small circumstances involved."

"But…"

Will stopped and turned toward her. "Brett made a mistake, Claire."

It took a moment before she could say, "You're remarkably forgiving."

"No. I was damn bitter about it—more so when Des decided she couldn't handle motherhood and hit the road. But—" his expression softened as he paused "—I found that bitterness fades when you have better things to focus on—like your kid."

There wasn't much to say in answer to that.

Will started walking again. "Brett has the

right to insist on parental rights, you know. And he hasn't. I owe him for that."

"He thinks you're afraid he'll still do it."

Will shook his head. "I know he won't." The three horses didn't move as Will and Claire walked toward them. "I admit, I was worried when he first moved back from Montana a few years ago, but we made our peace and I trust him. Now he needs to make peace with himself."

"So what do *I* do?" she said, more to herself than to Will.

"Damned if I know, Claire."

"I don't know, either," she said. "Part of me says do what he asks and leave him alone, but the other part… Well, let's just say I've never been known for common sense."

To her surprise, Will smiled as he ran a hand over the nearest horse's neck. "Which is why you're probably good for Brett. He needs someone who'll brush the bullshit aside and see things for what they are." He slipped the halter up over the horse's nose and ears, then buckled it. "I can see where he's avoiding getting involved with you because of Kylie and me. But—and I'm no shrink—I'd also bet he's doing it because he doesn't think he deserves to be involved with anyone who makes him happy."

"I think you might be right." Claire reached

out to pat the horse. The animal bobbed its head as she stroked it.

"Brett's always been hard on himself. Add a mistake like Des and, well, you get the picture."

Yes, she did.

Brett was denying himself a future. And by doing that, he was messing with hers.

REGAN CALLED ON HER cell phone just as Claire was pulling into her driveway an hour and a half later.

"You heard about my visit?" Claire asked as she got out of the car, slinging her purse over her shoulder and pushing the door shut with her free hand.

"I heard."

"I feel for Kylie." She tromped up the steps to the trailer as she talked.

"Yes, I know. But we have to play the hand we're dealt, as best we can. I think Kylie understands that now. We talked about ways of dealing with the issue without totally shutting Brett out of her life. Now we'll wait and see what she decides." Regan paused. "Will told me you came to talk about Brett." She waited, and when Claire didn't say anything, she added, "I'd suspected there might be something going on between you two."

"Now you have confirmation." Claire dropped her purse on the sofa and then headed for the kitchen. "I've decided to stay in Barlow Ridge for another year."

There was a long, ominous silence. "Because of Brett?" Regan finally asked.

"No. Because of the job, but it gives me time to decide about Brett."

"You know, Claire—"

"Oh, yes, I know," she said, without giving her sister a chance to finish. The odds were great things wouldn't work out with Brett, but even if they didn't, she wanted to stay with her job. If Brett didn't want to live close to her, he could leave.

"So what are you going to do now?"

"The unthinkable," Claire said. "I'm going to call Mom. I'll talk to you later."

She grabbed a soft drink out of the fridge, took a deep breath and hit the dreaded number one on speed dial with her thumb.

Ever efficient, Arlene answered on the first ring.

"Hi, Mom. How's life?"

"Very good, thank you." She sounded suspicious, as well she should be. Claire never called out of the blue.

"I don't think I'm going to graduate school."

"Why am I not surprised?"

"Because you know me?"

Arlene sighed.

"Hey, I found something I like to do, and I'm sticking with it."

"Claire," her mother said with exaggerated patience, "you can teach anytime."

"I can go to graduate school at any time, too."

"The longer you wait, the harder it is. I have firsthand experience." And she did. Arlene had put herself through graduate school later in life, earning her MBA while Regan and Claire were in grade school.

"I know what I'm doing."

"Then why did you call?"

Claire could picture her mother sitting at her desk, her glasses pushed up into her dark blond hair. Why had she called? "Reassurance."

"Rea…"

"Reassurance," Claire repeated gently. "I'm going to do this, but I don't want it to be adversarial, like with all the other things I've done."

"You do remember that I was *right* on most of the other things?"

"But this time *I'm* right, and I want some moral support, Mom. I know we're different. I know we don't see eye to eye. But…"

"Why do you need moral support, if this is the right thing to do?"

"Because I just do. I'm not like you. I can't simply grab the world by the tail and give it a shake."

Arlene snorted. "Since when?"

"What?"

"You've been doing that since you were a toddler."

"But not with you."

"I'm glad to hear something scares you." Arlene let out a breath. "All right. I will give you moral support. For now. Until I sense that you're making a major error. That should give you until next Wednesday."

A joke. Her mother had made a joke. Claire gave a silent sigh of relief. "Have you heard from Stephen?" she asked, changing the subject while she was ahead.

"Of course."

"But I thought…"

"We've come up with the perfect relationship. He stays in San Diego. I stay here. We visit once a month for five days, alternating locales."

"Mom!" Claire said, shocked.

"It works for us," Arlene said sharply. "You're always complaining about how I want you to be like me. Well, the same holds true for you. I like companionship in small doses. This works." And it also miraculously explained why Arlene had quit ragging Claire about her career choice well before the holidays.

"You're happy?"

"We're both happy. The only caveat is that during those five days I focus on us. No phones, no e-mail, no faxes. The other twenty-five days of the month, I can focus on business."

"If it works for you, it works for me. I'm just glad this is the reason you've been incommunicado. I had some wild theories going."

"No doubt," Arlene said with a sniff. "You always were creative."

"You do take weekends off?" Claire asked curiously.

"Some," her mother allowed. "I've finally trained a decent manager. If she stays on, I may increase my days away. One at a time. I guess I have to retire someday."

"No, Mom," Claire said, smiling. "Not you. You'll always have your finger in the pie."

"Thank you, Claire. And…" Arlene drew in a breath, then said just a bit too briskly, "I hope things work out for you in your job."

"I'll keep in touch."

UNTIL HIS BROTHER had called earlier that day, Brett figured his last parting with Claire had been exactly that. A last parting. He should have known it wouldn't be that easy with her, and he wasn't completely surprised when her car pulled up in front of his house.

"Hi," she said, testing the waters.

"Hi," he echoed in a less-than-encouraging tone.

"I've been doing some thinking."

"And talking to Will."

She looked surprised. "That, too."

"He called." And although Brett appreciated his brother's intentions—especially during such a rough time in Will's own life—Brett had made his position clear. He'd caused enough family damage.

The conversation had escalated into an argument and had ended with Will hanging up on him. Brett always had been able to punch his brother's buttons, and he hadn't lost his touch. If Will was mad, Will would leave him alone.

"So, I'm wasting my time, if I came here to talk about us?" Claire murmured.

"I know what I have to do."

"So do I," she said quietly, a note of resignation in her voice. She gave him a long look.

'Have you heard that I'm teaching here for another year?"

"No," Brett said, hoping against hope that she was messing with him.

"I like my job. I'm keeping it."

"How wise is that?"

"For me or for you?" she asked, idly twisting the ring on her left hand.

"Careerwise."

"Careerwise, it's an opportunity most teachers never get, so I think it's a fine move. I want to teach rural while they still *have* rural schools. And *we* still have some things to talk about." She tilted her chin. "Now we'll have plenty of time to do it."

"Claire," Brett said through clenched teeth, 'I don't need a good woman standing by me in my time of need."

"But apparently you do need to be a stubborn ass about this."

Whatever got the job done.

BRETT DID NOT WANT TO GO to the quilt show and community dinner, but when Jesse asked if he would be there, he heard himself say yes. If he and Claire were going to live in the same community, they might as well get used to bumping into one another.

Hell, he was never going to get used to it, and he knew it, so he was thankful when he managed to meet up with Jesse and Ramon outside the community hall, about a half hour before dinner started, without running into her.

"Have you seen the cars?" Jesse asked, bug-eyed.

"Not yet."

"Come on," the boy said, heading around the corner of the building toward the parking lot in back. "They're cool, and one guy let us crank the engine. They used to *crank engines!*"

Brett allowed Jesse and Ramon to point out all the features of the ten cars on display in the frigid air, and he had to admit they were nice specimens. After the cars, he dutifully asked the boys if they'd seen the quilts.

"Yeah. They're at the school," Ramon said, unimpressed. "We've seen 'em. I'd rather eat."

"The only cool one is Miss Flynn's," Jesse added. "It's purple and green and black. If I had a quilt, that's the one I'd get."

"Purple, green and black," Brett echoed. "Cool."

"They're not selling them until tomorrow," Jesse added. "You have time to see them." The *without us* was implied.

Brett nodded at one of the firemen who was

ending the barbecue behind the community hall as he and the boys headed for the entrance. "How're you getting home tonight?" he asked Jesse.

"We're dropping him at the end of his road," Ramon said. "And my mom wants to leave early, so we have to eat soon."

"Dad's home," Jesse added with a quick glance at Brett. "He had some work to catch up on, so he didn't come."

Big surprise. Brett followed the two into the community hall where a line was already forming. He'd grab a bite, then head home. Brett pulled his wallet out as they approached the cashier's table, where Bertie sat with a steel money box. "I'll pay for both these guys."

Bertie took the money and stamped their hands with ink smiley faces. The boys raced ahead, getting in line behind Marla and Deirdre.

"I heard she was staying," Marla said sharply. "And it's not my fault if she doesn't. I apologized."

"Well, I heard she wasn't staying," Deirdre responded.

The two women rounded on Brett, who hadn't even realized they'd noticed his presence. "You're her landlord. You should know. Is Claire staying or leaving?"

"Staying," he said abruptly.

Marla gave Deirdre a smug nod.

Brett ate dinner with the boys, and shortly thereafter the Hernandezes collected Jesse and Ramon for the trip home. Brett was on his way to the exit when he spotted Claire at the corner table with Phil, who had apparently finished his barbecuing shift and was now trying to light a fire under her.

"Hey, Brett?" Anne McKirk's husband waved him over to the bar. "I need to run home for a sec. Can you watch things here? Fifteen minutes tops. The other firemen are eating or cooking."

Or flirting.

"Sure," Brett said, even though he wanted to escape. A little community service wasn't going to kill him, and the McKirks were always there when Brett needed a hand with Phil's wells.

Twenty minutes later Brett was still selling beer and surreptitiously watching Phil put the moves on Claire. He shifted his attention for the umpteenth time, wanting desperately to get out of there. McKirk was not very good at telling time, and no one who wasn't buying beer was stupid enough to wander close as he had.

Phil swaggered up to the bar then, and since he was a fireman, Brett thought about abandoning ship. Until his soon-to-be ex-boss said, "Hey, no hard feelings. Right?"

Brett frowned. "About?"

"Claire. The best man and all that?" And then he had the audacity to wink.

Brett uncapped the beer and pushed it across the counter to Phil, who gave him a superior smirk and dropped a dollar in the tip jar. Brett felt like pounding him, but instead turned away and found himself looking into Anne McKirk's wizened face.

"How can you let that guy sniff around her like that?" she demanded.

"I think Claire can handle herself," Brett said in his best conversation-squelching voice.

"I know she can handle herself with Phil," Anne said, unfazed by his tone. "You're the one giving her trouble."

Damn it, had Claire been talking to *Anne?*

"She hasn't said a word," the woman snapped. "But I do have eyes in my head. That girl likes you. And, dumb son of a bitch that you are, you don't seem to be doing anything about it."

Brett scowled. "Maybe I'm not wild about her."

Anne snorted. "Maybe you think I'm stupid."

"Do you need a drink?" he asked. "And where's your husband, who stranded me here?"

"Give me a Pepsi." She plunked down a dollar. "And I don't know where McKirk is, but I know you'd better not let that teacher get away."

"You talking about that new teacher?" Justo Echetto, the sheep man, asked as soon as Anne had taken her Pepsi and stalked away.

Brett drew a slow, deep breath. "What can I get you?" he asked.

Echetto pointed at a bottle. Brett picked it up and poured a double, hoping the older man would shut up out of gratitude. The ploy failed.

"The kids are doing better in school, I hear. We should try to keep her." He looked at Brett as though he could get the job done.

Brett didn't know if Anne McKirk and Justo Echetto were serious or screwing with his head. And meanwhile, Phil was cozied up to Claire in a dark corner, and she was laughing at something he'd said. Neither Anne nor Justo seemed to notice that. They had to be screwing with him.

"Shift's up," McKirk said from behind him.

"Great." Brett wanted out of there. He

glanced over at the corner where Phil and Claire had been sitting, and was greeted by the happy sight of him escorting her toward the front entrance, a smug smile still on the jerk's face.

Brett clamped his teeth together so hard his jaw started to ache. He kicked around for a few more minutes, then collected his coat from a hook in the crowded entryway, feeling as if he'd done his social duty for the next five years—which was a good thing, since he didn't plan on socializing again for a long, long time.

It didn't matter who Claire left with. It was none of his business. He was going home to work on his biology lesson, like any red-blooded guy would do on a Saturday night.

A few seconds later he was listening to the ominous clicking of a nearly dead battery. Muttering a few innovative curses, he popped the hood and checked the connections. All good. It was definitely the battery, which had been sluggish earlier that day. He looked around. The street was crowded with vehicles, but there were no people around to help him. Even Phil and Claire were gone. He'd have to go inside and bum a jump from someone….

Screw it.

He'd leave the truck and jump it himself tomorrow with the one-ton. It was a cold night, but it was also less than a mile home. No big deal. His breath showed as he shoved his hands into his pockets and started down the street.

He inhaled deeply, telling himself that this was the reason he'd moved here. For the solitude. He was a guy who needed to be alone. A guy who didn't do well in relationships.

So it therefore followed that seeing Phil's truck parked in front of Claire's trailer should have no effect whatsoever on his state of mind. And there was absolutely no reason for him to amble down the driveway to take the path across the hay field, instead of the county road. And there was even less of a reason for him to open the truck door and reach inside to hit the panic button on the keys, setting off the alarm before easing the door shut again.

No. It was a totally childish thing to do.

And it felt damn good.

The trailer door banged open as soon Brett started down the path. There was cursing as the truck rhythmically shrieked its warning. Brett resisted the temptation to turn around and see whether or not Phil was fully clothed. He really didn't want to know. He just wanted the SOB to know that not everything was easy in life. Sometimes, little inconveniences happened.

And just as Brett was justifying his actions, he tripped over the ladder, which Claire had apparently moved for some unknown reason, and he went down hard. He was shaking his head, wondering if anything was ever, *ever* going to go right in his life, when a pair of shapely calves in purple tights came into his line of sight.

"What in the hell do you think you're doing?" Claire demanded. Just when Brett didn't think things could get worse, a loud explosion lit up the night, and damned if she didn't give him an accusatory look, as if he'd somehow caused it.

But his mind wasn't on Claire—or Phil, who'd been striding toward him, probably with the intention of smacking him in the face—but on the horizon.

"That's Jesse's place."

Claire brought her hand to her mouth. Phil had already turned and was heading for his truck.

"We need to get over to Jesse's place," Brett yelled as he scrambled to his feet.

"I'm getting the fire engine," Phil called over his shoulder.

"Someone else will get the engine," Brett shouted back, but Phil was already in his truck, gunning the motor. He swung the big rig in a backward arc, barely missing Claire's vehicle.

Brett looked at Claire. "I need your car."

"I'm coming, too."

He didn't argue. They pulled onto the county road and turned in the opposite direction from town. Phil's taillights were distant red dots. Brett drove as fast as he could on the thickly graveled road. An orange glow was already lighting the sky.

"Does anyone else live out here?"

"Just Jesse and his dad."

Brett negotiated the corners as fast as he dared, then turned into the drive, bouncing over deep ruts. Claire's car bottomed out, but Brett didn't slow down. Right now, he had to get to Jesse.

The closer trailer wasn't on fire. It was the one fifty yards behind it that was engulfed in flames.

The big question was, where was Jesse?

"I'll check the house," Claire said, before Brett uttered a word.

He had never felt his heart pounding so hard as when he leaped out of the car and started running for the burning trailer. Two big dogs were instantly on him.

"Jed! Bully! No!" Jesse screamed from

where he was crouched, too close to the burning trailer. He screamed the names again, and the dogs stopped.

Brett brushed by them, hoping they wouldn't sink their teeth into the backs of his calves as he approached the boy.

"Are you hurt?" he asked hoarsely, and then he saw why the kid was so close to the trailer. His father was lying on the ground. Jesse looked up, tears streaking trails through the dirt on his face. "I can't move him."

All the first aid Brett knew—don't move an injured man—was negated by another small explosion. A ball of heat rolled over them, and Brett heard Claire shriek his name from somewhere nearby.

A second later she was there, her arms wrapped around Jesse. "Come on," she said.

"No," the kid choked out.

"Brett will get your dad. Come on." She started dragging Jesse away from the fire. The flames were spreading to a nearby tree, crackling and popping over their heads.

Brett grabbed Jesse's dad by the armpits and started to pull. The last thing he was aware of before the final explosion was the distant sound of a fire engine.

About time, Phil.

BRETT KNEW HE WAS ALL right—he'd only been knocked to the dirt and he'd hit his head—but Claire couldn't keep her hands off him. McKirk, who was one of the local EMTs, was checking his vitals, trying unsuccessfully to make Claire keep her distance. Brett squinted up at her. "Jesse?" he asked, his voice thick. He'd inhaled a significant amount of smoke.

"He's fine."

"You'll live," McKirk said finally. "I need to see where the sheriff is." He stalked off, and Brett grabbed Claire's hand. Instinctively, she helped him to his feet. He only swayed for a second or two.

"What happened?" he asked.

"Looks like a meth lab," Claire said.

Brett felt anger welling up from deep inside. Jesse was sitting on the running board of a truck, a blanket wrapped around him, gazing at nothing. Tom Lane was stretched out on the ground, an oxygen mask covering his face. His eyes were open and he was staring straight up at the sky.

"Is he going to be okay?" Brett asked.

"He's coming out of it," an EMT said, "but I imagine he'll be doing some jail time. They're cracking down on these things."

Claire's hand closed over Brett's and he

squeezed her fingers. Squeezed. Hell, he was hanging on to her for dear life. He forced himself to let go.

And then he made his way over to Jesse, who suddenly seemed to realize he was there. The boy tried to smile. He almost made it. And then he was plastered against Brett's waist, hanging on for all he was worth.

"You ready to go home?" Brett asked.

"You mean, your house?"

"Yeah."

"What about my dad?"

"The EMT says he's all right. You'll be able to talk to him tomorrow."

"He's really all right?"

"Yeah."

The kid drew in a shaky breath and nodded against Brett's side. "I want to go home with you."

"Do we need to tell someone?" Claire asked, as the three of them walked to the car. Jesse was in the middle, the blanket still wrapped around him.

"The sheriff knows where to find us."

The trailer was now a smoldering heap of twisted frame and melted aluminum. The fire crew was still hosing it down, and Phil was shouting orders, apparently forgetting he wasn't in charge. Both guard dogs were lying under Tom Lane's vehicle, growling at anyone who walked near.

Brett opened the car door and helped Jesse in. Claire automatically slid behind the wheel, and then Brett settled in the passenger seat, letting his head rest against the cool window. He had a hell of a headache, but at least his family was safe.

CHAPTER FIFTEEN

THEY SETTLED JESSE on the sofa, covering him with blankets to keep him warm. He still didn't seem to understand what had happened, but the fire chief had called to tell them that Tom Lane *was* going to be all right. Jesse nodded after getting the news, and then asked Brett to sit with him. He did, until the boy fell asleep.

Brett only went as far as the kitchen then, even though he could have used a shower. Claire was waiting for him, her arms wrapped around her middle. He crossed the room to take her into an embrace, hold her close, make certain she was really all right.

She hugged him tightly, then eased herself out of his arms. Her face had a smudge of dirt and he wiped it off with the back of his hand.

"What happens now?" she asked.

Brett didn't answer. He shifted his attention to the living room.

"I'm going to see if I can get custody of Jesse," he said at last.

Claire's mouth popped open. "What?"

"He needs a stable home. I can give him that."

"This may not be the time to make such a decision."

"Why not? I figure, if Jesse's dad does something decent, like try to find a proper home for his kid, then the judge may look at him in a more favorable light when it comes to sentencing." Or at least that was the proposal Brett was going to make to Tom Lane. "And in the meantime, Jesse needs a place to stay."

Claire let out a quiet breath as she shook her head. "You can't make up for not raising Kylie."

"That's not it," Brett said impatiently. "I'm doing this for Jesse. I like him." Actually, what he felt was closer to love.

"So you have room in your life for a kid."

It sounded like a challenge, and Brett instantly rose to the bait. "Yes. I can raise a kid."

"Well, if you have room in your life for a kid, then you also have room in your life for me."

"Claire, it isn't a matter of having room."

"I think it is."

"Look," Brett said with an edge of anger in

his voice. "It's about Kylie. You two are close, and every time you're together, it'll bug her, knowing you're hooked up with me. I won't do that to her. She's been through enough. Hell, I won't do that to you, either."

Claire started for the door. "You're not giving your family a chance."

"They don't want a chance."

"Yeah?" She turned to face him, her hand on the doorknob. "Have you asked them their thoughts recently, after they've had time to process all this? Or would that be too dangerous?"

"What do you mean, dangerous?"

She pulled the door open, letting the cold air whip in around her. "If they forgave you, then maybe you'd have to take the brave step of forgiving *yourself*."

She spoke quietly, then turned on her heel and disappeared into the darkness.

"BRETT!"

The hairs rose up on the back of Brett's neck as Jesse's terrified scream echoed through the house. He raced into the living room. The boy was sitting bolt upright on the sofa, his face pasty-white.

"I thought you were gone," he said.

"I was saying goodbye to Claire—Miss Flynn."

"Did she go home?"

"Yes."

"Will she be back in the morning?"

Probably not.

"I'm sure she'll come to see you."

"What about my dad?"

"We'll call the hospital in the morning and get a report." Or the jail, depending on circumstances.

Jesse just nodded. "He's not a very good dad."

Brett couldn't argue with that.

"I never saw him until Grandma left, you know. Then they found him and made him take me."

"I think maybe he just didn't know how to be a dad. He didn't have much practice."

"He wasn't trying too hard to learn."

"You tried to save his life, Jess. That tells me you care about him."

"I do. But I…"

"What, kiddo?" Brett brushed the boy's hair back from his smudged forehead.

"Nothing." His eyelids were at half-mast again.

"You lie down and go to sleep. I won't leave.

If you wake up and I'm not here, I'll be close. I won't leave the house."

"What if Phil needs help with a calf?"

"I'll wake you up and you can come with me. You're a better rancher than Phil. Maybe he'll learn a few things from you."

Jesse smiled weakly and his head began to nod. Brett eased him down onto the sofa and arranged the blankets over him again.

Their clothes smelled of acrid smoke, which meant that the sofa would probably have a wicked scent by morning. Brett settled down in a chair and watched the boy sleep.

Raising Jesse wouldn't make up for not raising Kylie. One had nothing to do with the other. Or very little, anyway. Jesse needed a father and Brett needed a kid. There was no *replacement* involved. It was simply something that needed to be done.

For the first time in forever, Brett began to have a feeling that maybe something in his life was going to work out right, after all. And if one thing could work out… His head slumped against the back of the chair, and the next thing he was aware of was a loud banging on his back door.

It was still dark outside. He jumped to his feet, and after checking to see if the noise had woken Jesse, he walked quickly into the kitchen. He'd expected to see Phil or the sheriff through the tiny window, but instead his brother stood on the other side of the door. Brett yanked it open with a frown.

"We heard about the fire," Will explained as he stepped inside. Kylie was right behind him. Her face was pale, and Brett was astonished to see tears in her eyes.

"She was pretty worried," Will said. "Claire called and said you were all right, but Kylie wanted to see for herself."

"So you drove all the way out here?"

"I kinda wanted to see for myself, too."

Brett bit the edge of his lip as he shifted his gaze from father to daughter.

"I'm fine," he finally said. "You could have just called."

"Is that the little boy Claire told us about?" Kylie asked, gesturing at the blanket-covered form on the sofa.

"That's Jesse."

She swallowed, nodded. An awkward silence ensued.

"What happened?"

Brett indicated the kitchen chairs with a sweeping gesture, before closing the connecting door to the living room all but a crack.

Then he settled into his own chair and told the story.

"What happens to Jesse?" Will asked.

"I, uh, I was thinking that I'd see if he can live here with me. No one else seems to want him."

Kylie stared at him, her mouth pressed into a thin line. And then she leaned her head against her father's arm.

She didn't seem entirely happy about Brett's decision, which made no sense at all, since she had Will. What more did she need?

Brett swallowed. "I'm trying to help make things right, by giving Jesse a place to stay."

Kylie gave a silent nod, then got to her feet. She walked quietly into the living room and stood looking down at Jesse's blond head. Brett had no idea what she was thinking, why she was there. He met his brother's eyes, and knew confusion and pain must be apparent in his own when Will said, "I think she's coming to terms with the fact that life is unpredictable."

"You mean, she'd better get to know me while she can?" Brett asked with a touch of bitterness.

Kylie came back into the kitchen, easing the door partially shut again. "Dad, can I talk to Brett for a little bit?"

"Sure." Will got to his feet and went into the living room, closing the door behind him, leaving Brett alone with the most frightening person in his life.

Kylie remained standing near the door, her arms folded over her chest. "You remember that time when I came to find you at the Friday Creek Ranch?"

"Clearly." After more than a decade of self-imposed exile in Montana, he'd been laid off from his job and had moved back to Nevada to take the only ranch mangement position available. It was way too close to Will and Kylie for comfort, but beggars couldn't be choosers, and he had to admit he was curious about them, hoping they'd made good lives for themselves in spite of what he'd done. But he hadn't planned on actually seeing them. He had never quite gotten over the shock of riding in after a long day spent gathering cattle, wanting nothing more than a beer and a hot meal, only to be confronted by a younger version of Des, and realizing he was face-to-face with his daughter—who had hitched a ride to the ranch in a cattle truck!

Up until that point she'd been a shadow figure, but once he was in her presence, he was aware of one overriding emotion. Terror. This was his kid. She was real. And she wanted answers about her background. Like, why were her eyes brown and her father's eyes blue? Was she adopted? She'd figured Brett would tell her the truth without Will ever knowing, never guessing that she was actually talking to her biological father.

He had not responded well. Fear did that to a guy. He'd hauled Kylie back to her father— her real father.

"How could I forget?"

"You were pretty mean. You scared me."

"That's what I was trying to do."

"Because you didn't want me around?"

Yes. It was overwhelming. "I was afraid."

She chewed the inside of her cheek, pressed her arms more tightly around herself.

"I'd done a rotten thing to your dad. And to you," he said, gripping the back of one of the wooden chairs.

"Dad kind of…explained things."

Damn, he bet Will had enjoyed that. Telling the daughter who worshipped him about the mistakes he'd made. The mistakes her mother had made.

Kylie bit her lip, eyed him speculatively. "You were only two and a half years older than I am now when…" She faltered for a split second. "It happened."

"That's not an excuse."

"No. But it's an explanation." Tears were starting to well up in her eyes again and she looked at the ceiling. "Why did you move back?" she asked in a quiet voice.

"I got tired of being alone. I never found anyone to hook up with, have a family of my own." And looking back, at the women he'd dated, the choices he'd made, he wondered if he would have let himself do that. "I missed your dad and I was curious about you—even if I was afraid to admit it. So when the Friday Creek job opened up, I took it. I thought I could at least find out about you two, without intruding in your lives."

"Regan said you asked her whether or not we were happy, when she first met you—back when she and Dad were dating."

"I did."

The girl pulled in an uneven breath. "Now you have a kid to replace me."

"I can't replace you, Kylie. You were never mine."

She pressed her lips together. "I think Dad misses you."

"You think?" he asked solemnly, but his heart started beating faster, and he knew his eyes were probably getting damp around the edges.

"I know," she said. And then she walked into his arms, and for the first time ever, Brett Bishop got the chance to hold his daughter tight.

ALMOST AN HOUR LATER, Brett left his seat at the kitchen table to brew his world-famous instant coffee, leaving Kylie chatting quietly with her father. The three of them had talked for over forty-five minutes about…things. Nothing serious, just talk, and even though Brett knew they were all still working through issues, the fact that they could discuss everyday matters, like Kylie's grades, and Phil, made him realize that he'd honestly turned a corner in his life. Finally, after more than fifteen years, he no longer had the burden of living a lie. No more secrets to be kept, other than those that belonged in the family. And his daughter didn't hate him, which made his heart swell with happiness every time he thought about it.

But he couldn't help glancing out the kitchen window at the trailer. There were other things he still had to deal with. He wondered if it was too late.

After stirring coffee crystals into the hot water, he grouped the three cups together and carried them to the table without spilling. Kylie automatically reached for the blue cup. His cup.

She waited until he'd taken his seat before announcing, "Regan says Claire's probably in love with you."

Brett almost choked on his coffee. "Yeah?"

"That's what I hear." She took a sip. "So, what are you going to do about it?"

"I don't know." Brett glanced toward the living room.

"We'll watch Jesse," Will said.

Brett gave him a surprised look. "It's after midnight."

"Her light is on."

"Jesse might be kind of scared if he wakes up alone."

"Don't worry," Kylie said. "I'll talk to him."

"Thanks," Brett said softly. And then he grabbed his coat.

He was at Claire's door less than five minutes later. He hesitated only a moment before he knocked. The trailer had gone dark just as he'd trotted down his own porch steps, but he didn't feel like waiting for morning.

He knocked again, and was posed to rap a third time when the door swung open. Claire stood with her kimono gathered at the neck.

"Is Jesse all right?" she asked, looking alarmed.

"He's fine. Kylie and Will are watching him." The emotional speech he'd practiced on the walk over suddenly evaporated from his mind. "Claire, I'm so damn tired."

Without a word, she opened her arms and he stepped into them, gathering her close, burying his face in her neck.

EPILOGUE

Six months later

"SO YOU SEE," Jesse explained to Kylie with a serious expression, "we talked to the judge and then Brett explained to me how my dad giving him custody was a way of showing love, since he didn't know a lot about being a dad, and Brett does."

Kylie reached out and ruffled Jesse's hair. "I coulda told you that."

"But you didn't."

"Hey, some things you got to work out on your own or they don't mean a thing." She looked up as a truck pulled into the drive. "Shane's here. See you, Junior."

Jesse made a face at her, then scampered off as Ramon hailed him from the reeds near the creek.

Claire leaned closer to Brett as they watched the kids go in opposite directions. "Kind of warms your heart to see her picking at him like that."

Brett didn't answer, but his arm tightened around her.

"There's Phil," he muttered as a truck approached from the direction of the Ryker ranch. "What now?"

Brett was full-time manager of Phil's hobby ranch again, since Phil had forgotten to release the bulls on time for an early calving, due to an impromptu trip to Cancun, and then the hay crop had been disastrously harvested by the temporary help. After those two incidents, Phil had decided it was more cost-effective to simply keep Brett on. Apparently there was a limit to how much of a loss he was willing to take for tax purposes, especially when his neighbors were all snickering at him.

"Nothing. I invited him," Claire said.

"To a family barbecue?"

"The whole school is here," she reminded him.

"Yes, but how many were invited?"

Claire smiled and reached up to brush a bit of windblown dandelion fluff from her husband's hair. "All of them."

"I think you need to reevaluate your definition of family."

"Family, my love, is where you find it and

what you make of it." She pulled his mouth to hers briefly. "Don't you agree?"

He smiled down at her. "Wholeheartedly."

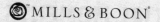

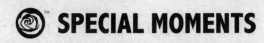

SPECIAL MOMENTS

Single titles coming next month

TRUST A COWBOY
by Judy Christenberry

Rancher Pete Ledbetter needed a wife – fast! After a summer romance he knew he was compatible with chef Mary Jo Michaels. But winning back her trust would be nearly impossible…

FAMILY IN PROGRESS
by Brenda Harlen

A romance with her sexy boss wasn't part of the deal – until a date led to an amazing kiss! Samara suddenly found she was falling for the wary widower and his irresistible kids…

DIAMOND IN THE ROUGH
by Marie Ferrarella

Miranda was as protective of her heart as she was of her family name – she didn't want some journalist digging into their business. Mike's pursuit of the truth could rob him of true love!

FALLING FOR THE LONE WOLF
by Crystal Green

Liam McCree was bad news for women. But Jenny's warmth and spirit made him want more than just a fling. Could these two opposites find a way to make a life together?

On sale 17th July 2009

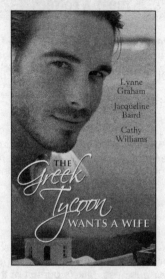

2 FREE

BOOKS AND A SURPRISE GIFT!

We would like to take this opportunity to thank you for reading this Mills
Boon® book by offering you the chance to take TWO more special
selected titles from the Superromance series absolutely FREE! We're als
making this offer to introduce you to the benefits of the Mills & Boon
Book Club™—

- ★ FREE home delivery
- ★ FREE gifts and competitions
- ★ FREE monthly Newsletter
- ★ Exclusive Mills & Boon Book Club offers
- ★ Books available before they're in the shops

Accepting these FREE books and gift places you under no obligation t
buy, you may cancel at any time, even after receiving your free shipmen
Simply complete your details below and return the entire page to th
address below. You don't even need a stamp!

YES! Please send me 2 free Superromance books and a surprise gift
understand that unless you hear from me, I will receive 4 super
new titles every month for just £3.69 each, postage and packing free. I an
under no obligation to purchase any books and may cancel m
subscription at any time. The free books and gift will be mine to keep
any case.

U9ZEI

Ms/Mrs/Miss/Mr ....Initials ....
BLOCK CAPITALS PLEAS

Surname ....

Address ....

....

....Postcode...................................

Send this whole page to:
UK: FREEPOST CN81, Croydon, CR9 3WZ

Available in July 2009 from Mills & Boon® Superromance

A Mum For Amy
by Ann Evans

Because of a Boy
by Anna DeStefano

The Rancher and the Girl Next Door
by Jeannie Watt

Doctor in Her House
by Amy Knupp

"...hear you were a wild man back ... the day," Claire said softly.

"...here'd you hear that?"

"...ut and about. You were a rodeo star...?"

"...eah, I was." Too close for comfort. Those ...s had ended up being the dark turning ...nt of his life and he wasn't going to discuss ...em. Period. Brett popped the cork back ...o the bottle. He pushed it across the table ...vards her.

"...e stood. "You keep it."

"...ou'll probably need it more than me." He ...cked it up and pressed it into her hands.

"...anks for the help," she said. "See you ...nd."

"...watched her walk down the path for a ...ment, admiring the subtle swing of her hips ...eath the swirly skirt she wore.

...aire Flynn was not going to be good for his ...eace of mind.